Dead Heading

Dead Heading

A Sloan and Crosby Mystery

CATHERINE AIRD

Minotaur Books
New York

This is a work of fiction. All of the characters, organizations, and events portrayed in this novel are either products of the author's imagination or are used fictitiously.

DEAD HEADING. Copyright © 2013 by Catherine Aird. All rights reserved. Printed in the United States of America. For information, address St. Martin's Press, 175 Fifth Avenue, New York, N.Y. 10010.

www.minotaurbooks.com

Library of Congress Cataloging-in-Publication Data

Aird, Catherine.
  Dead heading : a Sloan and Crosby mystery / Catherine Aird. —
1st U.S. edition.
      p. cm.
  ISBN 978-1-250-04113-5 (hardcover)
  ISBN 978-1-4668-3728-7 (e-book)
  1. Sloan, C. D. (Fictitious character)—Fiction. 2. Crosby,
Detective Constable W. (Fictitious character)—Fiction. 3. Police—
Fiction. 4. Missing persons—Fiction. I. Title.
  PR6051.I65D38 2014
  823'.914—dc23

                                                    2014003835

Minotaur books may be purchased for educational, business, or promotional use. For information on bulk purchases, please contact Macmillan Corporate and Premium Sales Department at 1-800-221-7945, extension 5442, or write specialmarkets@macmillan.com.

First published in Great Britain by Allison & Busby

First U.S. Edition: June 2014

10   9   8   7   6   5   4   3   2   1

For Torrin Wojtunik Macmillan
With love

CHAPTER ONE

'I don't believe it,' spluttered Jack Haines, the colour in his face draining away. 'All dead, you say?'

'Every last one, boss,' announced Russell Aqueel, his foreman. 'Well, all of them in number one and number two houses – the two farthest ones – anyway.'

'Good grief.' Jack Haines leant forward in his office chair and sank his head between his hands on his desk. He was a burly man and the chair creaked under his weight.

'The other greenhouses seem all right,' offered Mandy Lamb, the firm's secretary, automatically pushing a cup of coffee along the desk in front of him.

'They are. I've had a good look at the rest to be quite sure,' said Russell, a short, stocky man. He sniffed. 'First thing I did. Naturally.'

'But the young orchids and the special orders?' his employer asked tightly, lifting his head to look at the man.

'All dead,' said Russ. 'Every flaming one.'

'A flame would have been a help,' remarked Mandy Lamb detachedly, 'seeing as how it was the cold that killed them.'

'There was a frost last night . . .' began Russ.

'I do know that,' snapped Haines, his facial colour rapidly changing from grey to a rising red. 'You don't have to tell me. I've got a thermometer alarm by my bed, remember.' He stopped suddenly and said softly in quite a different tone of voice, 'Except that it didn't go off last night, did it?'

'I wouldn't know about that, would I?' said the foreman truculently.

'Go on, Russ,' said Jack Haines evenly. 'Tell me exactly what's happened.'

'When I came in this morning, first thing, both those greenhouse doors were wide open.' The man scowled at his employer. 'And before you ask, no, it wasn't me.'

'I didn't think it would have been, Russ,' said Jack Haines pacifically. 'So calm down.'

'But who on earth would do an awful thing like that?' demanded Mandy Lamb.

'Only someone malicious or careless, Russ,' said Haines bleakly.

'It could well ruin us, boss,' said the foreman. 'And where's the gain in that?'

'I wouldn't begin to know,' said Jack Haines tonelessly, although he thought he had a good idea.

Mandy Lamb shrugged her shoulders and said, 'On the other hand, anyone could forget to shut a couple of doors.'

Both men stared at her.

'Never,' said the foreman robustly.

'Not at a plant nursery,' sighed Jack Haines. 'It could kill the lot at this time of the year.'

'It has killed the lot,' pointed out the foreman soberly. 'Well, everything in those two houses, anyway.'

'What about all those plants Anthony Berra had in there for the admiral's garden?' put in Mandy Lamb suddenly. Waldo Catterick, an old sailor, was a favourite of hers.

'They're goners all right,' said the foreman. 'So is most of the stuff for Benedict Feakins, but not all of it though. He mostly wanted shrubs anyway, thank goodness, and they're still alive, being hardy. And Miss Osgathorp's special orchids were in the packing shed so they're safe enough.' He hesitated and then went on in more muted tones, 'But not Anthony Berra's other plants – the ones for the Lingards at the Grange. They're all goners too.'

Jack Haines groaned aloud.

'Dead as doornails, the lot,' said Russ. 'And there sure were plenty of them.'

'Who locked up?' demanded Haines suddenly.

'I did,' said Russ, adding with great emphasis, 'and I really did, Jack. Honest. Everywhere. The main gate was locked as usual when I got here this morning.'

'So someone got in somewhere else,' concluded Jack Haines.

'They sure did,' said the foreman instantly.

'But who?'

'Search me, boss, but I can tell you where. They came

through the fence that backs on to the field sure enough. You know, just where the compost heap backs up there. If you ask me . . .'

'I am asking you, Russ,' said Haines pointedly.

'It was a bolt croppers' job on the fence. That or wire cutters. Something like that anyway.'

Jack Haines pushed his coffee mug away and snapped into action. 'That makes it a matter for the police. Right, Russ, you go over to the Berebury Garden Centre, pronto, and then on to the Leanaig boys' place and see what you can pick up in the way of replacements before word of this gets out and their prices go up. So watch what you say to them all – especially Bob Steele at the garden centre. Oh, and call in at Staple St James Nurseries too. They may have something.'

'I'm on my way,' nodded the foreman.

'Sling me that phone, Mandy,' ordered Haines, 'and I'll get on to the police this minute. Well, what is it?' he said to Russ, who had paused at the office door, his hand on the handle. 'What are you waiting for?'

'Shall I call in at Capstan Purlieu Plants while I'm about it,' asked the man, 'and collect some replacement orchids?'

'Certainly not,' snapped Haines, his colour starting to rise again. 'Just get going. Now.'

Benedict Feakins was sitting with his wife at their dining-room table, lingering over a late breakfast that had included a couple of pain-killing tablets. He was going through his post whilst Mary Feakins was toying with a piece of dry toast. She had been doing this for some time.

After a few moments Benedict lifted his head from opening yet another bill to survey the garden through the window. While anyone else who was looking at it would only see a large patch of nondescript ground, loosely dug over and edged by some dispirited rhododendrons, what he saw in his mind's eye were banks of well-established flowering shrubs with an under-planting of hardy perennials, dotted about with something spectacular in the way of palms.

'I'll need a really good mulch to give everything a proper start,' he said.

'Benedict,' exploded Mary Feakins, 'how could you talk about mulch when I feel so sick!'

Benedict Feakins, who was unaware that he had spoken aloud, was instantly apologetic. 'Dearest, I'm so sorry.'

'And what I said – had you been listening – was that we need some more fuel for the boiler. It drinks oil.'

'So soon?' He brought his mind back to reality with an effort.

'Hot water doesn't grow on trees,' she said.

The pair hadn't been married long enough for him to find this remark anything but charmingly original. 'Very true.'

'It was all very well in your father's day,' she said, 'but we don't seem to have as much money as he had to run the place.'

'We haven't,' he said simply. 'Is it urgent? I mean, could it wait a few days until I've sorted things out a bit?' He waved at the little pile of post on the table. 'There are a couple of big bills in this lot.'

'Do you want your son to freeze to death?'

Benedict Feakins winced. The son in question had yet to be born but his welfare was already a priority in the household. He was all apologies. 'I'll get on to the bank,' he promised, 'and ask them what they can do about beefing up our overdraft. Don't forget we've got to go into Berebury today anyway to sign some papers for Simon Puckle.'

Simon Puckle was a partner in the firm of Puckle, Puckle and Nunnery, Solicitors and Commissioners for Oaths.

Mary Feakins, her morning sickness temporarily forgotten, gave a luxurious stretch and said, 'And then everything out here at Pelling will be really and truly ours?'

'It will, although,' he added conscientiously, 'naturally I didn't want Dad to die just so that we could inherit the place.'

'Of course not,' she responded swiftly, 'but he was ill and unhappy. He was never the same after your mother died, you know.'

'I don't suppose I would be if you were to die before me,' said Benedict fondly.

'Nonsense,' said Mary Feakins, her eyes sparkling mischievously. 'If I did, I bet you'd be married again within the year.'

'What,' he started up again, grimaced with pain and fell back in his chair, 'and let someone else look after young Benedict? Never!' He gripped the arms of the chair and this time moved with extreme caution as he tried to rise. 'I'm sorry but you'll have to do the driving into Berebury today. My back's still too painful.'

'What did you expect if you will dig up ground like

you did . . .' Mary Feakins' own attitude to pain in other people had started to change as her pregnancy advanced. 'You're not used to that sort of work and Anthony Berra seems to be.'

'We can't afford a professional garden designer. You know that's why I had to cancel his coming here to give the garden a proper grounding. But I really need to get those shrubs in soon,' he said earnestly, 'and I didn't know that digging was going to do my back in, did I?'

'You might have guessed.' She reached for another piece of dry toast. 'So how do you suppose with your bad back that you're going to be able to put these precious shrubs in the ground when you do get them?'

'I'll manage somehow,' he said through gritted teeth as another spasm of pain shot through his frame.

'You could always cancel that plant order for the front garden just like you put Anthony Berra off,' she suggested, not meeting his eye. 'They're going to cost an absolute bomb.'

'Then we'd miss a whole season of growth,' he said, waving a hand towards the window.

'I would have thought you could put a packet of seeds in instead. Some annuals there would look pretty.'

He shook his head. 'That would be no good in the long run. You'd only have to look at all this desolation for another winter.' He added another letter to the little pile on the table. 'We can't have that. Besides,' he smiled, 'you'll want somewhere nice outside to sit with young Benedict in his pram.'

'It was a pity your father was so keen on his cacti and nothing else in the garden,' she responded obliquely, 'and then you wouldn't have had to do all that work in the first place.'

'It'll look lovely this year as well next, I promise,' he said, blowing her a kiss.

'At least you don't take after him,' said his wife.

Benedict Feakins' head shot up. 'What do you mean?' he demanded hotly.

'In specialising in cacti like he did, that's all.' She shuddered. 'Nasty-looking things.'

'Prickly too,' said Benedict ambiguously. 'Mother didn't like them either but they gave Dad something to do and kept him happy enough after she died and that's what mattered.'

'He didn't really like gardening, did he?' she said, scanning the untended ground outside the window. 'Proper gardening, I mean, like you do. He liked fiddling around with little bits of things that looked as if they should have stayed in the desert where they belong.'

Benedict Feakins gave this some thought. 'I suppose not. Dad wasn't keen on the garden even before his hip got bad, but afterwards, of course, when he couldn't get about so easily the cacti were ideal. He must have spent hours in the greenhouse with them.'

Mary Feakins shivered. 'They give me the willies. Can we get rid of them before . . . before . . .'

'Before Benedict the Third arrives . . .' he finished the sentence for her, smiling. 'Of course we can. I might even get Jack Haines to take them in part-exchange.'

'That would be good.'

'I know what,' he said, 'we'll call in at the nursery on our way into Berebury and ask him.'

Mary Feakins changed tack suddenly. 'I suppose,' she admitted, 'you do need to be getting on with planting those shrubs anyway now. If you can manage it. But do be careful. You don't want the office saying you've got a self-inflicted injury like they do with sunburn.'

'The shrubs can't wait beyond the end of March,' he said. 'Ideally some of them should have gone in the ground last October . . .'

'But we weren't here in October, were we?' She looked round with pleasure at their dining room. 'We were making out in a grotty basement flat in Luston.'

Benedict Feakins acknowledged this with a quick jerk of his head. 'You were making out, Mary. I'm not sure that I was.' He looked out at the garden again in wonder. 'And now we've got all this.'

'You weren't expecting your father to die quite so soon, that's all.' She waved a hand in a gesture that took in the neat double-fronted Edwardian house. 'All this would have come to you one day anyway. You know that.'

'True, but you must admit that it couldn't have come at a better time.'

'For all three of us,' she said with manifest satisfaction. She got up from the table. 'Now, we really should be getting going . . .'

CHAPTER TWO

'Ah, there you are, Sloan.' Somehow Police Superintendent Leeyes was always able to make his subordinates feel that they had kept him waiting even when they hadn't done anything of the sort. It was, they felt, a gift. 'Two jobs for you this morning. Both out the same way, which saves time.'

'Sir?' He knew it would not be Sloan's time that the superintendent was saving but money. Police finances were as much under pressure as everyone else's these days and Sloan knew that saving his time never figured anyway.

'Both out Pelling way but not connected.' Superintendent Leeyes waved a message sheet in his hand. 'A missing person and trouble at a nursery.'

Detective Inspector Sloan groaned. Small children always spelt trouble, big time and all the time.

'A plant nursery, Sloan.'

He relaxed. That sounded better. Until the superintendent explained, that is.

'Surely that's hardly a crime, sir, leaving doors open,' protested Detective Inspector Sloan. He was the head of the tiny Criminal Investigation Department of 'F' Division of the County of Calleshire Police Force at Berebury and thought he knew the law as well as the next man. 'Not yet, anyway,' Sloan went on cautiously, since these days all governments seemed to be hell-bent on making more and more activities illegal.

Besides which, the detective inspector reminded himself hastily, this was the time of the year for his annual appraisal and it wouldn't do to put a foot wrong just now.

Superintendent Leeyes said, 'The owner thinks it is, Sloan. In fact, he's absolutely sure a criminal act is involved. Says he can prove it. And he's hopping mad about it.'

'Of course I quite understand how he must feel,' said Sloan untruthfully, subconsciously noting that the superintendent had used the word owner rather than householder, 'but even so . . . just an open door, I think you said . . .'

'Two doors opened and left open, to be precise,' said the superintendent, waving a message sheet in his hand, 'and a fence damaged.'

'Even so . . .' repeated Sloan, realising as soon as he'd said it that he should have been more circumspect. It didn't do to upset his superior officer at appraisal time. Although greenhouse doors left open with or without

18

guilty intent – even fences broken with undoubted guilty intent – wouldn't usually warrant the attention of a detective inspector, Sloan decided against pointing this out. 'And the missing person?'

'Old party not back from her hols,' said Leeyes. 'Gone walkabout, I expect.'

'Has she done it before?' asked Sloan. 'What do the family say?'

'She hasn't got any family. Lives alone,' said Leeyes, turning over the message sheet. 'It's a neighbour who's been in touch and no, she hasn't done it before.'

Detective Inspector Sloan sighed but said nothing.

'Even so . . .' harrumphed Leeyes, noting the sigh, 'I want you out there soonest.'

Sloan's unusual reticence was because there was something sinister pending at the Berebury Police Station as part of the appraisal element of his PDD – otherwise known as a 'Personal Development Discussion'. This was to be held with his superior officer quite soon. He hadn't been told exactly when it would be yet but it wouldn't do to jeopardise the interview by an unguarded response about a quite possibly disorientated old lady.

'Because,' went on the superintendent, the message flimsy still clasped in his hand, 'the owner of the nursery would seem to have had very good reasons for sending for us for something like that. And since as you know we're well under establishment these days . . .'

Sloan privately decided that they'd better be very good reasons indeed or he himself would want to know why. Since technically all law-breaking in the market town of Berebury and its environs, excepting traffic violations, eventually landed on his desk, he automatically took out his notebook. 'Just two open doors, did you say, sir, and a hole in a fence?'

'That's all that he seems to be complaining about. So far anyway,' trumpeted the superintendent. 'He said he'd tell us more when we got there.'

At this Sloan sighed again, his superior officer being given to using the royal 'We' only when he had no intention of doing any of the work himself.

'Right, sir,' he said without enthusiasm. 'I'll get out there straightaway.' The distinction between open and closed doors as far as crime was concerned was one beloved by insurance companies but disliked by those whose duty it was to frame charges – 'breaking and entering' was only one of them – when doors had been closed. Doors left open were quite a different ball game when it came to insurers and policemen alike.

'Two open doors and a broken fence so far,' repeated Leeyes, ever the pessimist. 'I'm told the man seemed a bit guarded on the phone.'

Sloan cleared his throat and in carefully neutral tones asked his superior officer if the police had any further information about either case. There were other – and indisputably really criminal – cases on his own desk awaiting his attention that were – would seem to be, anyway, he added a silent caveat of his own – more urgent than open doors and elderly ladies on the loose.

'Was there, for instance, anything stolen at the nursery, sir?' he enquired.

'No, Sloan, nothing at all.' The superintendent gave the message sheet another wave. 'It would appear from information received that theft would not seem to have been what whoever left the doors open had in mind since nothing would appear to have been taken.' He sniffed. 'What exactly was the object of the exercise is presumably too soon to say.'

'I'd better have some names,' said Sloan, taking a pencil out of his pocket and suppressing any references to gross carelessness that sprang to his mind. 'And their addresses, sir, please.'

'The missing person is an Enid Maude Osgathorp of Canonry Cottage, Church Street, Pelling,' said Leeyes. 'And man is Haines – a Jack Haines.'

'Jack Haines? Not the nurseryman?' Sloan's pencil stayed poised in his hand above his notebook.

'That's him. At Pelling too.' Leeyes, an urban man if ever there was one, sniffed. 'Back of beyond.'

'Ah.' Detective Inspector Christopher Dennis Sloan, who was known as 'Seedy' to his family and friends, had lived in the small market town of Berebury all his life. In his spare time he was a keen gardener and thus knew most of the nurseries for miles around. This one was out in the far reaches of the Calleshire countryside.

'None other. Proprietor of that big outfit on the Calleford road there.'

'What sort of doors?' asked Sloan, his attention now thoroughly engaged. This was different. Jack Haines was a nurseryman on a substantial scale, well known to professional and amateur gardeners alike and not above, when in a mellow frame of mind, dispensing his expertise to both. 'I mean doors to where exactly?'

'Greenhouses, Sloan.'

'Ah, I understand now.' Any gardener knew that that was something quite different too. 'Right, sir. I've got that. Greenhouse doors at the nursery.'

'Left open overnight, or,' Leeyes added ominously, 'deliberately opened during the hours of darkness.'

'I understand.' Sloan nodded, tacitly agreeing that this was different too. There was another distinction, as well, one between criminal activity that took place in the hours of darkness as opposed to in daylight – a distinction that went back to what was engagingly known as 'time out of mind' – but was still important in law.

'When no one was supposed to be there anyway,' amplified Leeyes, adding the automatic caveat, policeman that he was, 'or so the owner says.'

'I see, sir.' Because Sloan was an off-duty gardener himself he was beginning to be aware where this might be leading. 'And, of course, there was quite a frost last night . . .' He knew this because he'd only just pruned his own floribunda roses and when he had woken in the morning he had seen the hoary ground. He had hoped, then, that he hadn't done it too late in the season and wondered, as he did every year, whether he should have done the job in the autumn instead. Horticultural opinion was divided but 'the later the pruning the bigger the bush' was something on which everyone was agreed.

'There was. A really heavy one, too, for early March.' Superintendent Leeyes grunted and consulted the message sheet again. 'He says that Russell Aqueel – he's their foreman out there – came on as usual this morning at seven o'clock and found one entire greenhouse full of baby orchids and another one of young other plants killed off.'

'Not good, sir,' agreed Sloan. Nothing might have been stolen but even so there was undoubtedly loss involved. Heavy loss, certainly: crime, as well, if there had been a break-in. It was too soon to say. 'Were the doors usually locked? Or, rather, had they been locked last night?'

'You don't lock greenhouses,' said the superintendent irritably.

Detective Inspector Sloan forbore to say that you did if they contained valuable plants. He said instead, 'I'd heard that Jack had some young orchids that he's been growing out there. He's a bit of a specialist in them. Are they all right?'

'No, they're not,' Leeyes came back quickly. 'And judging from his present state of mind I should think he's pretty well lost the lot.'

'That's bad,' said Sloan. 'They must have been worth a packet.' He looked up and asked, 'Is Jack Haines talking about malice aforethought?'

'Jack Haines,' came back the superintendent impressively, 'is talking about sabotage. You'd better get out there and see him, pronto. And you can take that dim-witted constable, Crosby, with you. We may be short-staffed but I still don't want him here all day upsetting the civilian staff.'

'No, sir, of course not,' Sloan hastily agreed with this sentiment. Both men knew without saying that the superintendent was referring to Mrs Mabel Murgatroyd, the civilian staff supervisor, a lady of a certain age who took the view that uniformed policemen were an illiterate bunch who got in the way of the important work of the clerical staff.

When told about it, Detective Constable Crosby viewed the prospect of a journey far out into the hinterland with evident pleasure. Detective Inspector Sloan locked the seat belt of the police car into place with markedly less enthusiasm.

'There is no hurry, Crosby,' he said as the car took off at speed. 'The missing person hasn't been seen for three weeks and wilted plants don't run away. We'll go to the nursery first while any evidence that there might be there is still fresh.'

'Nobody dead, then?' said the constable.

'Not yet,' said Sloan dryly, averting his eyes from a near miss with a refuse lorry, all public service vehicles being anathema to the constable. 'It would seem that the only things that are dead to date are plant cuttings and I would like to keep it that way, please.'

It was something on his wish list he was destined to remember for a long time.

'That you, Anthony?' Jack Haines had reluctantly picked up the telephone to ring one of his professional customers and he wasn't enjoying the conversation.

'It is,' a throaty voice came down the telephone in reply.

'It doesn't sound like you.'

'Well, it is,' insisted the voice testily. 'I'm a bit chesty, that's all.'

'It's Jack Haines from the nursery here.' Haines groaned inwardly. The last thing he wanted was an Anthony Berra under the weather and in a low mood. 'I've got a bit of bad news for you, I'm afraid.'

'Tell me.' Anthony Berra was a thrusting young landscape designer beginning to be very popular with the landed gentry of the county of Calleshire and starting to be quite an important user of the nursery too.

'You're not going to like it.' Haines swallowed uneasily while he waited for the man to finish coughing. Although still with his name to make in the landscape design world, Anthony Berra was nothing if not business-like and rather formal into the bargain.

'How bad?' asked Berra shortly when he had recovered his breath.

'Bad.' Jack Haines told him about all the damaged plants in the greenhouses.

'Good God, man, you don't mean to say that I've lost the lot?'

Gloomily, the nurseryman admitted that the majority of the plants ordered by Berra for his client, Admiral Catterick, and all of those being grown for the Lingards at the Grange were now either dead or dying. 'And some of those for Benedict Feakins too.'

Anthony Berra took a deep breath and said frostily, 'I don't know what I'm going to say to the Lingards, Jack, if I can't get their Mediterranean garden fixed in time for their garden party in June. It was part of their contract with me that it would be.'

'I've been ringing round everywhere trying get replacements,' Haines admitted, 'but it won't be easy. Not at this time of the year.'

'I shouldn't think it will,' retorted Berra crisply, 'considering the effort I put in to ordering everything exactly as I wanted it for my planting plans for their new project. You don't pick up plants such as Strelitzia let alone Gardenia and Bouganvillia from any old nursery anywhere in East Calleshire.'

Half-heartedly Jack Haines muttered something about insurance.

'Mine or yours?' asked Berra on the instant.

'Yours,' said Haines gruffly. 'I've never even insured the orchids. I've lost all of them too.'

Anthony Berra wasn't interested in orchids and made that clear. 'What I'm interested in, Jack, is that greenhouse of yours that had my plants in it and no, I'm not insured.'

'Pity.'

'Actually,' drawled Berra a little unpleasantly, 'since I hadn't actually bought the plants yet I would have thought the loss was entirely yours. Not mine.'

'I grew them especially for you exactly to your precise order, didn't I?' responded Jack Haines, torn between keeping Anthony Berra as a customer and minimising his own loss. 'Especially those citrus trees and the palms, let alone the Mimosa.'

The landscape designer came back on the instant. 'I don't know who left your greenhouse doors open, Jack, and I don't care, but I can assure you it wasn't me.' There was an uneasy pause and then Berra went on in a more mollifying tone, 'It isn't quite as easy as that, anyway. You must know what these particular clients of mine are like. I should think the whole village does.'

Jack Haines had to admit that he did know what the Lingards of Pelling Grange were like and so did everyone else in the locality. 'Not exactly easy people,' he agreed.

'Especially the wife,' added Berra, opening up a little.

'Quite difficult, actually,' conceded the nurseryman. There weren't many people in Pelling who didn't know all about Major Oswald Lingard's new wife, Charmian, and her imperious ways. 'Comes of having the money, I suppose,' went on Haines. The second Mrs Lingard was rumoured to have brought a small fortune to the marriage. The restoration of the old and long neglected gardens was only one of the changes she was making at Pelling Grange. And to its owner, widower and former soldier, Oswald Lingard too.

'She thinks she only has to give an order for it to be carried out,' said the young landscape designer resentfully.

'And pretty pronto too,' added Haines, who knew the lady in question all too well. 'No hanging about with her.'

'She thinks she knows all about landscape gardening too,' muttered Anthony Berra, 'and believe you me she doesn't.'

'He's all right, though,' said Haines fairly. 'Been around in Pelling a long time, the Lingards have. I remember his mother. Nice old lady but hardly a bean to her name.'

'Oh, he's all right,' agreed Berra on the instant, 'although he's no pushover either what with having been in the Army. What his wife's going to say, though, if I can't get the work done on time I can't begin to think. It sounded to me as if she was going to invite half the county to her precious summer garden party just so that she could show them all her improvements to the old place. Not that they didn't need doing,' he added hastily in case the nurseryman should be thinking that he had been making work for himself at the expense of the owners of the Grange. 'The place was falling apart until she came on the scene.'

'No money around until then,' said Jack Haines, making what he hoped were sympathetic noises. Unfortunately the effect of these was somewhat lessened by Mandy Lamb's loudly calling out that his coffee was getting cold. 'Poor as church mice for years, the Lingards,' he added. 'Until now, of course.'

Anthony Berra's mind was still running on. 'You do realise, Jack, don't you, that my client is going to tell all her Calleshire friends that I've let her down. It's not going to do my reputation in the county any good if I do. Or yours,' he added ominously.

'As I told you, Anthony, I've already been on to two or three other suppliers to see if they can make good any deficiencies,' said Haines by way of mitigation. He didn't mention that he'd already had to swallow his pride and approach his three great business rivals for replacements. 'And they're being very helpful.' This was actually stretching a point since Russ Aqueel had not yet returned to the nursery at Pelling after going round them.

'I'm not having any old stuff,' snapped Berra immediately. 'I'll have to go over to the Lingards first to tell them and then I'm coming straight over to you to see for myself. If I put anything at all substandard in that garden it'll all have to come up again and the Lingards won't pay for that. The fact that the lady's loaded doesn't mean she's going to shell out for rubbish, you know. She's not silly.'

'It might just get you through this season, though,' suggested Jack Haines tentatively.

Anthony Berra wasn't listening. 'I'll just have to go back to the drawing board and revise my overall design, that's all, and she won't like that, I can tell you. Not one little bit.'

'I'm sure we can come to some arrangement about the cost of any replacements,' began Jack Haines.

Anthony Berra ignored this *amende honorable*. 'Do you have any idea at all about who could have done all this damage?'

'No,' said Jack Haines quickly.

Much too quickly.

CHAPTER THREE

Jack Haines, tubby and rather more than middle-aged, his complexion an unhealthy shade of red, was still spitting tintacks when the two policemen arrived at his office at the nursery. He barely greeted them before starting on his story. 'My foreman – that's Russ Aqueel, who I told the police about, swears he shut up all the greenhouses before he went off last night like he always does,' he told them heatedly. 'And he says there was no one around that he could see when he locked the main gate and went home.' He turned towards a youngish woman with auburn hair sitting at a desk behind him and said over his shoulder. 'That's right, Mandy, isn't it?'

'Yes, Jack,' she said in studiously uninflected tones, 'that's exactly what Russ says this time.'

'Happened before, has it, then?' asked Detective Constable Crosby chattily.

'No,' said Jack Haines.

'Yes,' said Mandy Lamb in the same breath.

'Which?' demanded Detective Inspector Sloan.

Jack Haines admitted grudgingly 'All right, I suppose it should be "yes". It happened once last autumn but there wasn't anything to speak of in that greenhouse at the time and in any case it wasn't frosty so it didn't really matter.'

'And was there now?' enquired Crosby brightly.

'I'll say,' Haines growled. 'Young orchids in one of them – worth a helluva lot of money; and a load of plants in the other that we were mainly growing especially for a local landscape designer.'

'Is your foreman always the last to leave at the end of the day?' asked Sloan. All policemen knew that workers who stayed around after everyone else had gone home sometimes did so for reasons other than earning Brownie points. If they worked in the office the crime of 'Teeming and Lading' came to mind; in the yard it was usually that of 'stocktaking' of an illicit kind.

'Well, the girls don't hang around after leaving time, I can tell you,' responded Jack Haines warmly. 'Some of them get picked up by their boyfriends and,' he raised his eyes to heaven and added piously, 'who knows who the others get picked up by. I certainly don't know and I don't want to.'

'And the men?' asked Crosby. 'Where do they go?'

'The Crown and Castle pub,' responded Mandy Lamb before her employer could speak. She pursed her lips. 'Every night. You'd think some of them haven't got homes to go to.'

'Greenhouse work is thirsty work,' chanted Jack Haines as if reciting a mantra. 'And hard work too, I give you that. They need to relax a bit after it. Wind down and so forth.'

'Including Russell Aqueel?' asked Crosby. 'Likes his drop, does he?'

The nurseryman nodded whilst his secretary, Mandy Lamb, rolled her eyes expressively.

'So you think some person or persons unknown broke into your grounds last night and opened a greenhouse door? Is that it?' Detective Inspector Sloan, not supplicant gardener now but working police officer, had his notebook prominent in his hand.

'Two doors, actually,' said Haines heavily. 'The two greenhouses furthest from the gate. The orchid one and the one with this year's young plants in.'

'Funny that,' observed Detective Constable Crosby to no one in particular.

'Nothing funny about it,' snapped the nurseryman on the instant, his colour becoming more choleric by the minute. 'It's very serious, especially at this time of the year. It'll put my customers' planting plans back a good bit, I can tell you, and that's only if I can buy in some new stock pretty pronto. It's much too late in the year to start growing any of it again from scratch here.'

'These greenhouses,' began Sloan, himself a greenhouse gardener manqué, 'what exactly was in them?'

'Number one was full of young orchids for any commercial customers who wanted them and number two had Strelitizia, Bouganvillia, Gardenia – that sort of thing – being grown for a posh new Mediterranean garden. Oh, and a lot of baby palms and some citrus trees. You name it, and we were growing on cuttings and raising

33

seedlings in it for sale to our commercial customers too.'
He groaned aloud. 'I've just thought . . .'

'Yes?' said Sloan.

'Some of those orchids in number one greenhouse are in our spring catalogue. We must have taken orders for them from all over the place.' He ran his fingers through what was left of his hair. 'I can't begin think what I'm going to do about that.'

'Then there's the rest of that special order from Anthony Berra for Pelling Grange,' his secretary reminded him. 'All those plants of his for the Lingards at the Grange were in there too. Don't forget that.'

'I haven't. I've told him already and he isn't happy.' Jack Haines groaned again and turned to her. 'Proper Job's comforter, aren't you, Mandy?'

'Just a realist, Jack,' she said, adding meaningfully, 'and someone round here has to be.'

'A special order?' queried Sloan sharply. The out-of-the-ordinary was always of interest to the police.

'It's for a local landscape designer,' explained Haines. 'The plants were being grown to order.'

'His order,' supplemented Mandy Lamb. 'Very fussy about it, he was, too.'

'A bit precious about his reputation, being local and on the young side still, is Anthony Berra,' conceded Haines, 'but he knows his onions. I'll give him that.'

'At least,' Mandy Lamb reminded him, 'the other orchids – those that we'd got ready for Enid Osgathorp to collect yesterday – are safely in the packing shed. The black Phalaenopsis, the single Oncidium and those big Cymbidiums – oh, and the two Dracula orchids . . .'

'Don't let her catch you calling her Enid,' said Jack Haines, momentarily diverted. 'She's Miss Osgathorp to you like she is to everyone else in Pelling and you'd better not forget it.'

He wasn't quite correct in what he said. To the police Miss Osgathorp was simply Enid Maude Osgathorp, aged 65, missing person, but Sloan did not say so.

'She seems to have forgotten to collect them anyway,' retorted Mandy pertly. 'She'd arranged to pick them up yesterday for some demonstration she was supposed to be giving somewhere tomorrow evening but she didn't turn up for them.'

Detective Constable Crosby looked around and asked with interest, 'Who are your nearest business rivals?'

'Rivals?' Jack Haines stiffened. 'I don't know that I've got . . .'

'All businesses have competitors,' said Crosby laconically, 'like all God's chillum got rhythm. Fact of life.'

Haines paused. 'Well, I suppose my nearest ones would be Staple St James Nurseries over towards Cullingoak and then there's always the Leanaig Brothers' place and the Berebury Garden Centre. I've heard that Bob Steele there has just started to go in for orchids himself.'

'And Marilyn,' added the girl behind him swiftly. 'Mustn't forget our Marilyn, must we?'

'Marilyn?' queried Detective Inspector Sloan.

'Just another grower,' said Jack Haines, stiffening, 'that's all.'

'Got another name, has she?' asked Crosby.

'Trades as Capstan Purlieu Plants,' said Jack Haines briefly, nothing mellow about him now, 'but I don't think any competitor would stoop to something like sabotage.'

'Except at Show time,' put in Mandy Lamb softly in the background.

'Showing's different,' said Jack Haines quickly. 'We're all rivals then.'

'No holds barred,' agreed Sloan, who knew all about Flower Shows from long experience. His own roses hadn't collected a prize at the Berebury Horticultural Society Summer Show yet but he lived in hope. He said, 'What about Girdler's place over Luston way? They've got a big nursery there.' Sloan, a keen gardener himself, knew that.

Haines sniffed. 'Joe Girdler's trying to breed the best rose in Christendom and good luck to him.'

'Right.' Actually Sloan was into roses himself but he didn't say so.

'Otherwise,' insisted the nurseryman, 'it's a pretty friendly trade.'

As befitted a man who had been in the Police Force all his working life, Detective Inspector Sloan took this last statement with a grain of salt, believing as he did that there was no such thing as a friendly trade. 'What about the other greenhouse? What did you say was in there?'

'Number one?'

'Yes.'

'Young orchids. And they're all dead. Every blooming one of them . . .'

'Except that they're not going to bloom,' murmured Crosby, sotto voce.

'God knows what they were worth,' said Haines, who hadn't heard him.

'This special order,' said Sloan. 'Was that for orchids too?'

Jack Haines shook his head. 'No, it's for this landscape designer I told you about. Name of Anthony Berra. He's got the contract for doing up a big old garden over the other side of Pelling on the way to Larking village and Berebury, like I said. It's been neglected for years.'

'Pelling Grange,' supplied Mandy Lamb, studying the fingernails on her left hand. 'Like I said, too.'

'Has he got enemies?' asked Crosby.

'I couldn't say, I'm sure,' said Haines stiffly.

'Have you got enemies?' asked Sloan.

'No,' said Jack Haines flatly.

'All God's children got enemies,' chanted Crosby almost under his breath, 'like they've got rhythm.'

'And Anthony Berra wasn't best pleased, I can tell you, Inspector,' went on Jack Haines, reverting to his own worries, 'when I told him what's happened to all his plants.'

'Very upset, I should say,' offered Mandy Lamb from the side-lines.

'I'd better have some names,' said Detective Inspector Sloan, tugging his notebook out of his pocket.

'He's called Anthony Berra,' said Jack Haines. 'His plants are . . . were . . . for one of those fashionable Mediterranean gardens that he's creating for Oswald Lingard over at the Grange in Pelling.'

'And Mrs Lingard,' put in Mandy. 'Mustn't forget her.'

'Why not?' asked Crosby curiously.

'She's the one with the money,' said the secretary simply.

'And Marilyn?' prompted Sloan.

'Marilyn Potts,' gritted Jack Haines between clenched teeth.

'She's an orchid specialist,' put in Mandy Lamb helpfully.

Jack Haines glared at her.

'One half of Capstan Purlieu Plants,' said Mandy, transferring her studies from the fingernails of her left hand to those on her right hand. 'The other half is Anna Sutherland.' She did not amplify this.

'I think,' said Detective Inspector Sloan, snapping his notebook shut, 'that before we go any further we'd better take a look at these greenhouses of yours. And then I'd like to have a word with your foreman.'

Jack Haines jerked his shoulder. 'I've sent him into town on an errand.'

'You have, have you?' said Sloan, making a mental note.

'In theory,' began Jack Haines, 'the last fingerprints on the door handles should be Russ's . . .'

'In practice,' Sloan interrupted him, suppressing his irritation, 'they may well belong to someone else.' Policemen, like doctors, didn't like being told what to do. All the same he would get Crosby to take any fingerprints off the door handles while they were at Pelling. It didn't seem a serious enough case to get a Scenes of Crime Officer out all this way, not with the economic climate being what it was. He snapped his notebook shut. 'My constable will soon be able to tell us that. Come along now, Crosby.'

The two greenhouses presented a sorry sight. In one,

serried pots of infant orchid cuttings had been burnt by frost and were clearly beyond aid. In the other, tender young plants had collapsed, their leaves now drooped over their potting compost like so many dying swans. Detective Inspector Sloan led the way inside, noting that the heating of the orchid house was not on. Above the pipes was a mist-maker from which little bursts of spray should have been emerging but weren't.

'No sign of forced entry, sir,' remarked Crosby, peering round. He started to apply his fingerprint gear to the door handle. 'The door hasn't been damaged at all.'

'No,' agreed Sloan, absently, his gaze still on the frosted orchids. They weren't his favourite plants but no true gardener could fail to be moved by the sight of so much wanton destruction.

'And there's no key in sight,' said the constable.

'It wasn't locked,' growled Jack Haines at his elbow. 'We've never had this sort of trouble before.'

Sloan nodded, unsurprised. In his experience very few stable doors ever got locked until after the horse had bolted.

'Now that we're alone,' said Jack Haines, nevertheless looking over his shoulder, 'there's something else you guys need to know.'

'Go on.'

He pointed to a device on one of the windows. 'I've got a frost alarm system rigged up in here. It's connected to a thermostat and should have rung in my bedroom and woken me when the temperature fell.'

'And it didn't?' said Crosby.

'It didn't,' Haines said heavily.

'Or you had been drugged,' suggested the constable brightly.

'No,' said Detective Inspector Sloan, going over and peering at a bimetallic strip. 'It had been disabled.' There wasn't a greenhouse in his own garden yet but that hadn't stopped him from studying the possibilities against the day when there would be. And then he would have such a thermostat in it. 'You can see that's it's been broken.'

'That must mean,' concluded Haines uneasily, 'that whoever left these two doors open knew what he was doing.'

'Or she,' said Crosby inevitably.

'An ordinary thief,' said Haines, carefully avoiding sexism, 'wouldn't have known what it was.'

Sloan was just about to make a proper examination of the other greenhouse when his personal radio spluttered to life.

'That you, Sloan?' boomed a distant voice from Berebury. 'Leeyes here. There's just been a call in from a Marilyn Potts over at Capstan Purlieu complaining about dead orchids. She's talking about sabotage . . . you'd better get over there as soon as you can.'

CHAPTER FOUR

Marilyn Potts surveyed a greenhouse that had once been full of thriving young orchids and now was nothing more than a home for the blackened stubs of dead plants fit only for the compost heap.

'All my chicks and the dam,' she moaned. 'Ruined. Every last one of them. Now I know how that Scottish chap felt. In *Macbeth*.'

'Macduff,' supplied the friend standing beside her.

'Anna,' Marilyn pleaded, turning in her direction, 'tell me it wasn't you who left the door open. Please.'

'Don't be silly,' snapped Anna Sutherland. 'Of course it wasn't. Besides, if it had been me who'd forgotten to shut the door I would have told you. You should know me well enough by now to know that.'

Marilyn jerked her head in tacit acknowledgement of this. Anna was invariably nothing if not forthright.

'Then who did?' she demanded. 'It certainly wasn't me.'

'I don't know. How could I?'

'There's only the two of us here,' Marilyn said tonelessly.

'You don't have to tell me that,' responded Anna Sutherland tersely. The nursery at Capstan Purlieu Plants was run by the two hard-working women and nobody else.

Marilyn made her way slowly up the greenhouse, looking to the right and left, and shaking her head in disbelief. 'Beyond aid – every last one.' She turned, her face stricken, and said 'And the dam – all the stock plants too.'

'Our seed corn, you might say,' agreed Anna bleakly.

'And I'm supposed to be speaking to the Staple St James Horticultural Society on orchids tomorrow evening, remember? Standing in for Enid,' wailed Marilyn Potts. 'How can I possibly do that now? Just talking about orchids will upset me.'

Anna Sutherland was bracing. 'Of course you can. Besides, they've already put a notice in this week's Berebury Gazette saying that old Enid's been delayed on her travels and that you're giving the talk instead. Take some slides or something – they oughtn't to mind too much. After all, you're doing them a favour and at short notice into the bargain.'

Marilyn shook her head. 'No, I needn't do that. Their secretary's quite sure Enid will have ordered some orchids for the evening and she's ringing round to find out where. Enid just hasn't come back from one of her famous trips.'

'It's all very well for some,' remarked Anna. 'I wish I could go abroad at the drop of a hat like she does.'

'She is retired now,' murmured her friend absently, still regarding her plants with a doleful face. She stroked one now as if the touch of a human hand could restore it to life. 'I guess old Doctor Heddon left her something when he died.'

'Where was it this time?' asked Anna as much to divert her friend as anything.

'The next-door neighbour wasn't sure – she couldn't decide from her note whether it was Carmarthen or Carinthia.'

'I thought it was only doctors who couldn't write clearly,' remarked Anna acidly, 'not their receptionists.'

Marilyn wasn't listening. 'I don't think that there's a single orchid left alive in the whole greenhouse.'

'Then I'll turn the heating and the humidifier off,' murmured Anna, pointing to equipment that were meant to keep the temperature of the greenhouse high and its atmosphere moist.

'You're always so practical,' complained Marilyn. 'Have you no soul?'

'You can see yourself that they're all dead,' said Anna, pointing to the plants on the staging. 'And not even you, Marilyn, can bring the dead back to life.'

'I know that,' said Marilyn with dignity, 'but don't you have any feelings?'

'Heating costs money,' retorted Anna, 'and from the looks of things we're going to need every penny we've got to get going again.'

'Get going again?' Marilyn stared at her. 'You must be mad. We can't catch up this year even if we started again now.'

'And if we don't get going again this year,' pointed out her friend, 'we've still got to live, haven't we?'

'I don't know that I want to,' said Marilyn, picking up a pot and staring moodily at the collapsed plant lying on the potting mixture.

'A few dead plants are not a good reason to give up living,' said her friend.

'A few dead plants?' shrieked Marilyn. 'How can you say that when every last one of this year's orchids that we've slaved over since they were potted is done for?'

'Some you win, some you lose, in this line. We've always known that,' said Anna calmly, 'and I must say it looks as if we've lost this time.'

'A greenhouse full of dead plants is a very good reason to give up trying to make a living from horticulture,' sighed Marilyn. She raised her head suddenly, turning an unhappy face in Anna Sutherland's direction as another thought struck her. 'You don't think, Anna, that someone somewhere is trying to tell us something, do you?'

Anna paused, her hand suspended over the heating switches. 'A business rival, you mean?' she said cautiously.

Marilyn shook her head. 'No, not one of them.'

'Well, Bob Steele is trying to get started with orchids and Jack Haines over at Pelling reckons to sell three times as many young orchids as we do even though his aren't half as good as ours,' said Anna.

'We can't be any threat to him, surely,' said Marilyn. 'He's big business by our standards.'

Anna shrugged her shoulders. 'Who knows how his mind works?'

'He mostly only goes in for the commercial market,' Marilyn said. 'And most of his domestic customers don't know what they're doing in the first place. They kill them quickly and then come back for more.' She grimaced. 'That's business. His sort of business, of course, not ours.'

Anna frowned. 'Anyway he sells so many other plants that I shouldn't have thought our orchids were any threat to his business. His catalogue is crammed full of all sorts of plants besides orchids.'

'What you mean is that he's not a specialist like we are.' Capstan Purlieu Plants concentrated on a few choice items for really knowledgeable gardeners. Actually they liked to think of their customers as plantsmen and plantswomen or even enthusiasts rather than mere gardeners.

'I mean that he's more of a knowing "nothing about everything" man while we're knowing "everything about nothing" women,' said Anna Sutherland eloquently. 'So who else wouldn't want us to succeed then?' she asked.

A little silence fell between the two women and it took a moment or two for Marilyn Potts to put a worry into words. 'Norman?'

'He wouldn't surely,' said her friend expressionlessly.

Norman Potts was – had been once, anyway – Marilyn's husband and their divorce had been notably spectacular in its acrimony.

'He would,' declared Norman's former wife vehemently. 'You don't know the half of what he would do.'

'And I don't want to,' said Anna Sutherland crisply. 'I'm your business partner, remember? Not your therapist.'

'If it was him,' hissed Marilyn, 'he's going to regret

it when the police get to him, let alone my solicitors.'

'Besides,' went on Anna, 'I'm a spinster, remember? As far as I'm concerned the secrets of the bedroom are meant to be secret. And stay that way,' she added for good measure. 'I don't need to know what else he could get up to.'

'You're a good friend, Anna, that's what, and I shall never forget that.'

'Talking of the police,' remarked Anna, lifting her head, 'they're arriving now. Look, they're at the gate.'

'Where did you say Capstan Purlieu Plants were, sir?' Detective Constable Crosby had asked Sloan while they were on their way.

'Keep going,' commanded Sloan tersely, his eyes glued to a large scale map of East Calleshire. He couldn't see the police car's sat-nav from the passenger seat and wasn't sure if Crosby bothered to listen to it. 'In about half a mile you should come to a little bridge over a stream and then you follow the right-hand lane until you get to the nursery.'

'Only if we don't meet anything coming the other way,' muttered Crosby. Single-track roads seriously cramped his driving style. 'I don't know how their customers ever find them.'

Lurking somewhere at the back of Sloan's mind was a saying that if you built a better mousetrap the world would beat a path to your door. Instead he pointed out that if someone had damaged the greenhouse at Capstan Purlieu then they at least had found their way there to do it. 'In the dark, too, probably,' he said.

'No one out here to see you in daylight,' countered Crosby, 'except sheep.'

'Where there's sheep there's a shepherd,' said Sloan, less bothered by the high hedges and narrow lanes of deepest Calleshire than the constable. 'Ah, I see a sign.'

A hand-painted wooden board rested on the road verge propped up against a tree. There was an arrow pointing ahead and the words 'Capstan Purlieu Plants' painted beside it in freehand. As the police car drew up in front of the nursery two women emerged from a cottage nearby to greet them. Crosby muttered 'Dr Livingstone and Mr Stanley, I presume,' but under his breath.

'Anna Sutherland,' said a tall, rather gaunt figure with her hair severely scraped back into a bun.

'Marilyn Potts,' said a shorter, plumper woman, standing slightly behind her, curly hair flopping about just above her shoulders. Both were dressed in workman-like trousers and grubby shirts.

'I hear you've had some trouble out here, ladies,' began Sloan formally.

'If by trouble you mean that we've lost half our livelihood for the foreseeable future,' said Anna Sutherland tautly, 'then yes, we've had trouble.'

'That's one way of describing the loss of a greenhouse full of valuable orchids,' supplemented Marilyn Potts, tears beginning to well up in her eyes.

'Trouble in spades then,' muttered Crosby, pleased with the gardening metaphor.

'Trouble with damage to some plants, I believe,' soldiered on Sloan, ignoring him.

'Trouble with all the young orchids growing in our

47

greenhouse,' said Marilyn Potts more precisely. She led the way to their greenhouse and pointed. 'As you can see for yourselves, every single one of them is dead.'

'Big trouble,' concluded Crosby, surveying the scene.

'Someone opened the greenhouse door last night . . .' began Marilyn.

'And left it open,' said Anna Sutherland.

'And then the frost got at them.' The tears in Marilyn Potts' eyes looked perilously near to streaming out as she fondled the remains of what had once been a living plant. She sniffed and the tears receded a little.

'Some person or persons unknown,' contributed Anna Sutherland, echoing, had she known it, Sloan's earlier sentiment. 'In other words, Inspector,' she said with emphasis, 'not either of us.'

'Definitely not either of us,' said Marilyn Potts, still sniffing. 'We would never have done a thing like that. Not in a hundred years.'

'I'm sure you wouldn't,' said Detective Inspector Sloan, although experienced policeman that he was, he was not sure of anything at this stage. It was too early to say. He scanned the greenhouse. 'Do you happen to have a thermostat in here to warn you of frost?'

'Too expensive,' said Anna Sutherland.

Marilyn Potts waved a hand towards the land at the side of their cottage. 'The hardy plants out there are all right. I've checked that nothing's happened to them.'

'Yet,' said her friend mordantly.

Detective Inspector Sloan took out his notebook and got down to business: police business. 'Can you quantify your loss?'

'A year's work,' said Marilyn Potts tremulously.

'That's if you don't count anything we may have to pay out to get going again,' said Anna Sutherland. 'Such as restocking.'

'Tell me,' said Sloan, 'do either of you have any thoughts on who might have left your greenhouse door open?'

'Caused criminal damage you mean,' said Anna Sutherland trenchantly.

'The perpetrator,' suggested Detective Crosby helpfully. It was word that had cropped up in his training that he didn't often have a chance to use.

There was an awkward little silence which Sloan, experienced policeman that he was, did nothing to break. After a moment or two Marilyn Potts said with almost palpable reluctance, 'It might just have been Norman.'

'Norman?' he said.

'My husband – my former husband – that is. Norman Potts.' She gave another little sniff and said, 'We parted brass rags.'

'Big time,' contributed Anna Sutherland.

'He wasn't happy about splitting the money after the divorce, you see,' explained Norman's former wife. 'He thought he should have had more of the final settlement than he did.'

Anna Sutherland gave a little snort. 'Wanted to reduce Marilyn to total penury, I expect.'

This, Detective Inspector Sloan, happily married man, knew all too well was quite often the main object of some ex-husbands and often more important to them than securing funds for themselves. He had no doubt that a forensic psychiatrist could explain this – but then, as anyone who had ever sat in a court of law could tell you – forensic psychiatrists could always explain everything.

'So that I would come crawling back, I suppose,' said Marilyn Potts. She gave a defiant shake of her head. 'But I'm not going to do that even if I starve.'

'Where does he live?' asked Detective Constable Crosby militantly.

'He used to live in Almstone when we were together but where he is now, I couldn't say for sure,' said Marilyn distantly. 'I don't know exactly where but I had heard it was over in Berebury near to a pub called The Railway Tavern.'

'That figures,' murmured Anna Sutherland enigmatically, turning to shift a large crate of plants to one side. She lifted this with great ease.

Detective Inspector Sloan made a note and asked, 'Would he have known Jack Haines' nursery over at Pelling by any chance?'

'I'll say, Inspector, very well indeed,' she said without hesitation. 'In fact, I know Norman went there when he was first trying to find me. I guess he thought I might be back there working for Jack at the time because he knew I was fond of orchids and Jack grows them too.'

'At least Jack Haines had the grace to warn her that Norman had been over to him at Pelling to ask him if he knew where Marilyn was,' interposed Anna Sutherland, hefting another crate and putting it on the staging. 'That was something.'

'But Jack Haines didn't tell him where you were, I hope,' said Detective Constable Crosby involuntarily. In his capacity as a young police officer he had abruptly been exposed to the world of domestic violence and, still a bachelor himself, he hadn't liked what he had seen of it.

Marilyn Potts gave a wan smile. 'No, not Jack Haines. He would never have done a thing like that, I'm sure.'

'Get real, Marilyn,' said Anna Sutherland. 'Norman could easily have found out where you were all the same. He might be a right menace but he isn't stupid.'

'There are always ways and means of finding someone,' contributed Crosby obscurely, a policeman only just beginning to find out about some of the sticky slug-like trails left by human beings on the surface of the planet.

Detective Inspector Sloan, who had been considering writing his report under the heading of 'Criminal Damage', decided that this remit might not be quite wide enough. 'Harassment' might well come into it as well: it was still too soon to say. He made a note of the fact that Norman Potts knew Jack Haines too. Two greenhouses of frosted orchids couldn't be a coincidence. Not on the same night.

Anna Sutherland said, 'There's no hiding place good enough for a battered wife these days.'

Sloan was a methodical man and so he ignored this and dutifully carried on. 'Is there anyone else whom you may have reason to believe bears either of you any ill-will?'

'You mean except Norman?' asked Norman's former wife.

'I do,' said Sloan, quite relaxed. Norman Potts might or might not be able to find Marilyn Potts but he had no doubt at all that, should they want to, the police could find the aforementioned Norman quite quickly.

'Not that we know of,' Anna Sutherland answered his question sturdily. 'Either of us.'

All that Detective Inspector Sloan knew was that that reply wasn't going to be good enough for Police Superintendent Leeyes. The superintendent's default setting was a toxic mixture of disbelief and irascibility.

CHAPTER FIVE

Anthony Berra's approach to his clients, the Lingards at Pelling Grange, was a sophisticated blend of regret and optimism. Fortunately it had been Oswald Lingard who had answered his ring at the front door.

'I thought I'd better come over as soon as I could, Major,' said the landscape designer, 'because I must warn you that there's been a bit of a problem with the plants that were being brought on for the new Mediterranean garden.' Berra hastened to explain about the open doors of the greenhouses at the nursery.

'Sabotage, do you think?' asked the major. His wife had wrought many changes at Pelling Grange but even she hadn't managed to prise Oswald Lingard out of his old tweed jacket. Patches of leather guarded the elbows but there had been nothing stopping the cuffs from fraying at the edges. 'Wilful damage and all that?'

'Could be,' admitted Anthony Berra, twisting his lips wryly. 'Too soon to say.'

'Lot of it about these days, you know, old chap. My apples are always getting stolen. Last year the blighters even pinched half my strawberries.'

'I think it's most likely to be someone with a grudge against Jack Haines,' replied Anthony Berra. He decided against going on to suggest that the strawberry thieves were more likely to have been of an avian rather than human nature.

He himself was dressed rather more carefully than his client although not much better. He didn't suppose for a moment that Oswald Lingard would notice – let alone care – how he, Anthony Berra, dressed but Charmian Lingard certainly would. It was part of the landscape designer's credo that people with money always knew about clothes and of necessity he tried to work with people who had money – hopefully quite a lot of it – so he always paid attention to what he wore and when.

'All of Jack Haines' staff, Major,' he said, 'are pretty certain that the gates to the nursery were properly locked up last night but you never can tell.'

'And employees being what they are they're not going to tell anyone if it wasn't,' concluded Lingard realistically, his time in the Army having left its mark on him in more ways than one. 'So where does this leave us, Berra? My wife will be coming back any minute now and she's sure to want to know.'

'I do have a plan . . .' began Berra.

Oswald Lingard wasn't listening. 'The restoration of the old garden here at the Grange means a lot to Charmian, you know. Very keen on it and all that.'

'At least the medieval herb garden is working well,' put in Berra. 'That's coming along nicely.'

'And then there's this big shindig she's planning. A lot of people'll be coming to that.' Lingard hunched his shoulders and gave a little chuckle. 'Bound to be. They'll all want to see what she's making of the place. And me.'

'Naturally,' agreed Anthony Berra smoothly, omitting any mention of the effect on the garden of his own work. Clients always wanted to think the good ideas had been their own. It was something he encouraged.

'After all,' went on the major reflectively, 'this garden has been pretty nearly derelict since before my great-grandfather's day. It was all right up until then, of course. Gardeners were two a penny until 1914.'

'One man to the acre then,' said the landscape designer. 'Those were the days.'

'We had four of them here until the Kaiser's war.' Lingard tapped his knee. 'And I couldn't do a darn thing myself when I got home – this bit of me hasn't been right since Helmand.'

'Oh, I understand that all right, Major,' responded Berra without hesitation, 'and as I say I've been giving that Mediterranean garden quite a lot of thought since Haines rang me. You remember that statue that Mrs Lingard brought home from Italy . . .'

'I thought she told you to call her Charmian?' interrupted Oswald Lingard.

'So she did,' murmured Berra. 'Now about the statue . . .' There had been no suggestion, though, that he called the major 'Oswald'.

'Rather jolly, I thought it,' said Lingard simply. 'I

know you yourself weren't very taken with it at the time, though.'

'It was just that I had trouble fitting it into my original design,' said Berra with perfect truth, the statue in question being of over-generous proportions and doubtful workmanship, 'but I've been thinking that now we're going to be without the plants that I'd planned to put in there, it could go in the bed to good effect. I'd got the ground all prepared in any case while you were away in Italy.'

Oswald Lingard gave a grunt. 'I'm sure that Charmian'll be pleased to have Flora, Goddess of something or other . . .'

'Bounty,' supplied Berra, 'bountiful' describing the statue's ample lines very well. 'And Jack Haines should be able to whistle up something colourful in the way of summer plants to fill the ground for this year and then next year we can put in the ones I had originally planned.'

'So it'll still look all right for the garden party, then?' The major sounded anxious. 'Charmian has set her heart on that being a success.'

'It will indeed, I promise you.' Berra gave what he hoped was a winning smile. 'Then, as I say, next year we can go for what I had organised in the first place.'

'You chaps will keep on talking about next year,' complained the major. 'You're as bad as that woman who was always saying that you should have come to see the garden last week when it was at its best or waited until next week when it would be even better.'

'Ruth Draper,' said Anthony Berra, who had heard this many times before.

It was at this juncture that Charmian Lingard swept in, a copybook picture of a lady gardener as found in the best fashion magazines: straw hat artfully tied on with a colourful scarf, elegant dress unsullied by soil and shoes that had never left the garden paths. She had that untroubled appearance of well-being only accomplished by a life totally untouched by money or any other worries. This was underlined by a chocolate-box complexion, designer clothes and excellent grooming.

'Did I hear Ruth Draper's name?' she said as she came in. She was carrying a wooden trug on which reposed a sheaf of greenery already half arranged for vases in the house. 'I'm not interested in last week or next week, Anthony. You know that. It's this week I want the garden right for. And every week, too, of course, but especially for the party.'

Berra smiled dutifully. 'And so it shall be, Charmian.'

She frowned. 'What are you doing here, anyway, Anthony? I thought you were going to be over at the admiral's today.'

'I'm going there as soon as I can.' He told her what had happened over at Jack Haines' nursery, spelling out the loss of the plants he had had grown there.

Charmian Lingard took this in her stride, difficulties always having been obstacles somebody else ironed out. 'Your problem, Anthony, not mine, but don't forget I'll be inviting your future in-laws and they'll be bound to want to see what you've done here.'

Anthony Berra was engaged to be married to the daughter of the Bishop of Calleshire. 'I know they will,' he said ruefully. 'But you'll be pleased that now I think we could fit Flora herself in the new garden after all . . .'

'I knew you'd come round to that in the end,' she said complacently, dumping the trug on the hall table. 'She'll look just right there with the peacocks on the wall behind her.'

Oswald Lingard grinned. 'I'm not sure what the old monks would have thought of her though, Berra, are you?' Pelling Grange had once been attached to a monastery despoiled by Henry VIII and occasional traces of the outline of the original garden had surfaced from time to time while the landscape designer had been at work. 'Or the Bishop.'

Berra smiled politely and pressed on.

'And I'll put some strongly coloured plants in the bed round her as a temporary measure for this year. I think a really good Centranthus ruber would look quite well against the grey of the sculpture . . .'

Charmian Lingard led the way into the drawing-room. 'Why not roses?' she asked as Anthony Berra had known she would.

'. . . and Cheiranthus cherie with deep red flowers and grey foliage. The one called "Blood Red" . . . '

'Why don't you people ever like roses?' persisted Charmian Lingard.

'Black spot.' Berra swept on persuasively, 'And there's a really striking Centaurea dealbata I'd like to try there. It's got deep pink flowers and a lightish green leaf.'

'I think roses would look even better,' said Charmian Lingard, a touch of steel creeping into her voice.

Anthony Berra, recognising this, gave in gracefully. 'Then, Charmian, I'll try some roses but they won't like the lime in the soil. We should go for varieties with good colours all the same, to lighten the stone of the statue. Now, I'll just need to take some measurements of Flora before I go so that we can get the dimensions of her plinth in proper proportion . . .'

'Flora among the flowers,' murmured Charmian Lingard sweetly. 'That sounds just right. Admiral Catterick hasn't got any statues in the Park, has he?'

'Not yet,' Anthony Berra grinned, reading her mind without difficulty. 'And,' he added, prompted by an eldritch shriek from the garden wall, 'he hasn't got any peacocks either.'

She screwed up her face in a child-like pout. 'He's got that sunken garden, though.'

'I don't think, Charmian,' said Anthony Berra gently, 'that the admiral feels in any way challenged by the work you're having done here. The Park is a very old-established garden with a character all of its own.'

'But ours was a monastery garden and you can't get any older than that.'

'True,' he said diplomatically, refraining from mentioning the Hanging Gardens of Babylon besides those of Persia and China and other plantings in antiquity, 'but I can't imagine the admiral minding that. Besides, I'm just keeping the Park ticking over for him now. Its glory days are over – and so are his too, come to that. He's an old man and not a well one these days.'

'I want him to come to the party all the same,' said Charmian Lingard, 'and see what I've done here.'

'I'm sure he will,' lied Anthony Berra.

* * *

Watched at a distance by both Anna Sutherland and Marilyn Potts, Detective Inspector Sloan and Detective Constable Crosby returned to their car parked outside Capstan Purlieu Plants.

'Now, Crosby, we need to get straight back to Pelling,' said Sloan briskly, 'and start enquiries about this Enid Osgathorp.'

'I don't know that I can remember the way backwards,' said the constable moodily. He had been hoping to drive back to the police station and its canteen.

'If, Crosby, baby elvers can find their way four thousand miles back to the Sargasso Sea without a route map, I think you should be able to manage it.'

He sighed. 'Yes, sir.'

Detective Inspector Sloan toyed with the idea of saying that the elvers then grew up to be adult eels but decided against drawing the parallel. He said instead, 'It makes sense to go back to that other nursery too while we're about it and have a word with Jack Haines about this Norman Potts. It'll save another journey.' Superintendent Leeyes had left him in no doubt that economy was the watchword at the police station these days even though 'Waste not, want not' was not usually a police mantra. Pleasing his superior officer, though, was high on Sloan's agenda all the while his assessment was pending. 'You can take the foreman's fingerprints while you're about it.'

'But there weren't any fingerprints on the door handles,' said Crosby, adding reproachfully, 'I did tell you that, sir. They had been wiped clean.'

'There is no need for that particular piece of information

60

to be disclosed at this stage of the investigation,' said Sloan, realising that he sounded stuffy even to himself. 'It is a basic principle of policing to give nothing away. Who knows what and who doesn't can be useful knowledge in an investigation.'

'Sorry, sir.' The constable sounded crestfallen. 'But we can ask Jack Haines why he didn't mention this character Norman Potts to us before, can't we?' said Crosby feelingly. 'He ought to have done.'

'Exactly,' said Sloan, who had already made a mental note of the fact. 'So just tell Control where we're going, will you?'

The constable applied himself to his personal radio while Sloan strapped himself in the car with a quiet sigh. Greenhouse doors left open and elderly ladies who had gone walkabout weren't quite the level of policing that he felt really came within the remit of the head of the Criminal Investigation Department of 'F' Division of the Calleshire County Constabulary, small though it was, and it rankled. On the other hand, what with his appraisal coming up so soon, this was no time to say so to anyone, least of all Superintendent Leeyes.

It was Crosby, though, who vocalised the sentiment. 'Who do they think we are?' he demanded indignantly. 'Maids of all work?'

'Maids of all police work,' rejoined the detective inspector crisply. 'Now get going, Crosby.'

Canonry Cottage at Pelling was in the middle of the village, the uncut grass in its front garden giving a clear sign to the world of the continued absence of its owner.

'Miss Osgathorp always lets me know when she'll be

coming back,' said her neighbour, a large woman in a flowery apron. It had been she who had rung the police. 'Because of getting in the milk and the bread for her.'

'So when . . .' began Sloan.

'That's just it, Inspector,' said the woman. 'This time she hasn't either done that or come back anyway.'

'Ah . . .' said Sloan, the thought idly running through his mind that large flowers on the apron would have suited the woman better than the tiny little ones that were there. Daisies, he thought they were. Poppies would have been better. Big, blowsy ones. 'What about her mobile phone? Have you got the number of that?'

'She wouldn't have one of them, Inspector. Said she'd spent all her working life answering the telephone for the doctor and she wasn't going to do any more telephoning than she had to.'

'No word then?' asked Crosby, already bored.

The woman shook her head. 'Not even a postcard and it's been three weeks since she went now. It's just not like Miss Osgathorp.' She pointed towards her fireplace. 'You can see that I've got a lovely row of postcards from her on the mantelpiece over there. Come from all over the place, they have.'

'Where had she been going?' asked Sloan.

The woman reached into the pocket of her apron, produced an old envelope and proffered it to the two policemen. On it was a word that began with the letters 'Carmarthen' and then trailed off into an almost illegible scribble, finishing with the signature 'Enid Osgathorp'. 'Search me. Mind you,' she added fairly, 'she doesn't always tell me where she's going, me not being someone to go about much. Proper traveller she's been since the old doctor died.' She sniffed. 'I daresay he left her something.'

'The old doctor?' queried Sloan.

The woman looked surprised that he needed to ask. 'Doctor Heddon, of course. Everyone knew him. Was our doctor out here at Pelling for years and Miss Osgathorp was his secretary and receptionist all the time he was here. Knew everyone, both of them.'

Sloan paused for a moment, seeking a tactful way to put his next question. He decided there wasn't one. 'Did she leave you a key to her house?'

The woman shook her head, unoffended. 'No. I was glad about that. She used to say "Norah, you don't want to be worried about my little old cottage. If it burns down, it burns down, and if burglars get in they won't find all that much there to take and I'm not leaving a key with anyone else either".'

Detective Inspector Sloan forbore to say that that aspect of theft hadn't deterred a lot of housebreakers he had known. He didn't mention either the feeling of outrage left behind by intruders, often worse than any loss of valuables. Instead he dispatched Crosby to take a look round the outside of the cottage next door.

The woman was still going on about her neighbour. 'Miss Osgathorp always said what you had to concentrate on when you got to her age was not being a nuisance to anyone so she wasn't going to be, not no-how. She was always one for spending her money on going places, not on buying trinkets that she didn't need. And that she certainly did, officer. Travel, I mean. If it wasn't one

63

country, it was another. Mostly ones with flowers.'

Sloan opened his notebook. 'Can you remember exactly when it was she went away?'

'Oh, yes,' said the woman called Norah very readily. 'It was the day after poor Mrs Beddowes done herself in.' She jerked her head in the general direction of the policeman. 'I expect you knew all about that what with you being in the police. The rector's wife.'

Detective Inspector Sloan didn't: this was partly because suicides weren't usually within his remit – PC York, the Coroner's Officer, usually dealt with the fall-out from those – but also because it was about three weeks ago that he, Christopher Dennis Sloan, family man, had taken some overdue annual leave. 'And when exactly did that happen?' he asked.

'That's just it, Inspector,' said the woman. 'Three weeks come last Friday. Balance of her mind disturbed, they said, though why she should do a thing like that, I can't think. Nice husband and three lovely children. She left a note,' Norah added lugubriously, 'but they didn't read it out at the inquest.'

'Miss Osgathorp,' prompted Sloan gently.

'Oh, she never stays away anywhere as long as this as a rule. She's her own woman, not like some,' here the woman sighed and let her gaze settle momentarily on a pair of indisputably male boots in the corner of the room, 'and so I suppose she can do just what she likes. Nothing to stop her.'

Sloan nodded. It was a sentiment with which the Force's Family Support Officer would have been the first to agree.

The neighbour was still going on. 'I wouldn't have thought nothing of it at first only this secretary of the Horticultural Society over at Staple St James rang me up because she couldn't get no answer from Miss Osgathorp's telephone. Seems she'd promised to go over there tomorrow night and talk to them about the orchids of somewhere or other. Indonesia, I think it could have been. Or Crete.'

'It could have been Crete,' agreed Christopher Sloan, the gardener in him momentarily taking over from the policeman. It was one of the places he meant to visit one day. 'I'm told the flowers there in the spring are something to write home about.'

'Never mind her not writing home, officer,' responded the woman with vigour. 'It's her not coming home that's beginning to worry me. It's just not like Miss Osgathorp to forget about giving a talk. Set a lot of store by that sort of thing, she did.'

'Did you see the going of her?' asked Sloan, hoping that Crosby would have had the sense to peer in a window or two next door while he was about it. Breaking into houses without demonstrable cause went down very badly with his superior officers and the Force's auditors, to say nothing of the press.

'Oh, yes. She went off like she always does,' said the woman called Norah. 'To catch a bus to Berebury and then a train to wherever she's going.'

'Did you actually see her go?' Sloan asked, possibilities such as a decaying corpse with a broken leg in an empty house coming into his mind.

'Oh, yes, I did that. I was just popping down to the

butcher's when I saw her go off towards the bus stop round the corner in time for the ten to ten bus on the Friday morning. With her suitcase. One of those with wheels that you can pull behind you. Besides,' she said, as if this clinched the matter, 'she waved to me as she walked down the road. And then that young Anthony Berra came by in his car. You know, the gardener man. He's going to marry the bishop's daughter in the summer. He pulled up when he spotted her and gave her a lift.'

Detective Inspector Sloan snapped his notebook shut at this. 'Then you'll let us know when she comes back, won't you? I expect she's just extended her holiday. Must like it where she is but I expect she'll be back in touch soon.'

Looking back later, he was the first to admit that this was one of the least good predictions of his career.

Not at the time knowing this, he set off to collect Crosby and met that worthy as he was coming back down the path of Canonry Cottage. 'Everything all right over there, Crosby?'

The constable shook his head and sounded puzzled. 'I can't quite make it out, sir. There looks to have been a bit of a break-in at the back of the cottage – there's a broken window to the larder with quite a lot of glass about and a bit of blood. All the other doors and windows are secure but someone's been in there through the front door as well but with a key. No doubt about it.'

'How do you know?' asked Sloan, suddenly alert.

'Come and take a look through the letter box, sir.'

Crosby led the way back up the path to the front door of Canonry Cottage and carefully pushed open the flap of the letter box with a pencil. 'See?'

Sloan bent down and took a look for himself. He saw what the constable meant. Letters that had been pushed through the letter box by the postman and landed on the doormat had been swept back as the door had been opened and stayed where they had then lain when the door had been closed again.

'Someone's been in this way, sir, I'm sure, and then come back out again.'

'With a key,' agreed Sloan.

The two detectives reached the same conclusions at the same time although they expressed them differently.

'Not a professional at the front,' decided Detective Inspector Sloan.

'An amateur at the back,' reasoned Detective Constable Crosby. 'Glass everywhere and blood on a sharp bit.'

There was, though, complete unison in what they said next.

'This'll need a search warrant, sir,' said Crosby.

'And Forensics,' said Sloan.

Superintendent Leeyes took a little persuading. 'A search warrant?' he barked. 'On what grounds?'

'A missing person whose house has been entered in her absence, twice,' Sloan said. 'Once with a key,' he added fairly. 'And once without.'

'So?'

'A key which she told a neighbour she hadn't left with anyone else.'

Leeyes grunted. 'That all you want?'

'A check of all the hotels and boarding houses in Carmarthenshire for an Enid Osgathorp would be a help, sir. She's retired and,' he said as an afterthought, 'as far as we know, travelling alone.'

The superintendent added something else. 'And presumably under that name.'

It was something else, agreed Sloan, which they would have to consider.

CHAPTER SIX

'More coffee, Jack?' Mandy Lamb hovered near the kettle, concerned about the unusual immobility of her employer. Jack Haines had sat, motionless, at his desk ever since the two policemen had left his office.

'What's that?' he jerked himself out of his reverie. 'Oh, no thanks.'

She pointed to a stack of letters. 'What about the post?'

He waved a hand. 'You see to it, Mandy.'

'Two whole greenhouses gone are going to set us back quite a bit,' she mused presently.

'You can say that again,' he said, a tiny bit more animated.

'It's bad, this loss, isn't it?'

'Very bad.' He continued to sit quite still, shoulders hunched.

'But it's not only the money, is it?' said Mandy perceptively,

69

automatically herself turning to the kettle on the counter in the corner. Jack Haines was a widower and, although Mandy was years younger than he was, she often found herself in the same position of sympathetic listener and maker of comfortable responses as many a wife.

'No,' he roused himself to answer her, 'although that's bad enough.'

Since he would not do so, Mandy Lamb voiced a name herself. 'Norman Potts?'

'No, not Norman,' he said roughly. 'Norman knows exactly where he stands with me all right. Always has ever since the beginning. Nothing's changed there.'

'You surely don't mean that it's Bob Steele who's worrying you?'

Jack Haines, impatiently pushing aside a pile of old seed catalogues, inclined his head into something approaching a nod. 'Sort of.'

'But the Berebury Garden Centre isn't really into orchids,' pointed out Mandy. 'They only do common or garden stuff.'

'I don't know what they're into,' Haines growled. 'Or up to. But I hope it's not what I think.'

'Sabotage?' said Mandy Lamb and frowned. 'You can't mean that, Jack.'

'Bob Steele came round the other day to see if we could spare him a dozen trays of Polemonium Jacob's Ladder for a customer. Said he was clean out.'

'I know. I saw him,' she said. 'Russ loaded them up for him. He paid for them all right – trade, of course.'

'That wasn't it.' Jack Haines took a deep breath. 'It's that I happened to drive past his place myself a bit earlier on that morning and could see quite clearly that he'd got hundreds of them on sale that day so he can't have needed any more.'

'Same variety?' Mandy Lamb might not know a great deal about plants but she did know that varieties mattered.

'Same variety,' he said. Mandy wrinkled her nose and since once again Jack Haines seemed unwilling to voice his suspicions, she said, 'So the Berebury Garden Centre is spying on us, is it?'

'I'd rather call it a fishing expedition myself,' said Haines.

She shook her head at him affectionately. 'You never did like calling a spade a spade, did you, Jack?'

'How do I know what to call it?' her employer demanded. 'Malicious damage, perhaps?'

'You don't think . . .'

'I don't know what to think but I do know that I saw Russ over there one day when I hadn't sent him.' He had begun to say something more when they were interrupted by the arrival of another visitor.

Minutes later Jack Haines was exhibiting rather more resolve than he had been doing with his secretary, but this time it was with an automatic well-mannered response to a customer. It was Benedict Feakins who had put his head round the office door. 'Got a minute, Jack?' he asked.

'Of course.' Jack Haines got to his feet, now every inch the helpful nurseryman. 'Come for your plants?'

'Not exactly,' said Benedict awkwardly. 'Well, in a way . . .'

'I'm afraid we've had some trouble overnight. Some of your plants got damaged, but some are all right,' began

Haines then, taking a second look at the man's bent back, he said, 'But you're not all right, are you? I can see that.'

'Too much digging, that's what did it,' the other man admitted. 'I was just getting the ground ready for all these shrubs you've got for me. It's getting late in the year for them as it is.'

The nurseryman gave him an indulgent smile. 'Weekend gardeners get a lot of back problems. They're not used to stoop labour.'

'Too right,' agreed Feakins fervently.

'Now your father, he had everything at the right height with his cacti.'

'His cacti are what I wanted to ask you about, Jack.'

'Don't overwater,' said Jack Haines immediately. 'A great mistake.'

'It's not that. It's that I – we – were wondering if you'd take them back in part exchange for my order. Mary doesn't like them and neither do I.'

The deliberate pause that followed was part of the commercial interplay that was innate in the nurseryman. 'I might,' Haines said slowly. 'What's the problem?'

Benedict Feakins flushed. 'You see I may have to keep you waiting for a bit before I can pay you for all the plants I ordered. It's lovely having Dad's house but the upkeep's proving a bit more than I bargained for and with a baby on the way . . .'

'I get you,' said Haines. 'Tell you what – you bring your dad's cacti in and I'll have a look at them for you.'

'Great. It would be good to get rid of them. To a good home, of course,' he added hastily lest Jack Haines happened to be as fond of them as his father had been.

The nurseryman looked at Benedict Feakins and grinned. 'You're not a chip off the old block, then . . .'

To Jack Haines' surprise Benedict Feakins stiffened, his face turning a pasty shade of white. 'No harm in a man's not liking cacti, is there?' he said dully.

'None,' said Haines hastily. 'It's just that your dad was so keen on them, that's all, and you don't seem to be.'

'I can't imagine that it's an inherited characteristic,' Benedict Feakins said stiffly.

'My father couldn't stand lilies,' volunteered Haines at once, 'and I love them. That right, Mandy, isn't it?'

'You do, it's only the cat that doesn't,' said Mandy Lamb tactfully. 'They're dangerous to cats, lilies. They really upset them.'

'Well, cacti really upset me as much as lilies do cats,' said Benedict Feakins more firmly. 'See what you can do about them, Jack, there's a good chap. There must be somebody out there who loves them more than I do.'

It was to the Park at Pelling that Anthony Berra headed when he left Jack Haines' nursery. He was going to see another client who had lost plants – Admiral Waldo Catterick this time. As he steered his car through the decaying entrance gates, he cast a professional eye over the grounds. This was a very different garden from that of Oswald and Charmian Lingard at the Grange. Theirs had once been monastic; this garden was that of a small manor with eighteenth-century grandeur superimposed on its original layout.

It had always seemed to him that whoever had lived here in the Park's glory days had not so much been anxious to keep up with the Joneses as having been making it quite clear that they considered themselves to be the top dogs of the neighbourhood themselves. It still showed in the ghosts of a parterre and carefully sited trees cleverly leading the eye towards a distant perspective. An old pergola, one side hornbeam, one side pleached lime, led to a sunken garden, all very overgrown.

Whoever the grandees of the past had been, they had long gone and only old Admiral Waldo Catterick lived here now. Elderly and arthritic, his horticultural demands were very different from those of the ambitious Charmian Lingard. The landscape designer was prepared to bet that the admiral never even got as far as the sunken garden these days.

Fortunately the house had escaped the worst excesses of the Baroque epoch and it sat squarely as it had always done in a sheltered fold in the land. Anthony Berra metaphorically shrugged his shoulders, only too aware that while a neglected house will stand for years, a neglected garden less than a decade. The admiral wasn't going to last for a decade. No way. Not now. Idly, he wondered who would live there when the old boy had gone and whether they would take an interest in the garden then. A widower for years, the man had no children that Berra knew of although he had heard that there had been a baby who had died.

He brought his car to a stop outside the front door and apologised for being later than he had planned, explaining that he had had to see someone else first. 'Did you get my message that I was very busy, Admiral? And would get here as soon as I could?'

'Signal received,' said the admiral, adding genially, 'You can't make headway in a heavy sea, my boy. I know that.' Elderly and arthritic the old sailor might be but he was still spritely.

'I'm afraid there was a bit of problem over at Jack Haines' nursery overnight,' began Berra, coughing. 'I've just been there to see the damage.'

The admiral regarded him with a pair of bright blue eyes. 'A bit of a problem, eh? That's what they said about the battle of Jutland too. Afterwards, of course.'

'Vandalism,' said Berra, who didn't know what he was talking about.

'Worse things happen at sea,' said the old sailor philosophically.

'I'm sure, but it's a confounded nuisance all the same,' said Berra. 'All those exotic plants I'd got lined up for you are thoroughly frosted and quite useless now. The shrubs are all right, though.' He coughed again.

'What you need for that cough, Berra, is to go sea. Take it from me, a dose of sea air clears the tubes.'

'Haven't time,' he said. 'Not in the spring.'

The admiral said, 'And I didn't waste my time while I was waiting for you.'

'No?' asked Berra warily. He and his client had very different views on what should happen in the garden at the Park.

'I've been thinking about scrapping those shrubs you got Haines to put by for me.'

Anthony Berra sighed. 'They're really very labour-saving, Admiral, and we did agree that low maintenance was what was needed here at the Park these days.'

'Can't wait for shrubs to settle in at my time of life,' he said with a touch of his quarter-deck manner of old. 'I'll be dead before they come into flower.'

'But, Admiral . . .'

'So I'm going to get you to order an extra load of bedding plants which I can enjoy from my sitting-room window this summer.'

Anthony Berra sighed again. 'You haven't been taking advice from Miss Osgathorp, have you? It's the sort of thing she would say. She might know about orchids but she doesn't know all her gardening onions.'

'Certainly not,' said the old man crisply. 'That woman's a downright menace.'

'In what way?' asked Berra curiously.

'Always poking her nose into matters that are no concern of hers,' said the admiral stiffly.

'I thought all old ladies were like that,' said Anthony Berra lightly. 'Especially the unmarried ones.'

'Doesn't understand the meaning of the Hippocratic Oath, either,' pronounced the admiral robustly.

Berra protested. 'But she wasn't the doctor.'

'More's the pity.'

'What do you mean?'

'Then I could have sued her.'

'Whatever for?'

'Dereliction of duty,' said the old man, sometime martinet.

Anthony Berra stared at him, wide-eyed, but the admiral said nothing more.

The two women who comprised Capstan Purlieu Plants' total workforce could not have been more different in temperament as well as in appearance. Anna Sutherland, spare and sturdy, was the total opposite of the shorter, chubbier Marilyn Potts. She was also clear-sighted and uncompromising. Marilyn Potts on the other hand seemed capable of confusing any issue to the point of complete incomprehensibility to herself and everyone else.

Except Anna.

'It's no good your hanging about here, Marilyn, mooning over every single one of your dead plants,' said Anna Sutherland implacably. 'You've got to go over and collect those orchids from Jack Haines whether you like it not.'

'I don't like it,' said Marilyn Potts mulishly.

'There's no sentiment in business. You should know that by now. You need those orchids for your demonstration tomorrow night and,' she added grimly, 'we need your fee for speaking. You've been told by the Society's secretary exactly where Enid Osgathorp had arranged for the orchids to be ready for her talk and all you've got to do now is go over to Pelling and collect them.'

'But from Jack Haines,' she protested weakly.

'He can't eat you,' said Anna.

'I don't know what Norman might have said to him when he went there looking for me.'

'What Norman might have said about you to Jack Haines or anyone else doesn't matter any more,' said Anna. 'Never did anyway,' she added under her breath.

'Norman used to say such nice things to me once upon a time,' said Marilyn, now near to tears again.

'Once upon a time is how all fairy tales begin,' said Anna Sutherland tartly. 'They usually end differently.'

'And now I suppose all his sweet nothings are like all my orchids. Dead and dying, the lot of them. Frosted.'

'The brothers Grimm didn't write much about flowers in their fairy tales,' Anna reminded her. 'Just Jack and the Beanstalk.'

'That was written by someone else,' objected Marilyn.

'I don't care who it was written by,' retorted Anna, 'you've still got to get yourself over to Jack Haines' place and pick up those orchids before tomorrow night.'

'He doesn't know yet that I'm standing in for old Enid.'

'Then you'll have to tell him, won't you?'

'Shall I ring him and let him know it's me who's going to be picking them up so that he can get them ready? And then I shan't have to hang around his place.'

Anna Sutherland gave an unladylike snort. 'Those orchids will be all ready and waiting for you when you get there, Marilyn, don't you worry. Enid would have had his guts for garters if they weren't and he knows she would – just as well as we do. I expect he's as frightened of her as everyone else.'

'Except you, Anna,' said Marilyn Potts, 'except you.' She looked up and caught a curious look on her friend's face. 'You're not afraid of anyone, are you?'

Anna's face relaxed. 'Not of anything in trousers, anyway.'

'Just as well,' said her friend drily, 'because there's one of them coming up the path now.'

Anna Sutherland looked over Marilyn's shoulder at the approaching figure. 'I wonder what our Anthony wants today?'

'Plants, I hope, and plenty of them,' said Marilyn vigorously.

It was indeed plants that the landscape designer was after. Anthony Berra arrived waving a list. 'Just checking if you've got any of these,' he said after punctiliously greeting them both.

'Not if they're orchids,' said Marilyn bitterly. 'We've lost the lot.'

'Not you too?' Berra launched into a graphic description of Jack Haines' losses.

'How very odd,' said Anna Sutherland. She frowned. 'Has some nutter got something against orchids, I wonder? Or him and us, perhaps?'

Marilyn Potts stayed silent while Berra went on, 'It also means I've lost all the plants Jack was growing for me for the Lingards as well.' The landscape designer grimaced. 'And you know what Charmian Lingard's like.'

'More money than sense, that woman,' pronounced Anna.

'Thinks money will buy anything,' chimed in Marilyn. She sniffed. 'Well, all I can say is that she hasn't lived long enough yet to learn that it won't.'

The sniffing became more pronounced and with tears welling up in Marilyn's eyes, Anthony Berra hurled himself into the conversation. 'Well, it seems that it's bad luck all round then.'

'Perhaps it isn't just bad luck,' said Anna Sutherland slowly.

'Well, it certainly isn't a coincidence,' agreed Berra. 'It can't be. Not two nurseries of orchids in one night. It makes you wonder what it could be that you and Jack have in common – besides growing orchids, that is.'

'Norman Potts,' said Norman's erstwhile wife, taking a deep breath. 'That's what.'

'Of course, Jack's stepson!' he whistled. 'I'd never thought of him,' he confessed. 'Ought to have done, I suppose, seeing he used to live and work there when Jack's wife was alive.'

'My once-upon-a-time husband,' responded Marilyn, whose mind seemed still bound up with fairy tales.

'But why should he or anyone else want to attack orchids?' asked Berra, looking mystified. 'I can't imagine any reason myself but then I'm not a psychologist.'

'If you ask me,' said Anna, 'reason doesn't come into it.'

'Is he pathological about them or something, then?'

'The only thing Norman Potts is pathological about is Marilyn here,' declared Anna Sutherland astringently.

'What about Jack Haines then?' asked Berra, still puzzled. 'Norman can't be pathological about Jack's orchids too, surely?'

'Can't he just?' said Anna. 'He always was anti-Jack after Jack married Norman's mother and he hasn't changed that I know of.'

'All I know is that Norman went over to Pelling a week or so back to see Jack Haines,' said Marilyn Potts. 'To try to find out where I lived.'

'It sounds as if he might have succeeded,' observed Anthony Berra, 'if he's the one who's dished your orchids. And Jack's.'

'Well, I haven't tried to find him,' added Marilyn acidly. 'I'd be quite happy if I never set eyes on him ever again.'

'Are you likely to?' asked Berra. 'I mean, is he local these days?'

'Last heard of living in Berebury,' she said, 'somewhere near a pub called The Railway Tavern.'

'Living off his ill-gotten gains, I daresay,' observed Anna Sutherland.

'She means half of our worldly possessions,' explained Marilyn. 'His and mine.'

'Immoral earnings,' said her friend Anna Sutherland trenchantly.

'Yes, of course,' murmured Anthony, a little embarrassed. He started to hand over the list of plants he had brought with him.

Anna plucked it from his fingers and scanned it quickly. 'Cercis canadensis – yes, we've got that; Photinia Red Robin – yes; Cotinus Royal Purple – lots of that; Lonicera etrusca – sorry sold out . . .'

'You got a customer on lime soil, then, Anthony?' said Marilyn.

'Too right, I have,' said Anthony Berra.

'We can't do you any magic potion for neutralising it. You'll have to go to Jack Haines or Bob Steele for that,' put in Marilyn, grinning.

'I know, I know,' he said good-humouredly. 'What you're saying is that Capstan Purlieu is a nursery not a plant centre. I haven't forgotten. Now, what about a good Abutilon, Anna?'

'We've got plenty. Take your pick. We've got a good line in lilies if you're interested?'

He wrinkled his nose. 'I don't like the scent much.'

'Remove the stamen, remove the smell,' said Anna wryly. 'I see you want a Cornus controversa Variegata too.'

'That's the Wedding Cake Tree . . .' began Marilyn, looking again as if she was about to cry.

'I hear you're getting married soon, Anthony,' Anna Sutherland interrupted her hastily.

He nodded. 'In the autumn. In the Minster over at Calleford by the bride's father.'

Anna, looking solemn, said, 'Don't let the girl have any Aegopodium podagraria in her bouquet or you'll never hear the last of it.'

'Anna,' said Anthony, throwing up his hands, 'you've got me there. Explain.'

'Bishop's weed,' cackled Anna.

CHAPTER SEVEN

It was at much the same time that morning when the solicitor Simon Puckle welcomed Benedict and Mary Feakins to his office in Berebury. That the solicitor was sitting behind a desk as he did so and not in an easy chair alongside his clients or even sitting beside them at a round table was thought by the junior members of the firm of Puckle, Puckle and Nunnery, solicitors, to be old-fashioned – even perhaps the making of a statement. That the desk had once belonged to Simon's grandfather only contributed to this image of antiquity.

At this moment, though, Simon Puckle was more concerned about Benedict Feakins' bad back than worrying about his own self-image.

'I'm all right, really,' said Benedict, nevertheless screwing up his face in pain.

'Sure?' asked Simon Puckle as his client lowered himself

into a chair with great caution. 'We could always do this on another day.'

'No,' said Feakins with unexpected vehemence. 'We need everything wound up today, don't we, Mary?'

His wife nodded her head at this, her mind elsewhere. There had been a promise of coffee when they arrived and – her morning sickness having receded – she was now quite hungry. There might be biscuits with the coffee . . .

'Just so,' said the solicitor. 'Now, as you know, probate has already been finalised – which was when you were able to take up residence in your late father's house at Pelling.'

'That means that everything is hunky-dory, doesn't it?' said Benedict Feakins. He essayed an uncertain laugh. 'No last minute snags or anything like that?'

Simon Puckle said, 'Certainly not.'

'Copper-bottomed at Lloyds and all that?' persisted Feakins.

'I assure you that everything is quite in order.' The solicitor was not prepared to state in so many words that the firm Puckle, Puckle and Nunnery were not in the habit of finding last minute snags in their work. Instead he made the point more subtly by moving swiftly on. 'Now we come to the peripheral matters, particularly the transfer of such securities as were held in your late father's name to yours. This, of course, will take time.'

'Everything always seems to take time,' complained Feakins wearily. 'The law's delays and all that. Shakespeare was dead right there.'

Simon Puckle did not rise to this either. 'There is also

the important point that the liability for the insurance of the property is now your responsibility rather than that of the executors and,' he added sternly, 'there can be no delay about that.'

'Are we talking big money?' asked Benedict Feakins warily. 'About the insurance, I mean?'

Simon Puckle glanced down at the contents of the file in front of him. 'Nothing inordinate.'

'I'm a bit strapped for cash at the moment, that's all,' admitted Feakins. 'Moving expenses and all that. But I expect I could raise a loan.'

'Perhaps an overdraft would be better,' suggested the solicitor mildly.

'We've reached our limit,' interrupted Mary Feakins. 'The bank won't let us have any more,' she explained naively. 'We went there first this morning.'

'I see.' Simon Puckle gave the young couple a long hard look. 'It is in my opinion a little early to be thinking of raising money against the property if that is what you had in mind and,' here he raised his eyebrows, 'if I may say so, a little unwise at this stage.'

Benedict Feakins was saved from answering this by the arrival of the solicitor's secretary with a tray of coffee. Mary Feakins gazed hungrily at a plate of digestive biscuits and half-rose in its direction.

'Ah, thank you, Miss Fennel,' said Simon Puckle pleasantly, as she poured out the coffee and handed it round. 'Perhaps you would be kind enough to stay as we shall need you as a witness to Mr Feakins putting his signature on these papers.'

'Of course, Mr Puckle,' she murmured, following the

coffee with an offer of biscuits all round. Mary Feakins took two.

'Now,' said Simon Puckle to his clients, 'do either of you have any other questions?'

'How long will it be before we – that is, I – can sell any of these assets?' said Benedict Feakins, his coffee untouched.

'When you have title to them,' said Simon Puckle crisply.

'And when will that be?' persisted Benedict.

'I think the correct answer,' said the solicitor, 'is that it will be in the fullness of bureaucratic time.'

Benedict Feakins groaned but whether this was from pain or disappointment at his answer Simon Puckle was unable to tell.

After his clients had left his office the solicitor sat at his desk thinking for a minute or two then he rang for his secretary. 'Would you please see if the manager of the Calleshire and Counties Bank is free to have lunch with me today, Miss Fennel?'

'The police are back, Jack,' announced Mandy Lamb unceremoniously as she ushered Detective Inspector Sloan and Detective Constable Crosby into the office.

'Come along in, Inspector,' said Jack Haines heartily. He pushed his chair back and came forward to greet them with every sign of pleasure.

It was Sloan's experience that a visit from the police was only ever welcomed by the victims of an offence. Villains seldom greeted him with the enthusiasm that met their return to Jack Haines' nursery at Pelling. Since the nurseryman and his other visitor were facing each other like a pair of warring dogs, it was obvious, too, that he and Crosby had arrived at a most opportune moment.

'And meet Mr Anthony Berra,' went on Haines, stepping back and ushering the two policemen into chairs. 'He's lost a load of plants too.'

'Only in a manner of speaking,' murmured Anthony Berra coolly. 'It's my clients who will be the losers in the long run. And Jack here, of course.'

'So,' hastened on the nurseryman, 'we're both very keen for you to find out who broke in and opened the greenhouse doors.'

'And why,' added Berra pithily. 'That's what I would like to know.'

'Are you two the only losers here?' asked Detective Inspector Sloan. 'No other victims?'

'I had stuff in there that I was planning to use in the gardens of Admiral Catterick but mostly it was for my clients, the Lingards,' said Berra, giving a little cough.

'And for young Benedict Feakins,' put in Haines.

Anthony Berra pulled a face. 'No, not for him any longer, Jack, I'm sorry to say. He says he's broke and can't afford me any longer.'

'It happens,' said Haines shrugging his shoulders. 'There are some other orchids in the packing shed awaiting collection by a Miss Osgathorp so they're safe enough and the other greenhouses and the hardy plants are all right. I've just checked them myself. As far as I'm concerned the biggest loss is the young orchids.'

'And as far as I'm concerned nearly half of my stuff for

this season was in that one greenhouse,' stressed Berra. 'The remainder is in one of the other greenhouses whose doors weren't left open . . .'

'Now, Anthony . . .' his voice died away as Jack Haines began a protest at this but thought better of it at the last minute.

'There was nothing at all of mine in the orchid one,' said Berra. He cast an enquiring glance in Jack Haines' direction. 'That's so, Jack, isn't it?'

Haines nodded.

Berra gave a twisted smile. 'And so there being "No Orchids for Miss Blandish" is not my problem.'

'You could say that, I suppose,' agreed Haines sourly.

'There were no orchids for our Mrs Lingard at the Grange, either,' said Berra lightly, 'since she wasn't going to have any orchids anyway.' He turned to the policemen. 'She's my client, you know, Inspector. The plants in number two greenhouse were mainly for her – their – garden. But not the orchids, thank goodness.'

Detective Constable Crosby suddenly stirred himself and asked the landscape designer if he'd got any professional rivals. Anthony Berra looked startled. 'Er . . . no,' he spluttered between coughs, 'well, none that I know of anyway.'

'Lucky you,' remarked the constable sardonically.

'I suppose that for the record I should say that there was a big London firm that also put in for the contract to restore the garden at Pelling Grange,' the landscape architect admitted, 'but seeing as I lived in the village anyway the Lingards awarded it to me.' He gave a boyish laugh. 'I suppose I came a bit less expensive too.'

'And lived on the spot,' added Haines generously. 'I'm sure that helps.'

'Also the Lingards know my future in-laws,' admitted Berra sheepishly, 'and I daresay that helps as well.'

'Quite so,' said Detective Inspector Sloan sedately. If there was one thing the police force did not usually suffer from it was nepotism. Most of the policemen whom he knew steered their sons and daughters away from serving in it as energetically as they could. And any such favours dispensed by the police could lead to a prison sentence.

For the policeman.

'It's not what you know, it's who you know,' chanted Crosby under his breath.

'Mustn't forget old Admiral Catterick at the Park,' put in Jack Haines. 'He's one of your clients too, isn't he, Anthony?'

'He is indeed,' agreed Anthony Berra warmly. 'He's a grand old boy. Been at sea all his life and doesn't know the first thing about gardens.'

'Leaves it all to you then, does he?' asked Crosby, an innocent expression on his face.

Berra said, 'Not quite, but I've been trying to get him to go over to labour-saving plants and so I'm mostly planting low-maintenance shrubs there. Unfortunately he's lost quite a lot of the more interesting plants that Jack here was bringing on for him too. There were some more in another greenhouse – one which doesn't appear to have had its doors left open either,' he added pointedly.

'Number three,' said Mandy Lamb before her employer could respond.

'This Miss Osgathorp you mentioned . . .' Sloan hoped

he was dropping this name into their talk with the same delicacy as a fisherman landing a dry fly on a trout stream. He wasn't sure if he had done.

'Fierce old biddy who gives talks,' responded Jack Haines immediately. 'Quite sound on orchids, actually.'

'Knows her stuff, Inspector,' agreed Berra. 'Bit of a battle-axe, though.'

'Well, she was the Dragon at the Gate for years and years, wasn't she?' put in Mandy Lamb from her desk at the front of the office.

'Come again?' said Crosby, looking meaningfully at a jar of coffee.

'She was Doctor Heddon's receptionist,' explained Mandy. 'Protecting the doctor from the patients.'

'I thought these days it was the patients who had to be protected from the doctor,' muttered Crosby, sotto voce, a few famous medical murders at the back of his mind.

'Last time I saw her,' said Berra ruefully, 'she told me exactly what I should be doing in the garden at the Grange. Thought I ought to be having a fernery there.'

'She is something of a pteridophile,' opined Jack Haines. 'She says ferns can manage without her while she's on her travels.'

'But I ask you, a nineteenth-century fernery in an old monastery garden!' Berra gave a short laugh. 'I can't see Charmian – Mrs Lingard, that is – wanting a fernery in her garden.'

'When exactly would that have been, sir?' asked Sloan. 'I mean, when did you last see Miss Osgathorp? Not Mrs Lingard.'

Anthony Berra frowned. 'It's a while since – it must

have been three or four weeks ago. Can't remember precisely when. I gave her a lift to the railway station. She was waiting at the bus stop but I was going into Berebury anyway and I picked her up and dropped her off at the sandwich shop two or three doors away from the station so she could buy something for the journey.'

'Going off on one of her famous trips, I suppose,' grunted Jack Haines.

'She did say where,' admitted Berra, 'but I can't remember where it was now. Not abroad, anyway. I do remember that much.'

With a fine show of indirection Detective Inspector Sloan took out his notebook and said, 'If you remember, Jack, we had promised to come back to interview your foreman . . .'

'I've told Russ,' interrupted Mandy Lamb. 'He's on his way over from the packing shed this minute.'

Anthony Berra stirred and said to Jack Haines that it was high time he was on his way and that he would pick up the plinth he wanted from the yard before he went over to see the admiral. He gave a valedictory wave of his hand to them all as he left whilst Detective Constable Crosby edged his way towards a corner of the office where there was a kettle and a row of mugs standing beside the coffee jar. He stood in front of these like a dog awaiting its dinner.

Jack Haines looked up as the door opened again. 'Ah, here's my foreman now,' he said. He turned to the newcomer. 'Good, I'm glad you've turned up, Russ. The police want to talk to you.'

'Any time,' said the man, shrugging his shoulders. He looked across at the two policemen and jerked his head in the general direction of the greenhouses. 'About this massacre, I suppose? Terrible, isn't it? There was weeks of work there – we'll never catch up, will we, boss? Not this season, anyway.'

Jack Haines shook his head and said sadly, 'No way, Russ. No way. Not now.'

'We need to know when you left here last night,' said Sloan to the foreman. 'It could be important.'

'Same time as usual,' said Russ Aqueel, shrugging his shoulders again. 'Must have been about half five. The others had knocked off prompt at five as normal but I came over to the office and signed off some timesheets for her ladysh . . . for Mandy here.'

Mandy Lamb tossed her head and gave a disdainful sniff in the background but said nothing.

'Then,' went on the foreman, 'I checked all the greenhouse doors and,' he added belligerently, 'I can tell you before you ask that they were all closed when I left. Every last one.'

'Sure, Russ,' put in Jack Haines uneasily.

'And number one properly watered and heated,' insisted the foreman, 'and steamy as it should be for the orchids. I checked the humidity in there before I locked the main gate and left.'

'In that case, sir,' said Sloan to the foreman, 'you won't have any objection to having your fingerprints taken by my constable here.'

The foreman thrust a grimy paw towards Crosby. 'Be my guest, mate.'

'After you've washed your hands if you don't mind,' said that worthy.

'There's a tap out the back,' said the man, turning. 'I'll be back in a minute.'

Detective Inspector Sloan sat back, saying casually to Jack Haines as if by way of conversation, 'You don't happen to know a man called Norman Potts, do you?'

The nurseryman visibly stiffened. 'Of course I know him, Inspector. He's my stepson,' he said between gritted teeth.

'Coffee?' said Mandy Lamb into the silence.

'I thought you'd never ask,' said Detective Constable Crosby.

'I had hoped I'd seen the last of him when his mother died,' growled Haines. 'But no such luck. He sued me for more of her estate than she'd left him. And lost.' He took a deep breath and asked, 'What's he been up to now?'

'Nothing that I know of,' said Sloan blandly. 'Should I?'

'Harassment, for starters,' said Haines. 'Came here wanting me to tell him where his wife – his ex-wife, that is – was.'

'And?'

'I told him to get lost.'

'And did he?' enquired Crosby with interest.

'Haven't seen him since,' growled Haines. 'Or wanted to, come to that. Like I said, I had hoped I'd seen the last of him. He's nothing but trouble as far as I'm concerned. And to his ex-wife too, from all accounts.'

'Tell me,' invited Sloan.

CHAPTER EIGHT

Detective Inspector Sloan had barely settled back at his own desk at Berebury Police Station before he was summoned to Superintendent Leeyes' office.

'Have you got anything else to add to this peculiar shopping list of yours, Sloan?' asked his superior officer testily.

'Not just yet, sir, thank you.' The reported iniquities of Norman Potts as a husband and stepson had slid easily off Jack Haines' tongue. They comprised a catalogue of domestic violence and included a threat heard by Haines to take revenge on a woman – and the legal profession – whom Potts swore to Jack Haines had stripped him of half his worldly wealth by way of a divorce.

Perhaps, noted Sloan, Norman Potts had already taken revenge too, on a nurseryman who had refused to play ball with a disgruntled stepson. The policeman didn't know that.

Not yet.

And Jack Haines certainly wasn't saying anything about that.

Not yet, either.

Sloan gave the superintendent an edited version of Norman Potts' reputation as represented by his stepfather and his former wife.

Leeyes grunted.

The detective inspector glanced down at his notebook. 'So, sir, I've put out a general call for this Norman Potts as a witness in connection with damage caused at the two nurseries.'

'In connection with,' Superintendent Leeyes rolled the phrase round his tongue appreciatively. 'I like it. Non-committal, and better than that old chestnut about helping the police with their enquiries.'

'Yes, sir.' In his time, Sloan been assaulted by men said to be helping the police with their enquiries and it hadn't been of any help at all.

'The press don't like anything non-committal,' said the superintendent with some satisfaction. 'By the way, Sloan, did I say that I've put you down for your personal development discussion for Friday morning?'

'Right, sir. Thank you, sir.' He swallowed. 'I'll make a note of that. And in the meantime,' Sloan plunged on, 'Crosby is checking on the other local nurseries to see if they've had any trouble too. Although,' he added realistically, 'I would have thought we'd have heard by now if they had.'

'Perhaps there's an orchid-hater at large,' suggested the superintendent. 'Can't stand 'em myself.'

'And in the matter of the MISSPER . . .' began Sloan. He wasn't very fond of orchids himself either but didn't think this was the moment to say so.

'I don't like Missing Persons cases, either,' trumpeted Leeyes immediately. 'Never have. In my experience they're neither fish, flesh nor good red herring. If you find them alive and kicking nobody gives you any credit for it. Worse than that, if they didn't want to be found in the first place, you get all the blame and if you find them dead, then you get all the blame too.'

'Up to a point, sir.' He coughed. 'There are one or two matters to be noted about Enid Osgathorp's absence, though. I think she is unlikely to have extended her holiday voluntarily since she had arranged to collect some orchids for a demonstration she had agreed to give tomorrow evening. They're still waiting for her to pick up at Jack Haines' place.'

Leeyes sniffed. 'They weren't caught up in the general orchid destruction then?'

'No.'

'I wonder why not?' he mused.

'I couldn't say, sir. Not at this stage.'

'And this battered wife . . .'

'We don't know that she was actually battered . . .' protested Sloan.

'Emotionally battered, then,' said Leeyes, who didn't normally admit to believing in the existence of the condition.

'Marilyn Potts,' said Sloan, 'was quite guarded about

him.' He hoped his personal development interview with the superintendent would be less challenging than this one.

'Do I understand that she's the one who is going to give this talk on orchids instead of the missing person?'

'That's what I was told, sir.'

'So you've haven't got very far, have you?'

'Not yet, sir,' said Sloan, biting down hard on any response at risk of jeopardising the aforementioned personal development interview.

The superintendent reached forward into his in-tray for a piece of paper. 'Well, you'll be pleased to hear that you've got your search warrant. You'd better go and have another look at Canonry Cottage before anyone else gets in there and muddies the waters.'

Mary Feakins reluctantly made the effort to heave herself out of her chair at the kitchen table of The Hollies where she had been taking a little rest between times. Then she walked towards the sink belatedly to begin washing up the breakfast dishes. She hadn't been able to face doing them earlier, bending over being a sure invitation to nausea. Today her routine domestic activities had been disturbed not only by the bout of morning sickness that had come on first thing but by their visits to the plant nursery and their lawyer in Berebury.

Until she reached the kitchen sink the only thoughts in her mind had been an imaginary confrontation with her doctor in which she was challenging him in the matter of morning sickness and his promises that hyperemesis gravida would not in the nature of things last for much longer.

She stood at the sink for a moment or two, hesitating while wondering whether bending over it now would still bring about another wave of sickness. There was a window above the sink and she allowed her glance to stray outside and into the back garden while she steadied herself against the working surface and tried to suppress the rising feeling of sickness. What she could see there was an unexpected pyramid of white smoke that suddenly billowed out into a cloud that obscured her view from the window. Just as quickly the smoke dispersed and she was able to take a second look and saw that it was rising from a burning pile of rubbish. Beside it was the figure of her husband who appeared to be furiously piling more and more things on the bonfire.

The washing up abandoned, she opened the back door and sailed across the garden towards the bonfire. 'Benedict Feakins, what on earth do you think you're doing out here?'

'Just having a simple bonfire,' he said, poking something under a pile of leaves. 'Nothing more, nothing less.'

'But look at what you're putting on it.' She frowned. 'That looks like a hairbrush to me.'

'It is,' he said, his back still bent almost double.

'And surely that's a toothbrush, isn't it?'

'Yes. It's only some of Dad's old things, that's all.' Benedict kept his head down and muttered, 'I cleared out his bedroom this morning. Everything there reminded me of him too much.'

She stared at him and then said in a softer tone, 'I didn't think you minded losing him so much as that.'

'Well, I did,' he mumbled, trying to straighten up, 'and that's all there is to it.'

'Sorry.' Mary Feakins stepped back a pace.

'I'm getting rid of all Dad's clothes too,' he said, a rising note in his voice. 'I just can't stand seeing all his things everywhere. They're going to the charity shop first thing tomorrow morning.'

'I understand,' she said, all womanly sympathy now.

'I can't explain the feeling,' he said in a choked voice. 'It came over me like a tidal wave yesterday and made me feel quite wretched.'

'There's lots of things that can't be explained,' said his wife cheerfully. 'Like my pica gravidarum.' From quite early on in her pregnancy, Mary Feakins had developed a marked predilection for cold herring. 'The doctor tells me that it's quite common.'

'Your craving fetishes are quite different, Mary,' he said seriously. 'This isn't like eating coal. It's more like . . . oh, I don't know that I can put it into words.'

'Don't even try,' she said kindly. 'Look here, I'll go back indoors and let you get on with it.'

'Bless you,' he said and obviously meant it.

Mary was bent over the sink again and was lowering some dirty plates into it when she was struck by a sudden thought. Wiping her soapy hands on a towel, she left the sink and went into their sitting room. Standing on the sofa table there was a studio photograph of her late father-in-law set in a silver frame. Lifting it carefully, she carried it out of the room and upstairs. Then she laid it safely under some spare sheets inside the linen cupboard. Benedict Feakins never opened the doors of the linen cupboard.

She was back at the kitchen sink in no time at all. Minutes later, a new and different thought in her mind now, she went back to the sitting room. The first time she had been concentrating on the photograph of her father-in-law but now she was looking for something that wasn't there but had been yesterday.

The urn containing Benedict's father's cremated ashes which were awaiting burial in Pelling churchyard was missing.

Detective Constable Crosby came into Detective Inspector Sloan's office and laid his notebook down on the desk. 'I've done the rounds of the other nurseries, sir, like you said. Seen the lot of them and none of them have had their greenhouse doors left open last night or at any other time. Joe Girdler hasn't got any greenhouses, anyway. Only roses. Rows and rows of them. Out of doors.'

'Him, I know,' said Sloan, quondam rosarian.

'The Leanaig brothers have got lots of greenhouses but no orchids and nothing at all happened at their place last night,' said Crosby. He suddenly realised that he needed to consult his notebook again and reached across Sloan's desk to retrieve it. 'Excuse me, sir.' He flicked over a page or two. 'Staple St James Nurseries only do hardy plants and the Berebury Garden Centre has greenhouses galore although only one with orchids in. They say they had no trouble last night but . . .' He fell silent.

'But?' prompted Sloan. In the last analysis a policeman relied on his sense of smell – that indefinable feeling that things weren't what they should be – a feeling that couldn't be put into words and some held couldn't be taught. It was something he was waiting to see if Detective Constable Crosby had.

'But their head honcho, Bob Steele, wasn't happy with the police coming there.' He wrinkled his nose. 'I could tell. He was edgy. Demanded to know why we'd come to see him before I could get a word in. Not a happy bunny.'

'Did you ask him if he knew Norman Potts?' Perhaps, after all, Crosby was developing that sense of smell. Aggressive interviewees always had an agenda of their own. Idly, Sloan wondered what it could be with Bob Steele.

The constable nodded. 'I did, like you said, sir. He told me he'd heard the name, that's all. He was quite cagey about it.'

'Or Capstan Purlieu Plants?'

'He knew them all right. Real specialists, he called the two women. Didn't sound as if he particularly liked them, though, or was bothered about them as competitors.' Crosby scratched his head. 'Called 'em small fry.'

'And Jack Haines and his nursery at Pelling?' said Sloan, deciding that it didn't sound as if the great gardening Goliath that was the Berebury Garden Centre was all that worried about the little David of the gardening world that was Capstan Purlieu Plants either. 'What did he say about him?'

'Bob Steele said he knew him too. He went a bit quiet when I started asking him a bit more about Jack Haines and he clammed up straightaway. He said he didn't know all that much more about either Haines or his nursery except in the way of trade.'

'And Enid Osgathorp?'

'Said he'd never heard of her but that there were a lot of old lady gardeners about, gardening being the new sex, and he couldn't be expected to know them all or t'other from which, could he?'

Detective Inspector Sloan lifted a sheet of paper off his desk. 'I can tell you that there is someone who has heard of her, Crosby. The receptionist at a hotel in the wilds of Carmarthenshire. She got in touch with us after getting our general request. She says they had been expecting a Miss Enid Osgathorp of Pelling to arrive there three weeks ago. She'd made the booking about a couple of months ago for a fortnight's stay, full board, earlier this month. She never showed up at their hotel, though.' Sloan read out from the piece of paper. 'The Meadgrove Park Country House Hotel.'

'Sounds posh, sir.'

'It's not bad,' said Sloan warmly, quoting from the paper in front of him. 'Five star, set in ten acres of landscape, extensive gardens, notable cuisine, fine wines and good fishing. You name it and it seems the Meadgrove Park Country House Hotel would appear to have it.'

'Does herself well, then, this Miss Osgathorp, when she's not at home,' concluded Crosby, whose landlady was notable for her cheese-paring.

'It would have set her back a good bit more than your average bed and breakfast,' agreed Detective Inspector Sloan. Holidays in the Sloan household usually had to be traded against the redecoration of the sitting room or saving for the long overdue replacement of the family car.

Crosby frowned. 'There was nothing very grand about that bungalow of hers in Pelling, though, was there, sir?

Looked very ordinary from the outside to me.' He sniffed. 'And on the small side too.'

'Perhaps,' said Sloan, rising to his feet, 'we shall find it very different from the inside. Let's go and see for ourselves now we've got the search warrant.'

Canonry Cottage, though, was as ordinary on the inside as it had been on the outside. It was furnished in the simple, spare style that had been popular forty years before and was – save for a light scattering of dust on the flat surfaces equating to three weeks without dusting – very neat and clean. Such ornaments as there were could only be described as tourist trophies – and that kindly.

The two policemen had entered with care aided by a set of keys only allowed out of the police station on a very secure basis, the distinction between master keys and skeleton ones being only a semantic one. They noted again the postal delivery that had been pushed back over the hall carpet when the door had been opened before. Sloan peered down at a postmark. 'Someone didn't come in here until almost a week after the missing person is said to have left,' he said, straightening up again, frowning. 'That's very odd.'

Detective Constable Crosby screwed up his face in thought. 'Then whoever came in had plenty of time, didn't they, sir, if they thought they had another week before she was due back home?'

'Or if they knew she wasn't ever coming back,' said Sloan softly. 'Had you thought about that, Crosby?'

'But . . .'

'That is, if she ever went away and they knew that too,'

said Sloan soberly. 'Remember Crosby, in police work all eventualities always have to be considered.'

'But two people saw her leave,' objected the constable. 'The woman next door and that gardener guy.'

'Two people said they saw her leave,' Sloan reminded him, 'which is something quite different. Better make quite sure she's not upstairs, Crosby.'

'Yes, sir,' said Crosby stolidly, dutifully peeling off and doing as he was bid.

'And watch where you're standing when you come back,' called Sloan after him. 'We know someone's been in and out of here through that back window as well as the front door and we need to take some carpet prints.'

'Yes, sir,' repeated Crosby. After a moment he said 'Why didn't that one go out of the front door instead?'

'Because, Crosby, the front door has a mortice lock. Presumably the missing person locked it behind her when she left and took the key with her.'

'But someone else came in and out with it,' said the constable, 'didn't they, sir?'

'It looks very much like it,' said Sloan, liking the situation less and less. 'Now, get upstairs, Crosby.'

Detective Inspector Sloan, himself sticking to the outer edges of the carpet, made first for a little bureau in the corner of the sitting room. It was unlocked. Donning rubber gloves and prising its lid open without leaving his own fingerprints on the wooden flap, he examined its contents carefully. Inside were a series of pigeon-holes and a little drawer. This drawer, too, was unlocked. It contained a few photographs of a child – one of which had 'Me at four' written on the back – and a locket. This had a lock of hair in it. The words 'Little Lucy Locket' welled into Sloan's mind from his sister's infancy – before he started to make notes.

'Anything there, sir?' asked Crosby, bringing Sloan's attention back to the matter in hand. 'Nothing to speak of upstairs except that I would say someone's had a good rummage through the wardrobe, everything else being neat and that a bit topsy-turvy. If that's where she kept her gin, it's gone.'

'Nothing out of the ordinary here, either,' said Sloan, replacing bundles of carefully tied domestic accounts in their pigeon holes one by one, 'except that I think someone's been looking for a secret drawer in here. Someone who didn't know about secret drawers in desks.'

Detective Constable Crosby, who obviously didn't know anything about them either, leant over Sloan's shoulder for a better look. 'Made a bit of a mess of the wood, didn't he, sir?' he observed. 'All those scratches . . .'

'Whoever it was brought a screwdriver with him – I expect he thought the bureau might be locked – but it didn't get him anywhere because I should say this bit of modern furniture hasn't got a secret compartment of any sort. They don't make 'em liked they used to,' said Sloan and stopped. He would have to be more careful about expressing that sort of sentiment, afraid that he was beginning to sound like the superintendent.

'So, sir,' said Crosby, screwing up his forehead into a prodigious frown, 'that means that someone's been in here just looking for something not someone.' His expression brightened. 'Unless the old lady's been abducted.'

'And perhaps not finding anything,' announced Sloan presently, after leafing through the last of the contents of the pigeonholes, 'although I should say that they – whoever they are – have probably been all through this bureau. There's nothing but receipted household bills and plant stuff in here, though some of the bundles have been put back upside down. Oh, and there are a couple of receipts for deposits for two pricey foreign holidays this summer. Very pricey indeed.'

'Some people have all the luck,' said the constable, who was saving up to go to the motor-racing at Spa-Francorchamps.

'We don't know, though, whether the intruders had any luck or not,' mused Detective Inspector Sloan, moving away from the bureau. 'They might well have found what they were looking for and taken it away. Either of them.'

'Or both,' said Crosby.

Sloan nodded absently as he paused at a framed photograph on the mantelshelf. It was of a group on a platform where a clergyman was presenting a bouquet and an envelope to a dumpy late middle-aged woman who was holding out one hand to receive them and shaking the clergyman's hand with the other. The words 'Happy Retirement, Miss Osgathorp' could be picked out on a banner at the back of the platform.

'Get on with circulating copies of the picture of this woman getting the presentation, Crosby,' commanded Sloan, picking up the photograph, 'and chase the railway people for a sight of their CCTV record of people entering Berebury station the day she was meant to be catching a train there now we've got a picture to go on.'

'When exactly would that have been, sir?' the constable asked, searching for a pen. 'Do we know?'

'We do. Norah, the woman next door, told us, remember? It was the day after Mrs Beddowes, the rector's wife, committed suicide. You can find that out quite easily.' Sloan paused and took another look at the man in the clerical collar in the photograph making the presentation. 'And that presumably is Mr Beddowes, the rector, widower of the deceased. We might have a word with him in due course. And with that landscape designer fellow – Anthony Berra – again. He seems to have been the last person to see Enid Osgathorp alive.'

'So far,' said Crosby lugubriously.

CHAPTER NINE

'Not much luck with those replacements, boss,' said Russ Aqueel, his foreman, leading Jack Haines out to the truck standing in the yard. 'A bit of this and that, that's all. Nothing like enough to replace what's been lost, though.' He shrugged his shoulders. 'As for keeping it all quiet, it's a laugh. The Leanaig boys guessed something was up straightaway when they saw what it was we were looking for and the people at Staple St James had heard already over the grapevine . . .'

'Some grapevine,' commented Haines richly.

'So I told Bob Steele at the Berebury Garden Centre anyway.' He studied his employer's face. 'I hope that's OK?'

'It's OK, Russ,' said Jack Haines quietly. 'I reckoned word would get around pretty quickly.'

'Bound to,' said the foreman, pausing.

'It's not every day that someone sabotages a firm's working stock, is it, Russ?' said Haines, giving the man a very straight look.

'Definitely not,' said Russ.

'The plants we were wanting . . .' prompted Haines.

'Bob Steele at the Berebury Garden Centre didn't have anything we wanted.'

'I didn't think he would have,' said Haines almost to himself. 'Not him.'

'But he did say that he had run out of Erysimum Bowles Mauve and if we had any to spare could I drop them over to him,' said the foreman.

'Sure,' said Haines dully.

Russ shot him a quizzical glance before going on. 'The Leanaig boys had quite a bit that would do for us and so did Staple St James Nurseries but both of them only had some of the things we lost – not all of them.'

Haines sighed. 'That figures. Anthony Berra was very precise. That's part of the problem.'

'I'd call him a right fusspot myself,' muttered the foreman.

'But none of them has had any trouble themselves, have they?' asked Haines quickly.

'Not that they said or I saw,' replied the foreman. 'I guess that it's just us.'

That it wasn't just Jack Haines who had had trouble overnight was not borne in upon him until Marilyn Potts arrived at his nursery.

Jack Haines had made his way back to his office deep in thought. He had only just sat down and Mandy Lamb had only just automatically put the kettle on when she looked out of the window and suddenly said, 'Here comes trouble . . .'

'There can't be any more trouble,' said Jack Haines, staying where he was.

'Have a look for yourself,' said his secretary.

He lumbered to his feet and went to the window. 'I don't believe it. Not her. I thought we'd seen the last of her.'

'Well, you haven't,' said Mandy Lamb, not without a certain relish.

'What does she want, do you suppose?'

'Half your worldly wealth, I expect,' she said pertly. 'That was what Norman wanted, wasn't it?'

'You don't have to tell me that,' he said, turning back to his chair. 'And it's not quite true anyway – what he wanted was all of his mother's worldly wealth, not half of mine.'

'Hello, Jack,' Marilyn Potts said cautiously, putting her head half way round the office door.

'Long time, no see,' said Jack Haines.

'I suppose I'd better throw my hat in first,' she grimaced, 'and see what happens to it.'

'No need for that,' he said gruffly. 'That's unless you've brought that no-good ex-husband of yours with you.'

'God forbid,' responded Marilyn Potts explosively. 'I've had enough trouble with Norman to last me a lifetime, thank you.'

'Me too,' grunted Jack.

'No, I've come to pick up Enid Osgathorp's orchids – I'm standing in for her at a talk she was supposed to be giving over at Staple St James tomorrow night because she seems to have gone walkabout.'

'So what's happened to our Miss Osgathorp, then?' asked Jack.

'No one knows. She'll turn up sooner or later I expect like the proverbial bad penny. She won't be happy when she hears what's happened to all my infant orchids, that's for sure . . . they're all dead and she reckons she's a bit of an orchid fancier.'

'Yours too?' Jack Haines' eyebrows shot up. 'God Almighty.'

Marilyn Potts launched into a histrionic account of the devastation at the nursery at Capstan Purlieu.

'Every last orchid,' declared Marilyn bitterly. 'There was the devil of a frost last night.'

'Don't I know it,' said Haines savagely. He peered at her closely. 'But let me ask you something else, Marilyn. Do you know Bob Steele at the Berebury Garden Centre?'

'Don't be silly, Jack. Of course, I do.'

'Has he been over to your place recently?'

She frowned. 'I think Anna said that he'd called round to pick up some Aeschymanthus a couple of weeks back. Said he'd run out of Mona Lisa.' She looked at him suspiciously. 'Why do you ask?'

'Nothing. I just wondered.'

'You lie, Jack.'

'I suppose I do,' he admitted. 'You see rumour has it that Bob Steele has plans to go in for orchids himself.'

'Rumours aren't everything.'

'He made an excuse to come over here to pick up some stock he didn't need.'

'He might have really wanted the Aeschymanthus from us,' she said doubtfully.

'He might,' agreed Haines, 'but I wondered if he was really casing the joints – yours and mine.'

'Whatever for?'

'Seeing how he could undermine the opposition, perhaps.'

Her voice rose to a high doh. 'Are you suggesting Bob Steele targeted our orchids?'

'He could have done . . .'

Marilyn Potts took a deep breath and drew herself up to her full height. 'I know you won't want to do anything of the sort but let's face it, Jack, the only person we know who hates both of us enough to wreak real damage on the pair of us is Norman Potts.' She swallowed. 'And you know that as well as I do so don't pretend that you don't because it won't wash.'

'If we look sharp,' said Detective Inspector Sloan, clambering into the police car, 'we might just be able to see those other two customers of Jack Haines who've lost their plants before we get back to the station.' He latched his seat belt into place, adding 'And that, I must remind you, Crosby, doesn't amount to a licence to kill.'

'No, sir. Of course not, sir.' The constable sounded injured.

'The Park at Pelling first,' decided Sloan. 'We'll see what the Navy has to say.'

The Navy in the person of Rear Admiral Waldo Catterick, R.N., retired, and as bald as a billiard ball, thought that there was altogether too much vandalism about everywhere these days and had the policemen seen the graffiti on the cricket pavilion?

'Not yet,' said Sloan ambiguously.

'Deplorable. Don't know what the world is coming to. Come along in anyway.'

'We're checking up on some unexplained losses at Jack Haines' nursery, including yours,' explained Sloan as they followed him down a corridor, the old gentleman's right leg giving an odd involuntary little kick forward as he walked. 'And out at Capstan Purlieu too.'

Sitting the two policemen down in a small morning room overlooking a lawn, the admiral leant forward and asked what exactly he could do for them.

Detective Inspector Sloan regarded the wizened face opposite him, made to seem smaller and older somehow by a nose so depressed as not to have a bridge. 'We're trying to make sure, sir, that there isn't anyone out there with a grudge against gardeners in general or any of Jack Haines' or Capstan Purlieu's customers in particular and I have been given to understand you are one of them.'

The admiral took the question seriously and said in a curiously high-pitched voice, 'None that I am aware of but as you will know yourself, Inspector, if you've ever been in command, you're bound to have upset somebody at some time or other. You can't run a tight ship without doing that.'

'Put him in the scuppers until he's sober,' chanted Crosby under his breath.

'Comes with the job,' said the admiral, who did not appear to have heard this.

It came with the police job too. Detective Inspector Sloan had upset a good many bad men in his time and said so.

'You're not in the Service to make friends,' barked Waldo Catterick in his best quarter-deck manner, 'although of course you do. Old shipmates and all that.' He looked up with a distinctly rheumy eye at the photographs of ships' companies that adorned the walls of the room. 'Most of them are dead now.'

You weren't in the police force to make friends either, thought Sloan to himself. On the contrary, often enough, it was in the nature of police work that enemies always outnumbered friends. 'We're also,' the detective inspector went on almost conversationally, 'looking into the disappearance of an old lady from the village. A Miss Enid Osgathorp. Do you know her?'

The admiral stiffened perceptibly, his back suddenly becoming ramrod straight. 'She used to work at the doctor's,' he said frostily, in tones that would have paralysed the lower deck, 'and that's all I can tell you about the woman.'

His body language, though, was saying something quite different to the police inspector, a man perforce experienced in these matters. Whether it was all he could say or not, the admiral refused to be drawn any further on Enid Maude Osgathorp. Perhaps, thought Sloan, a boyhood reader of Bulldog Drummond and similar clubland heroes, it wasn't done then to mention a lady's name in the Wardroom any more than it was in an Army Mess. He couldn't begin to think what today's young women would make of that.

Detective Inspector Sloan came away from Pelling Park with the uneasy feeling that he had missed something. Oddly enough he was sure it was nothing to do with the missing person but try as he might he couldn't put his finger on what it was that was eluding him.

'I expect he got them to walk the plank as well,' said Crosby as they left the Park.

'There's one thing for sure,' said Sloan, 'and that's that our missing person is not the flavour of the month. I think, Crosby, this is something we should be looking into. I wonder why the admiral didn't like her.' He tucked the fact away in the back of his mind for further consideration.

It was Mary Feakins who answered the doorbell at The Hollies, more puzzled than alarmed by a visit from the police. 'Benedict? Yes, he's here. He's off work with a bad back just now.' She led the way through to the kitchen where her husband was sitting uncomfortably wedged in a Windsor chair, his back cushioned against a hot-water bottle.

If his wife had been calm enough as Detective Inspector Sloan and Detective Constable Crosby arrived, Benedict Feakins certainly wasn't. He started to struggle to his feet. 'Police?' he echoed. 'What? Why?'

'Routine enquiry, sir,' said Sloan comfortably.

Feakins subsided back into his chair. 'What about?'

'I understand you had some plants being grown for you by Jack Haines,' said Sloan.

'Yes,' he agreed warily. 'But I changed my mind about them and I told Jack I didn't want them any more. To be quite honest . . .'

'Always a good idea,' said Crosby under his breath.

'I didn't think I – that is, we – could afford them after all.'

116

'Mortgage trouble, sir?' said Detective Inspector Sloan sympathetically. The state of their mortgage was a monthly topic with his wife in his own home.

Benedict Feakins shook his head. 'No, not that. I inherited this house when my father died but even so we're finding the upkeep's quite a struggle. I did tell Jack Haines that I'd still have the shrubs I'd ordered, though, and he seemed to be all right with that.'

'For the border in the front garden,' explained Mary Feakins. 'It was digging that up to get ready for them that did for Benedict's back.'

'We saw he'd been at it in the way in,' remarked Crosby conversationally. 'Didn't get very far, did you, sir?'

'I had to give after a bit,' admitted Benedict Feakins. 'I did too much at one go. I've been bent like a hoop ever since.'

'Easily done,' said Sloan, who grew roses because a policeman could tend them in small pockets of time and leave them at short notice when summoned to attend to malfeasance anywhere in 'F' Division. 'I see you've just had a bonfire too,' he remarked, looking out of the kitchen window and observing wisps of smoke rising at the bottom of garden. 'Back not too bad for that, then, sir?'

Feakins flushed and mumbled something about having some things to burn.

Mary Feakins cast her husband a sympathetic wifely look and then said, 'Inspector, I must explain that my husband was getting rid of some personal things of his late father's. He's only just lost him and he was finding it very distressing to have them still around and reminding

117

him of his recent loss so he decided to get rid of them.'

'Quite so,' said Detective Inspector Sloan. He rose as if to leave, something every policeman knew caused the person being interviewed to lower their guard. 'Well, since we don't at this time know why Jack Haines' greenhouses were damaged, we're just checking that none of his customers with plants in them had any personal enemies.'

The expression on Benedict Feakins' face was one of comic relief. 'Inspector,' he said solemnly, 'you can put me down as a latter-day Kim.'

'Sir?'

'Kipling's Little Friend of All the World.'

'Really, sir?' said Sloan. He'd always found that author's poem 'If' set an impossible standard of male behaviour and – worse – made a man feel a failure if he didn't measure up to it.

Crosby merely looked sceptical.

Benedict Feakins turned to his wife. 'That's right, darling, isn't it?'

'I don't think we're very popular with the butcher, the baker and the candlestick-maker just now,' she said obliquely.

Benedict turned back to the two policemen. 'As I said, we're finding living here a bit expensive, Inspector, that's all.'

Sloan nodded. 'Thank you, sir. We'll be on our way, then. Come along, Crosby.' He made another move to leave, paused and then he said casually, 'By the way, we're also quite concerned about someone who's gone missing from Pelling. An Enid Osgathorp. Did you know her?'

There was another change in the man's demeanour. He

sank back in his chair and seemed somehow diminished. 'Oh, yes, Inspector,' Benedict replied in a hollow voice. 'I knew her all right. She's been around in Pelling a long time. She worked at the doctor's.'

'Miss Osgathorp?' said Mary Feakins, coming to life suddenly. 'Wasn't she that odd old woman who came to see you one evening a while ago, Benedict?' She wrinkled her nose. 'I didn't really like her.'

Her husband moistened his lips and essayed a weak smile. 'Yes, that's her.'

'When would that have been exactly, sir?' asked Sloan.

'Oh, weeks ago now, Inspector,' he said.

'Don't you remember, darling?' interjected Mary Feakins eagerly. 'It was just before she went away.' She turned to the two policemen. 'She said she was going off on holiday somewhere the next morning and needed to see Benedict before she left. Quite insistent, she was.'

Her husband gave her a look of such great malevolence that she had never seen on his face before. It quite frightened her and she recoiled as if she had been stung.

'Really, sir?' said Sloan, seeing this look too, and turning back. 'Can you tell us anything more?'

'What do you mean?' he asked.

'Like why she came to see you, sir.'

He flushed. 'She came to remind me of something, that's all. And I hadn't forgotten anyway.'

A rapid change of subject was just another of the techniques that his old Station Sergeant had taught Sloan about questioning. He said now, 'Would you happen to know a Norman Potts by any chance, sir?'

Feakins looked blank. 'No. Why?'

119

'Another routine enquiry, sir,' said that officer blandly. 'That's all. Thank you, sir. We'll be off now.'

Crosby paused on their way out of the garden at The Hollies and looked at the newly dug earth. 'Long enough for a grave,' he observed, 'but not wide enough or deep enough.'

Detective Inspector Sloan was concentrating on something quite different. 'When we get back, Crosby, remind me to think of a legal way we could get a good look at what's in that bonfire. Remember, Benedict Feakins is someone else who knew that Enid Osgathorp was going to be away.'

'Someone else?' asked Crosby who hadn't been paying attention. 'Oh, yes. That gardener fellow who took her to the station – Anthony Berra.'

'And we really need to find out what it was that young man Feakins was burning on that bonfire, the one he got so agitated about and wasn't in too much pain to build.'

'He wasn't all that happy when his wife started talking about Enid Osgathorp either,' contributed Crosby. 'I could see that.'

'So,' said Sloan, 'we're just going to seem to drive away and lie up out of sight of the house and keep an eye on what our Benedict Feakins does next.'

What Benedict Feakins did next was to hobble out of his house at speed into the back garden and rake over the embers of the bonfire very vigorously indeed.

CHAPTER TEN

The Reverend Tobias Beddowes, rector of Pelling, received the two policemen in his study at the rectory there with nothing beyond a courteous greeting and a hasty warning not to fall over a bicycle aslant in the hall. The room was untidy to the point of disorder, the clergyman having to remove piles of books and papers from both chairs before the others could sit down.

'I apologise for the muddle,' he said, looking helplessly round the room, 'but I'm on my own with the two younger children now and things aren't getting done.'

'We were sorry to hear about the loss of your wife,' said Detective Inspector Sloan formally, grasping a conversational nettle ducked by most of his parishioners.

The rector shook his head. 'A very sad business. My elder daughter will be back soon, though, and that will help. She's very good. She'll see to things.'

'Been away, has she?' asked Crosby insouciantly.

'Honeymoon,' explained Tobias Beddowes briefly. 'Naturally, she and her husband couldn't get away straightaway after the wedding ceremony.'

'Naturally?' echoed Crosby as his superior officer stirred uneasily.

'Naturally there had to be an inquest,' sighed Beddowes. 'My dear wife . . . she died just before the wedding, you see. It was all too much for her, you know. The arrangements and the expense and all that just got on top of her.' He took a deep breath and said, 'Now, what was it you wanted to see me about, gentlemen?'

'It's a photograph,' said Detective Inspector Sloan, handing over the one he had abstracted from Canonry Cottage. 'I hope it won't distress you if your wife is on it too.'

The rector scanned the photograph of the presentation to Enid Osgathorp proffered by Detective Inspector Sloan and shook his head. 'No, my wife isn't on this. She didn't come with me that evening.' He lifted his head as if doing so was an effort and asked what it was they wanted him to tell them about the photograph.

'Miss Enid Osgathorp – is that her, shaking your hand?' asked Sloan.

'Yes indeed, Inspector, I can confirm that that is a picture of Enid Osgathorp taken in the village hall when she retired two or three years ago. She gave up work a little early because old Doctor Heddon had died and she didn't want to start afresh with anyone else, which is quite understandable. She had been with him for a very long time.' He went on looking at the photograph. 'Might I ask why you want to know?'

'Enid Osgathorp would appear to be missing from her home,' said Detective Inspector Sloan.

'Really? She does go away a lot of course, you know,' said the clergyman. 'She's become quite a traveller since she retired. I expect she'll be back soon.'

'She hasn't arrived at her destination,' said Sloan.

'Or left word,' added Crosby unnecessarily.

The rector raised his eyebrows. 'I don't think she would have left word anyway. She never said much about where she was going. She was always someone who kept herself to herself. A very private person, you might say.'

Detective Inspector Sloan, experienced policeman that he was, much preferred people who did not keep themselves to themselves. It could make detection more difficult.

'As to why she hasn't arrived,' said the clergyman, 'I'm afraid I can't help you. I think,' he added, smiling faintly, 'it would be fair to describe her as her own woman.'

'That, Crosby,' remarked Sloan as they walked away from the rectory and back to the car, 'usually means that the person they have in mind does what they like when they like.'

'Yes, sir, I'm sure.'

'Right, Crosby, go ahead and get some copies of that picture blown up and see what the sandwich shop has to say.'

'I can guess,' said the constable gloomily, 'that they serve dozens of old ladies every day . . .'

'Or,' Sloan completed the litany for him, 'that they can't remember yesterday, let alone three weeks ago.'

'That's right,' said Crosby.

'Don't forget we've got to find Norman Potts too. We'll try somewhere near the Railway Tavern pub in Berebury, down by the viaduct, first. That's where his wife thought he was living.'

'No, sir, I won't forget. He sounds a right bounder to me and the sooner we've got him, the better.'

'A policeman should not make judgements too early in an investigation,' Sloan reminded him. 'A prejudiced mind,' he added sententiously, 'is no good to an officer, and don't you forget it. Juries don't like it either. And in case you don't know it, they can detect a police prejudice half a mile away.'

'I won't forget, sir.' Crosby's face assumed an expression more commonly found on those of schoolboys reprimanded by their schoolteachers.

'And after we've started to look for the aforementioned Norman Potts, Crosby, you can check up with the bus company about how many tickets they sold on the ten to ten bus from Pelling into Berebury that morning.'

'But Enid Osgathorp didn't catch the bus, sir.'

'So it has been said by Anthony Berra,' pointed out Sloan, 'but we don't have any other witnesses to this yet. But anyone waiting at the bus stop might have seen or spoken to her and perhaps seen her being given a lift. Detection, Crosby, is largely a matter of checking every single thing. Remember that.' Sloan didn't know whether or not his attempts to train the constable in proper procedures would help in his own appraisal or not but there was no harm in trying. Surely Brownie points of any sort would help? On the other hand, on a bad day the superintendent was quite capable of blaming him for not catching Jack the Ripper.

'Yes, sir.'

'And find out how many of those at the bus stop used an old person's bus pass. Any other oldies there would have known Enid Osgathorp for sure.' He paused. 'Come to think of it, the whole village would know her if she had worked for the doctor.'

'Yes, sir.'

'Then, Crosby, you can see how far the railway people have got digging out their CCTV cassettes for us and how long they'll be about it.'

'They'll be semi-fast, I expect, sir.'

'Come again?'

'That's what they call their slow trains,' said Crosby, switching on the car engine.

'What you have to do, Sloan,' said the superintendent crisply 'is to make up your mind exactly what you're trying to do out at Pelling.'

'Yes, sir,' said Sloan, reminding himself that the upside of being back at the police station was the canteen there and he was hungry. The downside did not dare speak its name.

'The "in word" if I remember correctly,' the superintendent added, heavily sarcastic, since the idea that he would remember anything incorrectly was supposed to be thought risible, 'is prioritise. I just call it making up your mind.'

'Yes, sir,' said Sloan cautiously.

'Well?'

'I have. Made up my mind, I mean.' The detective inspector reminded himself to be careful with his choice of words. The superintendent was unpredictable at the best of times. 'The damage to the contents of the greenhouses out there and at Capstan Purlieu has been noted and I have been interviewing all those customers whose plants might have been targeted, but Enid Maude Osgathorp is definitely a missing person and perhaps at risk. Especially as some person or persons unknown would seem to have been in her cottage at some time,' he added carefully, 'and only presumably when she wasn't there.'

'Someone looking for something,' pronounced Leeyes swiftly.

'Or her,' said Sloan soberly.

'Or her,' agreed Leeyes.

'Twice,' said Sloan.

'You're not very clear, Sloan,' complained Leeyes.

'Presumably two people looking for something, sir,' said Sloan. 'But it would seem at different times and perhaps looking for different things. I don't know what. I think that both entries were probably effected after Enid Osgathorp had left but I don't know that either.'

'Ah, you've got a date for that, have you?'

'And her photograph, which we shall now be circulating,' said Sloan. 'We're on our way next to interview the last person known to have seen her and then I want to find out a bit more about a man called Benedict Feakins.'

'Leaving no stone unturned, Sloan, that's what I like to hear. Don't forget those damaged plants in the greenhouses out that way, even so. I don't like the sound of them. Not your run-of-the-mill damage.'

'I won't, sir.' He was tempted to say that that particular

126

problem could be downgraded since no one was at risk but decided against it. Tackling vandalism was always high on the superintendent's list of police priorities and so he definitely wouldn't want that put on the back-burner. The public probably found vandalism more threatening than the odd missing elderly party: they – and the newspapers – were certainly more vocal about it. 'I've got Crosby seeking the whereabouts of a man with a possible grudge about at least one of the parties concerned and the Scenes of Crime people are going over Canonry Cottage as we speak.'

'You have good reasons for saying all this, I take it?' said the superintendent, adding waspishly, 'Such as evidence.'

'I have, sir. Entry to Enid Osgathorp's cottage was clearly effected by two different methods – a key and a broken window.'

'So what stage are you at?' asked Leeyes, changing tack with disconcerting speed.

'Waiting for a report from the Scenes of Crime people,' Sloan answered automatically – and immediately regretted his speedy response. He should have taken more trouble with it: the superintendent favoured the considered reply. Being a bit late back with him was definitely preferable to an instant response.

'And what else?' his superior officer snapped.

'Replies to our enquiries, sir,' said Sloan, reaching for his notebook, 'including . . .'

'I don't want every last detail, Sloan,' he said testily, changing tack once again. 'Fill me in when you've got something concrete to report. I've got a meeting with the

Assistant Chief Constable about staffing before I can go home.'

Retreating as speedily as he could, Detective Inspector Sloan achieved his own office with relief. Crosby was waiting for him there.

'I've tracked Norman Potts down, sir,' he said. 'It wasn't difficult. He's listed as living just where his wife . . .'

'His ex-wife,' Sloan corrected him.

'Where his ex-wife said he would be, and that garden design bloke you wanted to talk to – the one who gave the missing party a lift into Berebury – he's over at Pelling Grange with his customers there just now . . .'

'I think he prefers to think of them as clients,' murmured Sloan, 'but never mind. Let's tackle him at his place of work first. I'd rather like to take a look at the garden at the Grange myself. It sounds interesting.'

Not only was Anthony Berra at Pelling Grange but his employers were in the garden with him when the two policemen arrived there. He was standing in the middle of a large flower bed that was empty save for a heavy plinth that he was lugging from place to place with some difficulty.

'Further to the right, Anthony,' called out Mrs Lingard, turning to the two visitors and saying plaintively, 'he will go on about the Golden Mean whatever that is.' She slipped effortlessly into hostess role as soon as Sloan explained his and Crosby's presence, while Anthony Berra lowered the plinth back where he had wanted it in the first place.

Charmian Lingard was now dressed in a suit of a mixture of light brown and blue coloured material, the lapels of the jacket of which hung so artfully that even Christopher Dennis Sloan, working husband, realised the whole ensemble was expensively understated. He made a mental note to remember it to describe it in detail to his wife, Margaret, and then just as quickly he made another decision not to. There was something about the fine cloth that bespoke of a different world.

'Anthony here,' Charmian Lingard went on, waving an arm, 'was just explaining his thinking about the new Mediterranean garden he's planting for us. It sounded so interesting. What was it, Anthony? Tall plants at the back, medium in the middle and short plants at the front . . .'

Crosby started to say something under his breath about rocket science.

'After that,' continued Charmian Lingard, who hadn't heard this, 'you have to choose flowers that flourish best in full sun, semi-shade and deep shade. Then flowers for spring, summer and autumn . . . and Buddleia at each end for butterflies.'

'All I really mentioned, Charmian,' protested Berra, 'was that the new Bergenias made good summer and winter foliage.'

She was undeterred and swept on. 'There was something you were saying about colour too, Anthony, wasn't there?'

The landscape designer looked embarrassed. 'Blues and yellows together, Charmian – hot colours massed in big clumps.'

Mrs Lingard said in a proprietary fashion, 'That wasn't all you said, Anthony.'

'This year, next year and five years on,' he said, rolling his eyes, man to man, in Sloan's direction.

'This year, next year, sometime never,' chanted Crosby. 'Cherry stones,' he explained to a bewildered audience. 'You know: tinker, tailor, soldier, sailor.'

'That will do, Crosby,' said Sloan repressively.

Charmian Lingard swept into the conversational void with a charming smile. 'Not, Inspector, that I am a five years ahead woman. It's this year for me, not even next.'

She would have been surprised had she known it how much she slipped down in Detective Inspector Sloan's estimation at this. In his credo, all good gardeners planned ahead. 'Quite so,' he said politely.

'But you say it's Anthony you've come to see, Inspector,' she said, turning to her husband. 'Come along, Oswald.'

'No need for you and the major to go, Charmian,' said Anthony Berra lightly. 'I didn't do it, Inspector, whatever it was, but I'll come quietly.'

'You took a Miss Enid Osgathorp to the station,' said Sloan.

'That's true.' He relaxed. 'So I did. I told you. Was that a crime?'

'Can you tell us again?' asked Sloan.

Charmian Lingard gave a tinkling laugh. 'It doesn't exactly sound like the Third Degree, Inspector.' Her only interaction with the police in life so far had been in the matter of fines for speeding (dealt with by the family solicitor) and parking tickets (paid for by an indulgent father). Her misdemeanours at boarding school had invariably been referred to the headmistress, a prudent woman very conscious of Charmian's family's worldly wealth and social connections. Somehow Charmian's transgressions there had therefore always managed to get left in the pending file. Any stepping over the line at her Swiss Finishing School had gone unrecorded.

'You see, we can't find Miss Osgathorp,' explained Detective Inspector Sloan, keeping his thoughts on the Third Degree to himself.

'Oh, I know her,' said Charmian Lingard, surprised. 'She was the funny old biddy who worked at the doctor's. What do the police want her for? Has she done something wrong?' She raised her eyes dramatically. 'Don't say she's a drug dealer?'

'She's been reported missing,' said Sloan baldly. 'And what we would like to do is to take some DNA material from your car, Mr Berra. With your permission, of course.'

'Sure,' said Berra. He waved an arm. 'It's over there.'

'How would that help,' intervened Charmian Lingard, 'if you haven't found her?' She examined Sloan's face. 'You haven't found her, have you?'

'No, madam. Not yet. We will, of course.'

'And I gave her a lift to the station,' said Anthony Berra to Charmian Lingard, abandoning his spade and leaping back onto the grass. 'And told the police so. She dumped her luggage on the front seat and sat on the back seat behind it. I think,' he said solemnly, 'she may have felt safer there. She has, I may say, always struck me as the archetypal spinster.'

'You can't be too careful if you're a woman on your own,' chanted Crosby sententiously. 'That's what we always teach the ladies.'

'That's what I tell my future intended too,' said Anthony Berra. He grinned. 'Not that she listens, I'm sure.'

'Where did you go after you'd dropped Miss Osgathorp off, sir?' asked Sloan.

The garden designer wrinkled his nose in recollection. 'A bit of shopping and then the bank, I think. Yes, of course, that's why I was going into Berebury that day anyway.'

'That would be the Calleshire and Counties, would it?' asked Crosby. 'On the Parade?'

'It would,' said Berra. 'My worldly wealth, such as it is, is in their hands.'

'Then where on earth did you manage to park?' asked Crosby with genuine professional curiosity.

'You may well ask, constable. In the Bellingham Hotel car park, actually,' said Berra. 'It's about the only free place but if you park there you have to eat there, so I did.'

Detective Constable Crosby nodded knowledgeably. 'That's what the notice in the car park says. "Park here, eat here".'

'So I did both,' said Anthony Berra neatly.

Detective Inspector Sloan raised something else on his agenda. 'Mrs Lingard, we are also looking into the break-in at Jack Haines' nursery. Just for the record, do you know of anyone who would have had a vested interest in the plants being raised for you not being available in time to be planted out properly?'

'I haven't offended anyone here that I am aware of,' she said stiffly, 'and Oswald's first wife is dead, if that's what you're getting at.'

Detective Inspector Sloan denied that it was.

'People can be quite jealous,' she went on with surprising bitterness, 'and of course one never knows with the old guard in any village.'

Sloan wasn't listening. He was concentrating on the meaningful look that Anthony Berra had cast in Oswald Lingard's direction at his wife's last remark. That old soldier, though, was taking good care not meet the other man's eye.

CHAPTER ELEVEN

Detective Inspector Sloan was still sitting in his office when Charlie Marsden, 'F' Division's Chief Scenes of Crime Officer, arrived back at the police station from Canonry Cottage at Pelling. Both Superintendent Leeyes and Detective Constable Crosby had long gone off duty. When Sloan had rung his wife, Margaret, to say he would be late back from work she had pointedly enquired the whereabouts of the other two.

'Gone home,' he admitted. 'Both of them.'

'The man in the middle,' she said, 'that's all you are, Christopher.'

'Someone's got to carry the can for the top and the bottom,' he responded, half-joking.

'Oppressed by those above and depressed by those below, if you ask me,' said his wife.

'So call me Common Man,' he said lightly.

'Have it your own way,' Margaret Sloan said, adding resignedly, 'it's a casserole, anyway.'

Not introspective, he decided that this did describe his state quite well. It described Common Man even better. Charlie Marsden, though, another man late for his supper tonight, could only be described as an enthusiast. Sloan found him cheering to listen to.

'Interesting little trip, Seedy,' reported the Scenes of Crime Officer, one professional to another. 'Challenging too. Gave the boys something to get their teeth into.'

'Tell me more, Charlie,' invited Sloan, leaning forward. 'All we had was a quick look.'

The man pulled up a chair and sat down opposite Sloan. 'You were quite right about there having been two entries. I can confirm that there have also been two quite separate searches in that cottage too, big time. With gloves on. That's what made it so interesting.'

'Big time for what, Charlie?'

'At a guess I should say papers of some sort. No sign of much disturbance in what we call domestic goods except that they've obviously been turned over by someone looking for papers. No ripping of sofas or cushions apart or anything flashy like that as you know . . .'

'Carpets not lifted?'

'Not that we could see but I would say that every single book has been opened and shaken about and then been put back on the shelf quite carefully by one of the intruders. Must have had plenty of time.'

'I think he or she . . .'

'They . . .'

'They probably had as much time as they wanted, Charlie, which is a worry in itself,' he admitted.

'Someone got in there with a key,' agreed Charlie Marsden tacitly.

'But you found no sign of actual theft, did you, any more than we did?'

'Not that we could spot. Nothing all that much worth taking there I should say . . .'

'Unless it's gone already,' put in Sloan automatically. 'We can't be too sure about that.'

'True, but there was nothing to suggest that there might have been great valuables there in the first place. You can always tell, you know.'

Detective Inspector Sloan did know. You only had to step into a house to get the feel for its owners. Just as his friend, Inspector Harpe, from Traffic Division, could tell a lot about the driver from a look at the car, he himself could usually tell what a house owner was like from the garden too. He leant back in his chair. 'So what was your take on the bungalow itself, then, Charlie?'

The SOCO considered this. 'I think it was lived in by one not-so-young but not-really-old party – I mean the place hadn't been grannified, if you know what I mean – no handles in the bath, no walking sticks, no special aids – none of that sort of thing but there was nothing very new there either and hadn't been for years, I should say. A bit on the shabby side but not so you'd notice. Lots of books about foreign parts and gardens. I'd say the owner was into travel – not one of those who devoted themselves to housework or collecting things.' Charlie Marsden knew about the downside of that way of life. His wife collected fine china and the big man was nervous about moving about in his own sitting room.

'There must have been something very valuable to the two people who went in there,' mused Sloan. 'Or that they had reason to believe was valuable, of course.'

'I can tell you a little about both of them,' said Marsden. 'Whoever came in through the pantry window was a bit careless . . .'

'We spotted the blood.'

'Better than that. A few hairs on the broken window. Useful stuff, hair.'

'Bully for you,' he said, metaphorically rubbing his hands. The hair of the dog that bit you had nothing on a single strand of human hair with its follicle still attached for the assistance it could sometimes provide in an investigation.

'His head must have touched the broken glass as he came in.' Charlie Marsden looked justifiably pleased. 'And, of course, we've taken the missing party's DNA from a hairbrush in her bedroom. Routine, these days.'

Sloan nodded. 'Good going, Charlie.'

'Thought you'd be pleased.' Charlie Marsden grinned.

'And I've got some DNA said to be hers from a car in which she was given a lift.' He corrected himself. 'In which she was said to have been given a lift.'

'And that's not all,' went on the Scenes of Crime man.

'Surprise me.'

'He who came through the front door with a key . . .' He paused and shot Sloan a quick glance. 'The male embraces the female and all that guff, you understand.'

'He or she is implied,' agreed Sloan solemnly. The

feminists at the police station were not women to be trifled with.

'He was very careful indeed. Not a single fingerprint or anything else anywhere but he carried out a very thorough search of the place all the same. We couldn't find a safe and presumably neither could either of them. If there had been any locked box then one or other of them took it away with them.'

Detective Inspector Sloan nodded. 'That figures.'

Charlie Marsden said, 'I guess that whoever the intruders were, they both had the same idea about where ladies keep their treasures. Well, their gin, anyway.'

'Back of the wardrobe,' said Sloan promptly.

'Too right. Both had had a rummage round there. No gin, though, but . . .'

'But what?'

'What looked like a very valuable book indeed on orchids. That had been thumbed through too, but with gloves on, of course.' He looked up. 'I think that's about all. It's a missing person case, I think you said?'

'With knobs on, Charlie. So did you find what I asked you to look for?'

'A spare key?' Charlie Marsden shook his head. 'No.'

'That's what's worrying,' said Sloan. 'The neighbour is adamant that she didn't ever leave one with anyone . . .'

'Which could mean,' the Scenes of Crime man finished the sentence for him, 'that whoever went in there with one took it off her.'

'I'm very much afraid so,' said Detective Inspector Sloan soberly. He swept his papers into a drawer and locked it. 'Not that I can do anything more about that tonight but I've got another job for you, Charlie. Just as interesting but different.'

'Surprise me again.'

'I want to know what was in a bonfire lit this morning in the garden of a house in Pelling called The Hollies. The name's Feakins.'

'We'll be round there first thing,' promised Charlie Marsden, making a note.

'Just give me time to get you a search warrant before you go,' said Sloan, 'and for heaven's sake keep a low profile. Make sure that the only pictures that get taken are yours – the last thing we want is the press publishing photographs of an old bonfire. Not at this stage, anyway. I want them to have one of the missing person first.'

'Another search warrant, Sloan?' barked Superintendent Leeyes the next morning. 'Whose house is it for this time?'

'It's not for a house, sir,' Sloan said quickly, the superintendent never being at his best first thing in the morning. 'It's for a bonfire – or rather the remains of one – in a garden belonging to one of the customers of Jack Haines at Pelling. He's one of those who have lost plants at Haines' nursery, which is interesting.'

'Don't say that they've started burning people at the stake out there,' Leeyes said, heavily sarcastic. 'Or that your missing person's gone up in smoke.'

'I don't know what has been burnt,' replied Sloan seriously, 'but there is a man there who was prepared to have a bonfire in spite of being bent double and in great pain from backache. He can hardly stand and yet he got himself out into the garden somehow yesterday afternoon to light it and scuttled back out there again pretty smartly after he thought we'd left.'

'And burn what exactly?'

'That is what we don't know yet, sir. Not until we've got a warrant and had a good look. All we do know is that it was not long after he and his wife got back from seeing their solicitor.'

Superintendent Leeyes, no fan of the Defence Counsel branch of the legal profession, gave a snort. 'You take their advice and they take your money.'

'There is something else,' ploughed on Sloan gamely. 'This man Benedict Feakins also got quite agitated when the name of the missing person was mentioned and as soon as we were out of his sight . . .'

'But not out of yours, I take it, Sloan?'

'No, sir. Crosby drove the car away while I kept watch.'

'And?'

'And Feakins staggered back out into the garden straightway,' said Sloan, 'and started raking about in the remains of the bonfire like a madman.'

'Hm.' Leeyes drummed his fingers on his desktop. 'Anything else to report?'

'We've been checking on other leads, sir.'

'Such as?'

'Crosby has confirmed Anthony Berra's story – he's the last person known to have seen Enid Osgathorp alive. He did visit the Berebury branch of the Calleshire and Counties Bank and he did have lunch at the Bellingham, just as he said he did. We're checking the street CCTV cameras now. No joy from the railway people though – they can't help us at all. No sighting of the missing person on their cameras at all and though she had a pre-booked ticket there is no trace of it having been checked or handed in.'

'And what now?' grunted Leeyes.

'Now, sir, I'm going to check on the recent death of Benedict Feakins' father,' said Sloan, 'just to be on the safe side, and then have another word with the old admiral. He made no secret of not liking the missing person but he wouldn't say why.'

PC Edward York, the Coroner's Officer, was very much a family man. Grey-haired and distinctly on the elderly side for a police constable, he had the bedside manner of an old-fashioned family doctor. Exuding muted sympathy, he attended to the bereaved with a skill honed over the years on the losses suffered by other people.

He was rather more forthright in the presence of Detective Inspector Sloan and Detective Constable Crosby. 'Feakins, did you say? Oh, yes, he came my way all right. An old boy who was found dead in his greenhouse out at Pelling not all that long ago?'

'That's him,' said Sloan.

'Usual thing – milk not taken in, newspapers piled up,' said York. 'Always a great help. I think it was the postman who went looking around the place for him the next morning and found him on the greenhouse floor.'

'Nice way to go,' remarked Crosby, who was only now getting used to seeing the bodies of people who hadn't gone in a nice way.

'Natural causes?' asked Sloan.

'Oh, yes,' said the Coroner's Officer immediately. 'Post-mortem but no inquest. Heart packed up, if I remember rightly. All quite straightforward – from my point of view, anyway. Family very upset, naturally, but they lived away. The usual story – the parent didn't want to be a nuisance and the younger generation didn't want to seem overly concerned because the old man was so keen on keeping his independence for as long as he could.'

'A common problem,' nodded Sloan. His own mother wasn't frail yet but would be one day and perhaps would be like that too.

PC York said, 'The son told us that a regular telephone call every Sunday evening was about all that his father would agree to.'

'Solomon Grundy died on Saturday, buried on Sunday,' remarked Crosby inconsequentially.

Detective Inspector Sloan scribbled a note to himself. 'No sign of the son being overcome by remorse or anything like that?'

The Coroner's Officer, a man experienced in these matters, shook his head. 'His reaction seemed perfectly normal to me or I would have remembered. He was shaken, naturally, but he identified him in the ordinary way.'

'Thanks, Ted,' said Sloan. 'That's been a help.' He shuffled some papers about on his desk until a copy of the photograph of Enid Osgathorp at her retirement presentation surfaced. 'By the way, should this old lady ever come into your view . . .'

'Dead or alive,' interposed Crosby.

Sloan decided to rise above this and carried on. 'Let me know pronto, will you, Ted? She's gone missing.'

PC York regarded the picture with interest. 'Will do. Haven't seen her yet.' He tapped the photograph with his finger. 'I can tell you, though, who the clergyman in this snap is. I saw quite a lot of him not all that long ago. That was at Pelling too. Name of Beddowes.'

'The one whose wife committed suicide,' nodded Sloan. 'Yes, that's him at her retirement presentation handing over something to Enid Osgathorp. We've already seen him.'

'Very unfortunate, that suicide was, what with the daughter's wedding pending at the time.' He frowned. 'I think I heard that they went ahead with the ceremony after the inquest but that it was a very quiet do in the end.'

'Understandable,' said Sloan.

'Lot of gossip out there at the time, of course,' said York, a man used to working with gossip. 'It goes with the territory.'

'Small villages are like that,' opined Sloan.

'It didn't amount to anything,' said York, 'because of course I looked into it. The gossip, I mean.'

'Naturally.' Detective Inspector Sloan, mentor, made a mental note to talk to Crosby sometime about the importance of policemen properly evaluating gossip without spreading it – but not here and not now.

'The daughter blamed herself for wanting a proper wedding reception and honeymoon and all the works but I must say there didn't seem anything very out of the ordinary about their plans to me.' PC York had three married daughters and knew the scenario well. 'Quite the opposite, actually.'

'Didn't want anyone complaining that the Easter

offering was being misspent, I expect,' said Sloan knowledgeably. His mother was a great churchwoman and he knew exactly what was expected of a clergy family: a more stringent economy than that which was practised by the congregation.

'Reception in the church hall, with the parish ladies doing the refreshments,' recounted York. 'And the church flowers rota ladies doing the decorations. Lavender and peonies, I expect.'

Detective Constable Crosby's head came up. 'Not roses all the way?' he said, bachelor that he was.

'Lavender for devotion and peonies for joy and prosperity,' said the Coroner's Officer promptly. 'The language of flowers.'

'Girls come expensive,' said Sloan, who only had a son and was sometimes grateful for this. His wife, Margaret, insisted that this sentiment would only last until the said son was old enough to buy his first motorbike.

PC York was still thinking about the rector's daughter. 'And she could hardly not get married in church anyway, could she? Not with having a clergyman for a father and all that.' The man grinned and said, 'After all, the rector couldn't very well offer the bridegroom a ladder and fifty quid to elope with his daughter, now could he?'

'No,' agreed Sloan. That presumably went for the father of the girl that Anthony Berra was marrying too, especially since her father was a bishop. 'The family insisted to me that she'd been very worried about the cost of the wedding,' he said, casting his mind back to his visit to the Rectory.

PC York stroked his chin. 'She could have been

worried about the expense although I can't imagine why. They'd even got a friend taking the wedding photographs, although I wouldn't advise that myself.'

'Headless bridesmaids,' grinned Crosby.

York pressed on with his narrative. 'You see, the mother had been saving up for it for ages. They showed me her cheque-book. Lots of withdrawals in cash with "Wedding Fund" written on the counterfoil. The only thing is that nobody could find any money stashed away anywhere when she died. Looked everywhere, they did.'

'Perhaps she put it all on a horse,' suggested Crosby jovially. 'Double your money and all that.'

'Were they regular withdrawals?' asked Sloan more pertinently.

'First of the month,' said York. 'Without fail. As the daughter told me afterwards, there should have been enough money there to have had a proper photographer, which, I may tell you from bitter experience, is saying something.'

Sloan tried to remember some of the details of Mrs Beddowes' suicide. 'We were told that there were letters . . .'

PC York nodded. 'There were. I handed them over to old double-barrelled.'

'Mr Locombe-Stableford,' interpreted Sloan, who felt that the decencies should be preserved in the presence of the young.

'Him,' said the Coroner's officer, referring to Her Majesty's Coroner for East Calleshire. 'He didn't read them out at the inquest which is his prerogative. He just said that he was satisfied that the deceased had taken her own life while the balance of her mind was disturbed and gave that as his verdict. That was when the press lost interest.'

'So you don't know what was in the letters then,' ventured Crosby.

The Coroner's Officer cast him a pitying look. "Course I do, sonny. It was me that unpinned them from her pillow, wasn't it?'

'So what was in them, Ted?' asked Sloan swiftly.

'Said no one was to blame for what she had done then and now but herself and to remember her with compassion no matter what.'

'And what do you suppose she meant by that?' mused Sloan. 'Then and now.'

York shrugged his shoulders. 'Your guess is as good as mine.'

'And what had she done?' asked Crosby curiously.

'Committed suicide,' said York. 'You're not supposed to do it.'

'No,' persisted Crosby, 'I mean what had she done that made her commit suicide?'

The Coroner's Officer shrugged his shoulders. 'Who knows? Disturbed minds aren't easy to read in spite of what the shrinks would have you believe. She'd meant to do it all right, though. She'd travelled over half the county for weeks buying small lots of tablets here, there and everywhere.'

'Determined then,' concluded Crosby.

'The family were still insisting that she'd been worried about the cost of the wedding,' said Sloan, turning his mind back to their own visit to the rectory. Perhaps he should go back and ask if the deceased had known Enid Osgathorp too. He immediately answered his own thought. Of course, she would have done. The rector's wife would have known a lot of people but the doctor's receptionist must have known everyone. And all about them too, probably. Well, everything on their medical records anyway.

'I think,' declared Detective Inspector Sloan obscurely, 'what we are dealing with now are live doubts rather than dead certainties – but this may change.'

CHAPTER TWELVE

Mandy Lamb was usually able to cajole Jack Haines back into his usual good humour but not this morning. Even a continuous infusion of coffee did nothing to raise his spirits. Her employer still sat, listless and preoccupied, at his desk.

'Russ came in earlier looking for you,' reported Mandy.

Jack Haines sighed. 'I'd better see him then.' He pushed a desk diary aside. 'Mandy, you haven't seen Norman about lately, have you?'

'Not for yonks, Jack, thank goodness.' She pulled a face. 'He's not your most lovable character.'

'Margot was fond of him,' said the nurseryman.

'She was his mother,' pointed out Mandy Lamb.

'He couldn't do anything wrong as far as she was concerned,' sighed Jack Haines. 'Everything was all right until she died.'

'That's mothers for you,' said Mandy Lamb who was still single and childless.

'And I reckon I treated him well enough until he got greedy,' murmured Haines, almost to himself. 'Really greedy.'

'You treated him very well,' she said emphatically. She paused and then added, 'Better than he treated you.'

'Stepchildren usually have chips on their shoulders,' he said. 'Goes with the territory, I suppose.' He sipped at the latest mug of coffee, braced his shoulders and said, 'I suppose I'd better get back to business. What does Anthony Berra want now?'

Mandy scrabbled about among the papers on her desk. 'I've got his list somewhere here. Ah, got it!' She handed over the sheet of paper to him. 'He's on his way over now.'

'I suppose in view of what's happened we'd better pull out all the stops for him.' Jack Haines scrutinised the paper she had given him.

Mandy said, 'He's still got that hacking cough. He doesn't look all that well. I hope he's looking after himself.'

'I think we can do most of these,' said Jack, still looking at the list.

'If not,' she said mischievously, 'we could always ask Bob Steele if he could send us some of them.'

'Over my dead body,' he growled, his face turning an apoplectic shade of crimson. 'I'm not going down on my bended knee to that man for anything. Anything at all. Is that understood?'

'Yes, Jack,' she said sedulously, turning back to her own desk. 'But according to Russ the man's happy enough to come to you for almost anything.'

'That's as maybe,' he said enigmatically. 'And mind

what you say about Bob Steele in front of Russ. I'm not happy about him either.'

They were interrupted by the arrival of Anthony Berra. 'I hear the admiral's ordered just what he wants as usual,' he said ruefully.

'He has,' said Haines, adding peaceably, 'He's old, of course.'

'And difficult,' sighed Berra.

'Handling him must be good practice for your dealing with the Bishop, Anthony,' said Mandy Lamb briskly. 'I hear your future father-in-law is no pushover.'

'That's nothing – you haven't met his wife,' groaned Berra. 'I call her Mrs Proudie behind her back. Terror of the diocese from all accounts. By the way, Jack, I've just come from the Berebury Garden Centre and Bob Steele said again he was sorry to hear about your troubles and if there was anything he could do, to let him know.'

'That'll be the day,' muttered Haines, half to himself, his complexion again turning an unhappy shade of red.

'Upset you, has he?' concluded Berra. 'No sentiment in business and all that?'

'You could say something of the sort,' Haines managed through clenched teeth. He waved a list in his hand. 'I'll get Russ to look out these plants you want.'

'Thanks. I'll have them as soon as you can get them – our Charmian will have my guts for garters if anything more goes wrong with her precious Mediterranean garden. I must have been mad to agree to do it for her.' He broke off to cough.

'I hope that's not catching,' said Mandy Lamb pointedly, edging away.

He stared at her and said stiffly, 'Certainly not.' Just as quickly his mood changed and he said, 'I've just thought of a good quote for my new business card that I'd like to run past you.'

'What's that, then?' asked Jack Haines, who didn't believe in advertising.

Anthony Berra said '"A good garden is a painting come to life". What do you think of that, Jack?'

'I think,' said the nurseryman firmly, 'that you should tell them the truth – which is that a garden is hell's half acre with everything in it fighting for survival night and day.'

'Not "A lovesome thing, God wot" then?' put in Mandy Lamb.

'Certainly not,' said Haines.

'A man doesn't bite the hand that feeds him,' said Berra obscurely.

'Coffee, Anthony?' As always when dissention threatened, Mandy Lamb took refuge in her universal remedy.

Jack Haines said, 'A cobbler should stick to his last and you should stick to yours, Anthony. Garden design, not playing with words.'

'I'll remember that,' said the other man slowly, turning to go. 'By the way, Jack,' he asked, 'had you thought of your stepson as a possible orchid killer?'

'Yes,' said Jack Haines shortly. 'I had.'

Detective Constable Crosby stood up when Sloan got back to his office. 'Where to now, sir?'

'Where indeed?' murmured Detective Inspector Sloan.

Nothing with its roots in Pelling seemed to fit: in his book, events so far seemed more Rubik's Cube than jigsaw.

'The canteen?' suggested Crosby hopefully.

'Why not? At this stage, Crosby, it's as good as anywhere else.'

The canteen at the police station served an all-day breakfast. The meal could not be further from the 'five-a-day' mantra of the healthy eating brigade. Sloan regarded the bacon, eggs, sausage, mushrooms, tomatoes, baked beans and fried potatoes with enthusiasm, only wondering in passing whether the fried mushrooms, tomatoes and beans could be deemed as three of his 'five-a-day' allotment of healthy fruit and vegetables. He decided not.

'I brought some toast as well,' said Crosby. 'I hope that's all right.'

'Good thinking,' said Sloan. When later in the day his wife Margaret enquired whether he had eaten at work, he could admit with some truth that he'd had some toast. It was not the whole truth, of course, which was important. He reminded himself that not saying anything was a form of lying. But the whole truth at Pelling was something that was beginning to bother him because he seemed to be no nearer to it today. Or to establishing whether the absence of the missing Enid Maude Osgathorp, whose home had been broken into twice, had any connection with frost-damaged plants at Pelling and Capstan Purlieu.

'There's only one thing we really know about Enid Osgathorp,' he mused aloud, 'apart from the two break-ins at her house and that we know she's been missing for over three weeks.'

Detective Constable Crosby, having been brought up

not talk when his mouth was full, for a wonder remained silent.

'That's that she wasn't the flavour of the month,' carried on Sloan, demolishing a sausage. 'There is a certain absence of warmth whenever her name is mentioned although Anthony Berra sounded quite neutral when he told us he had given her a lift into Berebury.'

'That reminds me, sir,' said Crosby, when he had swallowed and regained the power of speech. He parked a piece of toast on his plate while he reached for his notebook. 'I checked on that. I found two old ladies who had also been waiting at the bus stop that day. They remembered him stopping and picking her up.'

'But not them?' said Sloan. 'He didn't give them a lift too?'

'Just her.'

'Perhaps they didn't like her either,' said Sloan idly.

'That man Benedict Feakins sure didn't have any nice feelings about her,' Crosby said. 'He looked like a frightened rabbit when her name cropped up.'

'And the admiral actually admitted he didn't like her,' said Sloan. There was something at the back of his mind niggling him about the admiral – something from way back that he felt he was missing but he couldn't think what it was.

'So that lets him out of anything that's been going on,' decided Crosby, attacking a rasher of bacon.

There would be a moment, resolved Sloan, when he would have to explain the concept of double bluff to the constable but, the man's attention now being centred on the bacon, this didn't seem to be it. Instead he said, 'All the same, Crosby, I think we'll have another word with him later.'

'Don't forget, sir, we haven't traced the husband of one of those women at Capstan Purlieu yet,' said Crosby. 'Norman Potts.'

'That's true, although we don't know where he fits in the picture – or even if he does. Perhaps we'd better get on with that too.'

'Nobody liked him either – at least, not his stepfather or his ex-wife,' said Crosby.

Someone had once listed the reasons for murdering people: gain, conviction, elimination, the lust of killing, revenge, jealousy . . . Not being liked didn't seem to be one of them. The absence of war from the list had struck Sloan as strange at the time he first read it but that was presumably different. Those intent on making war had always said so throughout history, hadn't they?

'More toast, sir?' Crosby, hovering, interrupted his train of thought.

Without thinking, Sloan's hand stretched out for it. He said absently, 'There's really only one thing about Enid Osgathorp that we do know for certain and that's that she knew everyone in Pelling by virtue of her occupation as keeper of their medical records.'

'And those two women out at Capstan Purlieu as well,' pointed out Crosby. 'She knew them too, because one of them is standing in for her at that talk she was supposed to be giving tonight.'

'She must have known the rector's wife, anyway,' concluded Sloan, 'talking of whom it would be interesting to know where she had stashed her wedding fund money. Not in the bank, anyway, because she'd taken the money out of the bank each month, not put it in there.'

'And she couldn't have put it anywhere in the house,' concluded Crosby, 'because the husband and children would have found it by now if she had.'

'True.'

'Perhaps it got stolen?' suggested the constable.

'Then we would have heard about it,' said Sloan, qualifying this immediately by adding, 'unless someone in the family had nicked it. We mightn't have been told in that case, families being what they are. Unlikely, though, I admit.' Struck by a sudden thought, he said, 'If the question of probate has come up, we could always check with the family's solicitor to see if he's found it. Otherwise, Crosby, we might have to consider that Mrs Beddowes had been giving the money to someone else . . .'

'What on earth for?' asked the constable, who was now tackling the bacon.

'What, indeed?' said Detective Inspector Sloan rhetorically, 'but in my book, regular cash payments out of someone's bank account over a long period about which nobody else knows anything spells only one thing.'

'What's that, then?' asked Crosby.

'Blackmail,' pronounced Sloan succinctly, 'especially if it's followed by suicide, so I think we'll see if we can track down all that money of Mrs Ann Beddowes' next. Whether we are dealing with a suicide followed by a murder is something else that has to be considered.'

Crosby chewed his toast for a moment and then

said, 'Ann Beddowes couldn't have murdered Enid Osgathorp . . .'

'No, Crosby,' he agreed, letting out an exasperated sigh. 'She couldn't because she was already dead before Enid Osgathorp went walkabout. What I'm pretty sure about now is that someone else has done, though, and that one of the break-ins to her house was carried out by that someone else looking for the evidence that led to the blackmail.'

CHAPTER THIRTEEN

'Back again, Anthony? You're earlier than usual this morning.' Charmian Lingard appeared in the grounds of the Grange at Pelling as if by magic as the garden designer was working there. She was wearing trousers so well-cut that they shouted as having come from a London couturier. They were of a light brown check, the outfit being topped by a plain cream blouse of expensive simplicity.

'Nothing like as soon as those poor old monks would have been at their first office when they lived here. They had to get going really early.' Anthony Berra straightened up and leant on his spade. 'I wanted to get Flora's plinth settled in.' He gave the statue an affectionate pat. 'I'm just finishing checking the levels of the base so that I can fix her properly. It's very important to get her standing up straight.'

'I quite agree,' said Charmian Lingard whose own

excellent deportment had been refined at the Swiss Finishing School. 'We can't have her doing a Leaning Tower of Pisa act. Not here.'

'She'd look drunk and that would never do,' agreed Anthony solemnly.

'You're teasing me, Anthony.'

He reverted to business. 'I'm hoping to get everything ready before I go and then I'll have to leave the concrete round the plinth to set. I'm going set off next and do another round of nurseries to see if I can replace some of the plants we've lost . . .'

'You've lost,' she corrected him, a touch of steel in her voice.

'I've lost,' he conceded at once, hiding a grimace. 'I've already been to Jack Haines' place and over to the nursery at Capstan Purlieu . . .'

'I've heard of them. One of them's a bit fierce, isn't she?'

'I wouldn't want to tangle with Anna Sutherland myself,' admitted Anthony Berra, adding hastily, 'very sound on her subject, all the same. But I'll have to try some other places too. And you'll be pleased to hear that I've drawn up a new planting plan.'

'You don't waste much time, do you, Anthony?'

He essayed a smile. 'It's not so much time and tide that wait for no man, Charmian, as the length of time the plants are in the ground that matters.' He added, grinning, 'And we do have a deadline, don't we?'

'You know we do and I know you're teasing me again,' said Charmian Lingard sweetly. 'The garden party. I'm already working on the draft of the invitation to the printers. I'm really just waiting for the proof to come back

160

and then I can give them the go-ahead.' She gave a sigh of great satisfaction. 'It's going to be a great occasion. I do hope I can persuade the admiral to come. He's such a game old chap and I'm sure he'll turn up if he can. Besides, he must know the bishop and his wife.'

'And everyone else who matters in Calleshire,' added Anthony Berra, but under his breath.

'It's a bit like being in church, sir, isn't it?' whispered Detective Constable Crosby. 'Sitting on these hard chairs and being so uncomfortable.'

The two policemen were in the waiting room of the offices of Puckle, Puckle and Nunnery, Solicitors and Notaries Public, of Berebury.

'What you are sitting on, Crosby,' Sloan informed him, 'is what is known as a flea chair.'

The constable jumped to his feet. 'I have never had fleas and I don't want them now.'

'But if you had, Crosby, they wouldn't have jumped off you and onto these wooden chairs because they haven't got cushions on them for the fleas to settle on. You may sit down again.'

Crosby resumed his seat with a certain caution.

'You don't need to worry,' said Sloan kindly. 'They're hall chairs and they're what the hoi polloi were supposed to sit on while they waited for the local nobs to ask them what they wanted.'

'We're not hoi polloi,' objected Crosby. 'We're different. We're sworn police officers.'

'Just so,' agreed Sloan as Miss Fennel appeared and said that Mr Puckle would see them now.

'As you know, Inspector,' said Simon Puckle pleasantly, 'I can't give you any information about any client – not without a court order, that is.'

'We were just wondering,' Sloan said to the solicitor, 'if that applied to the affairs of deceased clients. I understand that death cancels all contracts.'

Simon Puckle frowned. 'Inquest reports, probate records and court judgements are all in the public domain . . .'

'Let alone what they put in the newspapers,' grumbled Crosby who felt he had been misreported after making his first arrest. 'Everyone sees that.'

'That is,' carried on the solicitor urbanely, 'they all become available in the public domain in due course.'

'The law's delays,' murmured Crosby, sotto voce, still put out over the mention of fleas.

'What we are looking for,' explained Sloan, 'is missing money.'

'Theft, you mean?' Simon Puckle's eyebrows went up.

'Not necessarily.'

'In that case you might need a forensic accountant rather than a solicitor.'

'What I want,' said Detective Inspector Sloan in a straightforward manner, 'is to know what the late Mrs Ann Beddowes did with the money that she took out of the bank every month.'

'Nobody else seems to know,' contributed Crosby in an antiphon.

Simon Puckle sat back in his chair and steepled his fingers while he gave the matter some thought. After a moment he said, 'Presently neither do I. Nor indeed does anyone else to whom I have spoken.' He coughed. 'As her executor I have a duty at law to establish the extent of her estate and . . .'

'No joy?' suggested Crosby.

'Not so far,' he temporised. 'And I think I am in a position to tell you also that her family haven't been able to help in this respect. There is no trace of where it went every month although I still have the requirement to establish that it hasn't been salted away somewhere and thus requires to be included in her estate. If it has simply been disbursed by the deceased in any way whatsoever it is not my responsibility as her executor to know on what. In my capacity as her executor I am only concerned with what remained in her estate at the time of her death.'

'And it's not there?' asked Sloan, rising to take his leave. Solicitors, he had been told, unlike policemen, measured their time in minutes.

Simon Puckle shook his head. 'Not to my knowledge, Inspector.'

'Come along then, Crosby,' said Sloan. He paused with his hand on the door, struck by a sudden thought. He thanked the solicitor and then said, 'If you can tell us that perhaps you could tell us something else.'

'Perhaps.' Caution was obviously the watchword with Simon Puckle.

'The late Doctor Heddon of Pelling. Did you act for him?'

The solicitor nodded. 'Our firm were his executors and we duly submitted details of his estate for probate.'

'And these aren't secret?'

'No. Probate was granted in due course.'

'We would like to know how much money he left to Miss Enid Osgathorp. How do we find out?'

Simon Puckle said, 'I can tell you that myself, gentlemen. He didn't leave her anything at all. If I remember rightly – I could check for you if it's important – everything went to a niece of his in Calleford.'

As the two policemen walked back from the solicitors' premises through the streets of Berebury to the police station, Detective Inspector Sloan remarked to his subordinate, 'So that's someone else who didn't like Enid Osgathorp either.'

'Simon Puckle?' said Crosby.

'Doctor Heddon,' said Sloan. 'Enid Osgathorp had worked for him for years and years out there at Pelling but he didn't remember her in his Will.'

'I'll have worked for the Chief Constable for years and years,' said Crosby stoutly, 'but I bet he won't remember me in his Will either.'

For a long moment Sloan toyed with the idea of trying to explain to the constable the concept that he worked for the well-being of the populace as a whole, not that of the superintendent, but just as soon decided against it as being too abstract. Instead he said, 'We know that Enid Osgathorp had a large enough income in her retirement to support a long series of exotic holidays abroad and luxurious ones in this country although she still lived very simply when she was at home.' The fact reminded him that they still hadn't got any further with identifying the blood and hair on the broken glass at the back of her house. He resolved to give this his attention as soon as he could – not that he knew where to begin. All that he could deduce was that whoever it was who had come in through the front door with a key was more likely to have got it from Enid Osgathorp somehow, somewhere, than whoever had come in through the broken window at the back. This could hardly be described even by an optimist as progress on that investigative front.

The police station came into view as they turned the corner. 'My guess,' continued Sloan, 'is that the money to finance her lifestyle came from people such as the late Mrs Ann Beddowes by way of blackmail, which is why the money can't be found, and that is also probably why the poor woman committed suicide.'

'But she was the rector's wife,' protested Crosby.

'That, I am afraid, Crosby, does not automatically convey blamelessness, although,' he added grimly, 'it does make the appearance of blamelessness very important as far as her husband's parishioners were concerned.' His own mother, a great churchwoman, always reminded him that Caesar's wife was a woman above suspicion but even that was something, police officer that he was, that he had always taken with a pinch of salt.

The superintendent greeted his return without enthusiasm. 'The fact that nobody liked the missing person, Sloan, is not evidence.'

'But it may be relevant . . .' began Sloan.

'She sounds to me like that "fat white woman in gloves",' interrupted the superintendent.

'Enid Osgathorp was short and thin,' pointed out Sloan, somewhat mystified and not knowing where this was leading. 'Everyone has said so.'

165

'"Who walked through the fields missing so much and so much",' quoted Leeyes. 'It's a poem, Sloan.'

'Ah,' said Sloan. That explained it. Once upon a time the superintendent had started to attend a series of lectures on modern verse but had left declaring to all and sundry that poems weren't what they used to be when he was a lad and what had happened to the works of Sir Henry Newbolt? Sloan thought what was more important from a police point of view was whether they too – like the fat white woman in gloves – were missing so much and so much.

And, if so, what.

Answer came there none and Sloan made his way back to his own office. There was a report on his desk awaiting his return. Crosby was waiting for him there too.

The report was from Charlie Marsden, the Division's senior Scenes of Crime guru. He wrote that, as instructed, he had examined the remains of a bonfire in the garden of The Hollies at Pelling, the home of Benedict and Mary Feakins. He had retrieved a half-burnt gentleman's hairbrush and the handle of a toothbrush from the embers, the fire being out but its remains still warm by the time he and his team had got there. He had also found traces of fibres and substances that could have been ivory, horn or bone, and did Detective Inspector Sloan want them sent for forensic examination.

'Not half,' said Crosby when he had read this too.

Charlie Marsden had appended a footnote to the effect that Benedict Feakins had appeared very anxious when he and his men arrived and kept on saying that he had only been burning some items that had belonged to his late father because he found it upsetting to have them around and that wasn't illegal, was it? 'I assured him that it wasn't,' wrote Charlie, 'since under my understanding of English Law a man could do what he liked provided there wasn't a law against it, unlike some benighted countries where you could only do it if the law allowed you.'

'It doesn't sound as if Feakins was cremating Enid Osgathorp,' said Sloan mildly, leaving aside Charlie Marsden's world view. 'It's not something you usually do in full view of the neighbours and he would have had to park the body somewhere out of sight and smell for the best part of three weeks which wouldn't have been easy.'

'Someone's done it somewhere, though,' observed Crosby. 'If she's dead, that is.'

'I asked the bank to let me know if she had made any withdrawals since she went missing,' said Sloan in passing. 'And they haven't so far. The trouble is if she was only using her credit card any purchases wouldn't show up quite yet.' He pulled his notebook towards him. 'What I want to know is why should Feakins need to dispose of anything on a bonfire at a time when any sort of movement gives him so much pain?'

'And why get so twitchy if he hasn't done anything wrong?' Crosby responded. 'That's important.'

'You must always remember, Crosby, that the appearance of guilt does not prove guilt,' said Sloan, an early lesson by his own mentor fixed for ever in his mind. It was something juries need to be reminded of too.

'Yes, sir. I mean no, sir.'

'It looks to me as if he was trying to destroy evidence of his father's DNA,' remarked Sloan thoughtfully.

'I can't think why he should,' said Crosby.

'Neither can I,' said Sloan seriously, 'but if for a moment we suppose that our Miss Osgathorp was blackmailing both him and Mrs Beddowes we ought to be able to find out why.'

'And why he's so frightened now.'

'There's something else you're forgetting, Crosby.'

'Sir?'

'If they are victims, then you can bet your bottom dollar that they're not the only ones.' He pushed the report to one side. 'Our trouble, Crosby, is that we've got a jigsaw with too many pieces and we don't even know if they come from the same puzzle let alone our having a pretty picture to go on.'

'That's makes them too easy,' opined Crosby. 'Anyone can do a jigsaw with a picture.'

'Then,' said Sloan with a touch of asperity, 'you tell me what deliberately frost-damaged plants, a missing woman and one who has taken her own life have in common.'

'If anything,' said Crosby, adding casually, 'Oh, I rang the admiral's house like you said. No point in going out there just now, sir. The woman what does for him said he's just been taken in hospital. He's gone and broken his hip.' He grinned. 'I asked her "Did he fall or was he pushed" and she said it had just broken but he wasn't in any pain. Hard luck for the old boy, though, all the same, isn't it?'

Crosby got no further. Detective Inspector Sloan brought

one of his hands into the palm of the other with a loud smack in what he was later to describe as a light bulb moment. 'That's it!' he exclaimed softly. 'Of course. I should have thought of it before.'

'Thought what, sir?'

'What William Shakespeare told us. He said "Consumptions sow in hollow bones of man".'

'Beg pardon, sir?' said Crosby, even more bewildered.

'The car, Crosby,' Sloan snapped, springing to his feet. 'Now!'

CHAPTER FOURTEEN

'Still no sign of Enid coming back,' said Marilyn Potts over at Captain Purlieu Plants. 'I've just rung her house in case she's got home after all and could give her precious talk herself tonight but there was no reply.'

'She's probably stuck on a donkey in Petra,' said Anna Sutherland.

'Not Petra,' said Marilyn. 'She's been there. Not enough flowers for her in Jordan, anyway. Now, if you'd said she was marooned on a mountain in Anatolia, that would be more likely.'

'It wouldn't surprise me,' said Anna darkly, 'if she was one of those vandals who pinch rare seeds while they're there.'

'Wrong time of the year for seeds,' said Marilyn ambivalently.

'Rare plants, then. Have trowel, will travel. Don't

you remember that unusual cyclamen she brought back last year from above the tree-line somewhere in Turkey?'

'I don't know if Customs look in sponge bags,' said Marilyn doubtfully, 'but I wouldn't put it past them.'

'And I wouldn't put it past Enid to try to smuggle something interesting back here and then ask us to grow it on for her. Goodness knows why she doesn't have a greenhouse of her own.'

'Greenhouses,' declared Marilyn, 'need watching. And don't we know it,' she added mournfully.

'Our Enid never misses a trick,' said Anna. 'Not never.'

Marilyn Potts gave a great sigh. 'And now I must make a few notes for the Staple St James people tonight.'

'You don't need any notes, my girl. You could talk about orchids standing on your head. And all evening too.'

'But not necessarily the ones we've got in the shed for tonight. Enid must have ordered those six special ones from Jack Haines for a reason. I'll have to try to work out why.'

Anna Sutherland gave one of her high cackles. 'Don't you start on the language of flowers.'

'Why ever not?' Marilyn giggled. 'If it came to that, I could always send Norman a bouquet of lobelia.'

'Malevolence,' interpreted Anna. 'Good thinking.'

'Mock orange . . .'

'Deceit,' said Anna.

'And bilberry,' said Marilyn.

'Can't remember,' admitted Anna.

'Treachery.'

'Just the job,' concluded her friend. 'That's him – malevolent, deceitful and treacherous. And don't we know it.'

'Do get a move on, Crosby,' urged Detective Inspector Sloan.

'Yes, sir. Of course, sir.' Crosby had followed Sloan at a dog trot out to the police station's car park and into their police car. 'Where to, sir?' he asked as he started the car's engine.

'Berebury Hospital and don't hang about.'

Had it not been for the set look on his superior officer's face, Detective Constable Crosby might have been inclined to retort that he never hung about when at the wheel but one glance at the expression on Sloan's countenance was enough to ensure that he stayed silent as the car ate up the distance between the police station and the hospital. At one point he was tempted to ask what the hurry was all about but he held his tongue. After a few minutes he was rewarded with a terse explanation.

'What I want to do, Crosby,' said Sloan, 'is to get to the hospital before they put the admiral under.'

'I see, sir.' The constable pressed his foot down on the accelerator a little more firmly.

'They'll be giving him an anaesthetic any minute now so they can set his leg and I must talk to him first.'

'I'm sure, sir,' said Crosby. He made a token pause at a roundabout, cutting in neatly ahead of a sports car to the manifest surprise of its young driver.

'And I'm sure of something else,' murmured Sloan,

more to himself than to Crosby. 'But I need to know for certain.'

Detective Constable Crosby waited until more of the road had slipped by and then ventured a question. 'Is it important, sir? I mean, seeing the admiral now.'

'Anaesthetics can do funny things to the memory and also,' he added caustically, 'can be a gift to the defence.'

'Am I being a bit slow, sir?' Crosby asked humbly.

Detective Inspector Sloan essayed a small smile. 'I think that in the motoring sense, Crosby, that would be a first but we're not talking fast cars now, are we?'

'No, sir.'

'And you're not being slow. If anyone's been slow it's me. It's the admiral's leg that's broken for no reason and without pain that's made me remember.'

'Remember what, sir?' Crosby caused the police car to round a blind bend with impeccable respect for any cars that might have been oncoming and straightened the vehicle up at just the right moment afterwards.

'Timon of Athens.'

'A Greek gentleman would that be, sir?'

'No, Crosby, just a character in a play.'

'But with hollow bones, I think you said.'

'He was a man with many friends. Too many friends,' Sloan said ambiguously, as some more of the play came back to him. It had been a youthful schoolmaster who had seen fit to bring it to the attention of a group of pubescent boys in a lesson called 'Relationships' but really to do with the facts of life: the dangerous ones. English literature had had nothing to do with it; sexually transmitted diseases everything.

'You can't have too many friends, surely,' objected Crosby, who found it difficult to make them, based as he was in modest lodgings.

'It depends on the friends,' said Sloan dryly.

'In Athens, were they, these friends?'

'What? Oh, no, just in this play by William Shakespeare called *Timon of Athens*.'

Detective Constable Crosby promptly returned his whole attention to the steering wheel, while Detective Inspector Sloan went back in his mind to when he first heard that bit of the play read out. It was the shape of the admiral's nose that should have told him in the beginning. What was that quote? 'Down with the nose, down with it flat, take the bridge quite away.' The admiral's nose had had no bridge.

'Which door, sir?' asked Crosby, swinging the car through the hospital entrance gates with a flourish and bringing it to a standstill in a bay marked 'Ambulances Only'.

'This will do,' said Sloan, leaving the constable to find out for himself whether the authority of a policeman on duty ranked higher than that of an ambulance man with a patient on board. Once inside the hospital, though, and presented with a long direction board, Sloan wasn't sure where to go next. As far as he was concerned it was a toss-up between 'Orthopaedic' and 'Geriatric' wards.

Opting for the orthopaedic ward, he was met at its portals to his relief by a woman in nursing uniform. In Sloan's experience people in uniform had the weight of authority behind them and as a rule knew what they were doing. This one admitted to having a patient called Waldo

Catterick in her care and certainly knew what she was doing.

This was refusing to let him onto her ward. 'Until visiting time,' she said flatly, 'and then only if the patient is feeling like visitors.'

'It is important that I see him before he is operated on,' said Sloan. 'Very.'

'It is important that he has his premedication before then,' she countered, adding in an acidulated tone that mocked his own, 'very.'

'Really important,' he pleaded.

This she showed no sign of responding to.

'Please, sister,' he said.

'I really cannot have a patient disturbed at a time like this,' she said austerely, the majesty of the nursing profession meeting the majesty of the law head on.

He tried another approach. 'Not even if it's a matter of life or death?'

The distinction between the two was obviously less important in the medical world than the police one since it cut no ice with a ward sister accustomed to daily matters of life or death. She said, 'It is important that the patient goes to the operating theatre in a calm state of mind and,' here she gave a minimal smile, 'I cannot imagine that a visit from the police could be other than unsettling.'

It wasn't, thought Sloan, so much a case of irresistible force meeting immoveable object as of Greek meeting Greek. He decided on a different – and definitely duplicitous – ploy. 'I could always arrest him,' he said to the ward sister, even though he wasn't sure that he could.

He made to take a pair of handcuffs out of his pocket. 'Neither you nor anyone else, sister, can stop me doing that in the performance of my duty as a police officer.'

'All right then,' she conceded, yielding very reluctantly, the majesty of the law prevailing over the Florence Nightingale ethos at last. 'I'll give you a minute or two with the patient. No longer, mind. And don't upset him.'

It was all he needed.

Admiral Waldo Catterick was lying on the bed, a pale blue flowered hospital operation gown giving the old sailor an oddly feminine appearance and one quite at odds with his grey beard.

'There's something I need to know about Miss Enid Osgathorp,' said Sloan without prevarication.

A pair of china blue eyes stared back at him. 'A nasty piece of work,' responded the admiral without hesitation.

Sloan pulled up a chair and sat down beside his bed. 'Tell me why. I need to know.'

The old man gave him a shrewd look. 'Will it stay between you and me?'

'I'll do my best but I can't make any promises.' There were other, higher, authorities than his and truth – the whole truth – came into their reckonings well ahead of such trifles as personal privacy, career and reputation.

The beard lifted and fell, signifying its owner's understanding of this. 'She tried to blackmail me about having had what we called one of the venerable diseases,' he said. 'Oh, not directly but I knew quite clearly what she meant.'

'They were old in history,' offered Sloan. This much he did know. And he knew too, that judgements were for the courts, not the police. And perhaps – who knows? – to Saint Peter.

'Oh, they're treatable now but it wasn't so easy in my day, Inspector. You're too young to remember.' He shifted slightly in the stiff hospital bed and then went on, 'I caught a dose of the clap out east when I was a young man and it's on my medical record. And,' he added dryly, pointing to his broken leg, 'you might say that I'm now paying the wages of sin.'

The young schoolteacher had skirted round most of these in his talk on relationships but Sloan could see some of them embodied in the patient before him now.

'That was enough for the Osgathorp woman, of course,' he said. 'She knew, all right, and could prove it.' He sighed. 'Every nice girl loves a sailor. That was the trouble.'

Detective Inspector Sloan tacitly agreed with him. 'And now, Admiral, she's been missing for three weeks, which is our problem.'

'She'll turn up,' said Waldo Catterick. He echoed an old hymn. 'Jesus can't possibly want her for a sunbeam.' Something approaching a grin crossed his weather-beaten face. 'You're too young to remember that expression too.'

'I should have worked out where the woman was getting her information from before,' said Sloan, concentrating on the job in hand.

'It shouldn't surprise you in my case,' said Catterick frankly. 'All admirals have been midshipmen once upon a time, you know, just as all bishops have been curates in their day.'

'What did you do about it?' asked Sloan, leaving aside this nugget of conventional wisdom.

'Took the tablets.'

'I mean, about Miss Osgathorp.'

He gave a high laugh just as a nurse approached with a tray with a hypodermic needle on it. 'Like the Duke of Wellington, I told her to publish and be damned.'

'But she didn't,' said Sloan, eyeing the nurse and getting to his feet to go.

'Of course not, Inspector. Then everyone would have known what she was up to with everyone else's medical records at her fingertips, wouldn't they? It would have quite spoilt her little game and I counted on that.' The blue eyes twinkled. 'I was right too.'

'But you didn't tell us that she had attempted to blackmail you so that we could have done something about it,' pointed out Sloan astringently.

'Then everyone would have known, wouldn't they?' said the old man simply.

'Just a little prick,' said the nurse, advancing with her hypodermic syringe at the ready.

Sloan left hastily before the admiral could catch his eye.

CHAPTER FIFTEEN

'So every single patient on the doctor's list at Pelling could have been being blackmailed by this woman?' barked Superintendent Leeyes back at the police station. 'Is that what you're trying to tell me, Sloan? And not very clearly, if I may so.'

'Theoretically, sir, but actually it would only be worth her while . . .'

'If it was her, remember,' intervened the superintendent.

Only the prospect of the Annual Assessment and his Personal Development Discussion coming up very soon stopped Sloan from quoting Erasmus in the matter of going where the evidence led – another kernel of wisdom brought to his attention by his philosophical old Station Sergeant. Instead he went on, 'Quite so, sir. That being so, obviously there would only be any point in her trying it on with those who knew or had reason to believe that there was something discreditable on their medical records.'

'But we don't know who they are, do we? That it?'

'We don't know yet, sir,' said Sloan patiently. 'And we have no idea how many there are of them either.' He'd been running over in his mind his own medical history, hoping that it didn't have anything in it worse than acne. Mind you, as he remembered, that had seemed very shameful at the time. Prompted by this thought, he went on, 'And we don't know at this stage exactly what medical information there could have been on their records that made them vulnerable to blackmail.'

'Plenty, I daresay, human beings being what they are,' said Leeyes, a natural cynic if ever there was one.

Detective Inspector Sloan, experienced police professional that he was, could only agree. He didn't need a statistician to tell him that quite a large percentage of the population had something to hide. He knew that already.

The superintendent drummed his fingers on his desk. 'But that woman, Enid Osgathorp, would have known all about their little medical foibles by virtue of having access to their records. That's what you're telling me as well, isn't it?'

'If it was her, sir,' he said, tongue in cheek.

'I take your point,' said the superintendent loftily.

'And I'm very much afraid that at least two people weren't like the admiral and didn't refuse to play ball.' He was tempted to add that it took two to tango but thought better of it.

'And therefore presumably paid the price of silence instead?' said Leeyes.

'Just so, sir. Two people who didn't tell her to publish

and be damned, anyway.' There had been something engagingly straightforward about the old sea-dog at Pelling. Sloan hoped the operation on his hip was going well.

'Two, you said?'

'The SOCO reported that there are signs of two separate break-ins at Enid Osgathorp's house after she'd left it.'

'Looking to see if she had evidence of their weaknesses there,' concluded Leeyes, who was wont to equate illness with culpability – and always with failure. 'And finding it, do you suppose?'

'I don't think that there would have been any evidence there to find,' said Sloan, who had been thinking about this. 'She didn't need evidence. Such that there was would have been on their medical records anyway or Enid Osgathorp wouldn't have known about it. Presumably the records – hard copy or computer – were safe enough from anyone else.' He hoped that this was true. The records were in government hands, which, he thought realistically, wasn't by any means the same thing as being safe from prying eyes. 'The victims would have only needed to be sure that she was aware of their medical histories. They wouldn't have needed proof because they, too, knew it would be there – written on their records.'

'And they themselves naturally knew them, as well, of course,' said the superintendent, stroking his chin, a sure sign that he was thinking too. 'So there wouldn't have been any question that she hadn't got her facts right.'

'Exactly, sir.' Sloan coughed. 'There is, though, the

possibility that they wanted to be sure that there was nothing in her house that led directly to them.'

Leeyes shuffled some papers about on his desk. 'And are you telling me that one of the people who broke in has killed her?'

'All that we know for certain,' Sloan said steadily, 'is that she's been missing for three weeks now and that we can't as yet trace her whereabouts. Of course we now also know that some person or persons unknown would seem to have a motive for silencing her.'

'Do you have anyone else in your sights, Sloan? Besides the two unknown breakers and enterers of her cottage, I mean?'

'Not the vicar's wife, anyway,' he said. 'She was dead before Enid Osgathorp is said to have left – did leave – but I'm fairly sure she had been one of her victims.'

'Wonder what she'd been up to?' Leeyes asked, with something approaching a grin. 'Mrs Beddowes, I mean.'

'I couldn't say, I'm sure, sir,' said Sloan austerely. He paused and then said, 'Benedict Feakins is still up to something but I don't know what.'

'Then find out,' commanded Leeyes automatically.

'He seems to be short of money, which could be accounted for by blackmail, and he shied away like a frightened pony when Enid Osgathorp's name was mentioned. But he doesn't strike me as having the bottle to do away with a kitten, let alone an elderly party, although,' he added fairly, 'desperate men can be driven to take desperate actions.'

'He was one of those who lost plants at Jack Haines' nursery too, wasn't he?' mused Leeyes. 'So, you said, did that old admiral. What you need to be looking for, Sloan, like Charles Darwin, is the missing link.'

'Sir?'

'The one between the missing party and all those dead orchids.'

'There may not be one.' Charles Darwin had known there was a missing link before he started looking for it. Sloan did not.

The superintendent swept on. 'There was someone else too, whose plants were damaged . . .'

'A couple called Lingard,' supplied Sloan. 'No sign of any financial pressure there but there wouldn't be anyway.'

'Why not?'

'The wife's got money so it wouldn't easily show up if she'd been shelling out to the Osgathorp woman.'

Leeyes thought about this for a moment. 'What about those two women at the nursery at Capstan Purlieu? Where do they come in?'

'They lost plants all right, although they didn't seem to have been growing them for specific customers so we couldn't explore that aspect further. I would have said there was no money there for a blackmailer anyway, besides which they're blaming a disaffected husband. I'm going to interview him as soon as we can locate him.'

Superintendent grunted. 'Anyone else?'

'The nurseryman Jack Haines – he lost plants too, of course; quite a lot of them, including a greenhouse full of orchids. He seems to have got something on his mind but I don't know exactly what. It could be blackmail too.'

'Sounds as if someone doesn't like him either,'

commented Leeyes. 'Wilful damage to those greenhouses must have a reason.'

'Yes, but we don't know what it is. Any more than we know why the orchids at Capstan Purlieu were trashed. Anthony Berra says he doesn't know either why his plants should have suffered – we're seeing him again next. Haines' stepson, who is also the former husband of one of the women at Capstan Purlieu, is the only one in the frame for the greenhouse jobs so far. But as I said we haven't caught up with him yet.'

'It's about time you did,' said Leeyes. 'And found out if the missing person had any connection with him or Jack Haines.' He bared his teeth at something approaching a smile at an impeding witticism. 'We can't have anyone leading us up the garden path, can we?'

'No, sir,' said Sloan, taking this as his leave to depart.

'We're going back to Pelling next, Crosby,' announced Detective Inspector Sloan to the waiting constable, 'to have another chat with the last person admitting to having seen Enid Osgathorp alive.'

'So far,' said Crosby elliptically.

They found Anthony Berra in the garden at Pelling Grange. The Lingards were out but he was still working on the new border. 'I'm just getting the frost tolerant plants in,' he said, kicking some soil off his spade. 'This business at Jack Haines' greenhouses has really knocked my planting plans back.'

'I'll bet,' said Crosby, who didn't know his crocus from his Crocosmia. 'Big job you've got on here,' he added, looking up and down the long bare stretch of ground.

'Too right, I have,' said Berra.

'Just a few questions, sir,' said Sloan.

'Fire away.'

'There were three women waiting at the bus stop but you only picked up Enid Osgathorp.'

Anthony Berra wrinkled his brow. 'You didn't know our famous Miss Osgathorp, did you, Inspector? It looked to me as if the other two did because they stepped back when she got into my car. It seemed that they weren't too keen to join her.'

'Not popular?' So far, Anthony Berra would appear to have been one of the few people not to have openly criticised the missing woman.

'To put it kindly, Inspector, I think the power of being the gateway to the doctor sometimes went to her head.'

'Power corrupts,' observed Crosby. He started to say something in that connection about his superintendent until quelled by a fierce look from Sloan.

Berra threw him an amused glance. 'So they say,' he murmured.

'But she knew you well enough to get into your car?' persisted Sloan.

'She knew my bad chest even better,' the young man said wryly. 'And that my cough isn't infectious, which everyone else seems to have difficulty in believing.'

'Can we just run over what happened next?' said Sloan. 'You said you went to the bank and had lunch at the Bellingham. What else did you do?'

'What I always do when I go into Berebury – trawl through all the charity shops.' He grinned. 'I collect old gardening artefacts and that's where you find them – if you're lucky. I picked up a Victorian dibber there once and my collection's never looked back. You'd be surprised at what turns up in those sorts of shops.'

Detective Inspector Sloan, a policeman and thinking like one, made a mental note that these days while most High Street shops had automatic tills which recorded the time and nature of all transactions, your average charity shop was staffed by elderly and probably unobservant volunteers. He was about to ask for more details of Berra's shopping trip when his personal phone rang.

It was the Division's Chief Scenes of Crime Officer Charlie Marsden, sounding quite excited. 'I've just heard back from Forensics about those items we collected from the Feakins' at The Hollies. Guess what else was in the remains of that bonfire?'

'Surprise me, Charlie,' said Sloan.

'I bet I will,' chortled Marsden. 'Fasten your seat belt.'

'Go on.'

'Cremated ashes. Forensics weren't quite sure but they thought it was a full set, so to speak.'

CHAPTER SIXTEEN

'The Hollies, Crosby,' ordered Sloan, speedily taking his leave from the Grange. 'We are about to hold what I am told the Army call an interview without coffee with Benedict Feakins.'

They found the man again sitting huddled motionless in his chair in the kitchen at his home.

'He didn't sleep at all last night so I took him to the doctor this morning,' explained Mary Feakins as she ushered the two policemen into the room. 'He advised him to keep moving but Benedict says that's still too painful.' She raised her voice slightly. 'You've got visitors, Benedict.'

Benedict Feakins started to struggle to his feet and then fell back into his chair, the colour in his face draining away. 'What is it now?' he asked running his tongue over patently dry lips.

'Your bonfire,' said Sloan.

'What about it?'

'What exactly were you burning on it?'

'You should know,' he retorted with a flare of anger. 'Your people came and took all the embers away. God knows why.'

'Tell me,' ordered Sloan peremptorily.

'As I said yesterday, just old things.'

'Such as?'

'A hairbrush.'

'Whose?'

'My father's – my late father's.'

'Why?'

'I didn't want to use it myself.'

'What else?'

'His toothbrushes.'

'You're sure they were his?'

Benedict Feakins looked at him blankly. 'Of course I am and I certainly wasn't going to use them myself.'

'What was wrong with using your waste bin?'

'Nothing, but I was having a bonfire anyway.'

'In your condition?'

'I've already told you that I just couldn't stand having Dad's things around. That's all.'

'There were traces of fabric in the bonfire,' said Sloan, taking out his notebook and making as if he was looking up a page.

'So?'

'I'm told there is evidence that you had been burning clothes as well,' carried on Sloan.

Detective Constable Crosby stirred. 'You can't argue with laboratories.'

He was ignored by both men.

Feakins' jaw jutted out. 'Old underclothes that couldn't very well go to the charity shops. No harm in that, is there?'

'Got a guilt complex about your father dying alone, have you?' That, Sloan knew, was unfair.

'No,' Feakins protested in anguish. 'Well, yes, I suppose I might have. Something like that, anyway,' he added, latching on to the suggestion with suspicious speed.

'And how, Mr Feakins,' said Sloan sternly, 'do you account for the presence on that bonfire of cremated ashes?'

The man mumbled something about them being his father's and wanting to be rid of them too.

Detective Inspector Sloan suddenly switched his questioning away from the bonfire. 'When did you last see Enid Osgathorp?'

He started. 'Exactly when I told you I did. Just before she went away.'

'How often did you usually see her?'

'From time to time,' he said uneasily.

'Why?'

'She knew Dad and she used to call round to see how I was getting on.'

'Did you go to her house?'

'I have been there.'

'Why?'

Feakins became more flustered. 'She liked talking gardening. Old ladies do.'

'True,' said Sloan, leaning forward. It was at this point that his notebook tumbled off his lap and onto the quarry tiles on the floor. It slithered in Feakins' direction. The man automatically looked down and as he did so Sloan took a look at his scalp. 'Nasty cut you've had there,' he said. 'How did you do that?'

'It's nothing,' he said, raising his hand to brush his hair back.

'I suggest you did it on the window you broke while effecting an entry to Miss Osgathorp's cottage after she left for one of her trips.'

'No,' he shouted. 'No, I didn't. It wasn't me.'

There was a muffled sound behind him. Sloan spun round and was just in time to catch Mary Feakins as she fainted and fell towards the floor.

'And so, sir,' Sloan reported to Superintendent Leeyes the next morning, 'I sent for the doctor for Mrs Feakins and arranged for her husband to report here to be interviewed under caution. He's not going anywhere – he can only hobble as it is. He said he'll be bringing his solicitor but Simon Puckle is in court this morning so it'll be this afternoon.'

'Sentencing in the Corrigenda case,' said Leeyes knowledgeably. 'The leader of the gang should get twelve years for fraud.'

Detective Inspector Sloan was not interested in that case, beyond being glad that they'd got another villain nailed. He'd learnt long ago not to take on problems that weren't his. 'So, sir, I'm going to take the opportunity of checking up on Norman Potts while I've got the time.'

The less salubrious end of the market town of Berebury was seafaring writ large in the history of the largely rural county of Calleshire: old seafaring, that is, the river having silted up in an earlier century. Its level had long ago become too low even for the barges that had once plied their trade between the town and the coast. Its dwellings, though, had been designed in response to the activities of the pressgang. This was in an age when a prison sentence had been viewed as a desirable alternative to service in the Royal Navy.

The cottages there had been built beside narrow lanes leading to a veritable rabbit warren of twisting alleys and blind corners, all designed to thwart those seeking to kidnap men to crew naval ships. These avenues of escape lay between cottages huddled cheek by jowl with each other with only an apology for a garden. Here and there dwellings had been upgraded, window-boxes and double-glazing added and old doors replaced with shiny new ones, but the general effect was still of dilapidated antiquity.

The coming of the railway had brought navvies to build bridges and carve tunnels and they had succeeded the old seamen in the little dwellings. The most individual building in the vicinity in which the two policemen found themselves was the public house called the Railway Tavern. It was on a corner of the main street and was slightly different in appearance from the other buildings by virtue of having coloured glass windows and old saloon doors. The last known address of Norman Potts in Ship Street was only a few doors away and the two policemen found it easily enough. There was no sign of gentrification about the outside of his house; indeed it had a generally neglected look about it.

Detective Constable Crosby gave the front door what he always thought of as an official knock. When this did not produce any response he knocked again, but louder this time.

'Perhaps,' suggested Sloan mildly, 'the man's out at work.'

'Or lying low,' said Crosby militantly.

'Go round the back and see,' ordered Sloan, 'while I have a word in the pub. Then with a bit of luck we can clear up the orchid business and get on with finding out exactly what happened to Enid Osgathorp.'

'Yes, sir.' The constable disappeared down an alleyway further down the road and Sloan took himself to the Railway Tavern.

The landlord was busy attending to his beer machines when Detective Inspector Sloan entered the saloon bar. 'We're not really open yet,' he began, his voice dying away as Sloan reached for his warrant card and showed it to him. He examined this before saying, 'Licensing hours are different now, you know, Inspector.'

'We're looking for a Norman Potts,' began Sloan without preamble.

'Join the club,' responded the landlord unexpectedly. 'Said he'd be in last night to settle up and did he come? No is the short answer. He didn't.'

'What about the night before?' asked Sloan, seeing that was really what lawyers called the material time as far as the opened greenhouse doors were concerned. 'Did you see him out and about then?'

The landlord screwed up his face in thought. 'He was in then quite early but he didn't stay. Slid off before I could have a word with him about what he owes me. Saw me coming over and scarpered, I expect.'

'Got a lot on the slate, has he?'

'And some,' said the landlord, adding briskly, 'although what it's got to do with the police I don't know, I'm sure. Has he been in trouble then?'

Detective Inspector Sloan laid his warrant card flat on the bar counter. 'I'm not sure either that it has anything at all to do with us but we'd like a word with him, that's all.'

'Wanted for questioning,' sniffed the landlord disparagingly. 'That's what that's called by the mealy-mouthed. Can't say that I'm all that surprised.'

'We just wanted a word, that's all,' said Sloan truthfully, the police force being collectors of information not purveyors of it.

'Well, I can tell you for starters that he lives alone and moans a lot,' said the landlord who appeared to be nursing some personal grievance. 'He's got a chip on his shoulder as big as a sack of potatoes.'

'About what?'

The landlord gave the handles of the beer machine a final wipe. 'Stepfather threw him out and then his wife did the same. Can't say I blame either of them. You name it and he's complaining about it. Miserable sod.'

'Like that, is it?' said Sloan. 'What work does he do?'

'None if he can help it, I would say,' said the landlord. 'Officially he's employed by the local authority when it suits them and when they can't get anyone better. Markets and Parks department seeing as he said he used to work in a nursery.'

'That figures,' said Sloan, getting ready to leave.

'Can you tell me something,' said the landlord, 'seeing as you're a copper?'

'Try me.'

'There's a man committed a crime in here the other evening but I don't know what to call it.'

'Go on.'

The landlord pointed to a pair of drab curtains hanging by the window. 'See those?'

'Yes,' said Sloan. 'What about them?'

'And the radiator under the window?'

Detective Inspector Sloan sighed. 'Of course.'

'The other evening one of my customers – he's a plumber – put his hand round the curtain and slid his key into the bleeder valve. Must have loosened it just enough to make it leak a bit.'

'So?'

'So next morning I notice water on the floor and send for him, don't I? The bastard says I've got a leak and charges me a score for repairing it.'

'I'd call that grievous harm to your pride and pocket,' said Sloan briskly. 'Now, tell me if Norman Potts is out and about today.'

The landlord jerked his shoulder in the direction of the man's house. 'He should be in all right – at least I haven't seen him go out this morning.'

Detective Inspector Sloan thanked the publican and made his way back there. Crosby was waiting for him outside the front door looking distinctly uneasy.

'The back door was unlocked, sir, so . . .' his voice faltered and died away.

'So?' said Sloan.

'So I went in . . .'

'You did what, Crosby?' exploded Sloan. 'Don't you know that that's something that you have no right to . . .'

'And he's in there, sir,' interrupted Crosby. 'Norman Potts, I mean – at least I think it's Norman Potts – because it's a bit difficult to tell who anyone is with a face like it is. He's dead, sir. Very.'

CHAPTER SEVENTEEN

Superintendent Leeyes took the news as a personal affront. 'Norman Potts? Hanging? Where?'

'From a beam in his kitchen,' replied Sloan literally. 'They're all quite ancient buildings down by the old harbour and there are lots of beams in them.'

'I don't want an architectural survey, Sloan,' Leeyes bellowed down the telephone from the police station. 'I want to know if it's suicide.'

'Too soon to say, sir, although the rope was lashed over the beam all right,' said Detective Inspector Sloan. 'As I said, it looks like suicide. I can't say for certain at this stage if it is, though, but Doctor Dabbe is due here any minute . . .'

Leeyes grunted. 'I hope he doesn't kill anyone on the way.' Doctor Hector Smithson Dabbe was not only the consultant pathologist to the Berebury Hospital Group but acknowledged to be the fastest driver in the county of Calleshire. He was Crosby's only known hero.

'There is one thing, sir . . .'

'Yes?'

'There are a couple of orchids on the dresser.'

'I hope, Sloan,' said Leeyes loftily, 'that you're not going to start talking about flower power now.'

'There were no other flowers in the house, sir, and there is no garden to speak of here since these are old fishermen's cottages.' He paused, wondering how to put a new thought to the superintendent without damaging his own prospects for promotion for ever. 'There was something, though, that seemed quite purposive about the way the orchids were set out on the sideboard. As if where they were had a meaning . . .' Sloan decided against saying that their position reminded him of the placing of candlesticks on an altar. There were those at the police station, he knew, who had been known to doubt aloud if Superintendent Leeyes had ever stepped inside a church, let alone been christened. Some of them, bitter men, had also been heard to express the conviction that his parents had never been married either.

'Saying it with flowers again, eh?' said Leeyes. 'Is that what you're trying to tell me?'

'Not exactly, sir, but it was mostly orchids that were damaged in both nurseries and the deceased – if he is Norman Potts, as we suppose – is the former husband of one of the growers.'

'Are we talking remorse?' enquired Leeyes. 'Couldn't live with what he'd done – that sort of thing.'

'It's too soon to say, sir.' It was too soon to jump to

any conclusions either but Detective Inspector Sloan was not going to voice that particular thought. Not with his Personal Development Discussion in the offing. 'There does seem also to be some question of his owing money to the publican along the street.'

'Has he got a record? Always worth a look, you know,' pronounced the superintendent magisterially. 'You can't unchequer your history.'

'We're looking into that now,' said Sloan, reminding himself not to sound too defensive or to start talking about any Rehabilitation of the Offender legislation designed to do just this. That always upset the superintendent. As far as he knew in history, blots on the family escutcheon remained there even unto death. Heralds were adamant on this. So was Superintendent Leeyes.

'And find out who benefits from his death while you're about it,' commanded Leeyes. 'Someone must.'

'Of course, sir,' murmured Sloan. That was something he himself always thought of under the heading of 'churchyard luck'. The Assistant Chief Constable, a man with plenty of Greek and even more Latin, always phrased it even more neatly as *cui bono*? It was an aspect of every suspicious death that he, a professional detective, always followed up as a matter of routine.

'Was there a note?' asked the superintendent more mundanely, bringing him back to earth.

'Not that we have found in a superficial examination of the property,' said Sloan with precision. He ventured to say that the cottage did not seem to be one where flowers – especially exotic ones – might ordinarily have been expected to be found.

'Are you trying to tell me, Sloan, that instead of a note the orchids are meant to be a message in themselves?'

'There is a definite connection between the deceased – if the deceased is Norman Potts as we suppose – and both of the nurseries whose doors were left open and the orchids in them killed,' Sloan reminded him. 'That at least we know – with his stepfather and his former wife, neither of whom had a good word to say for him.'

Superintendent Leeyes sniffed. 'Funniest suicide note I've ever heard of, Sloan. Orchids on the sideboard.'

'If it is a message, then it would have the advantage of not having had to be written by hand,' pointed out Detective Inspector Sloan, 'and therefore there is no handwriting to be examined.' It also meant that the orchids could have been put there by anybody – anybody at all – but he did not say so to the superintendent. Instead he made a mental note to have the plant pots photographed exactly where they were and examined for fingerprints or, better still, DNA.

There was a pause while the superintendent digested this. 'I suppose,' he said grudgingly, 'you'd better deal with the whole business before you get back to that missing person inquiry in Pelling and the damaged nurseries there. After all, it's nearly three weeks since the old lady disappeared so it isn't exactly urgent and you say the man Feakins isn't going anywhere.'

'Yes, sir. I had just hoped that we could clear up the matter of the damage to the greenhouses while we were about it before we got back to looking for Enid Osgathorp.' He toyed for a moment with the idea of saying something about the best-laid plans of mice and policemen but he wasn't sure if the superintendent would appreciate the reference especially as it ended with something about aforementioned plans, as the poet had it, being apt to 'gang aft agley'.

'How did he do it?' asked the superintendent.

'It would appear at first sight that he stood on a chair and then kicked it away,' said Detective Inspector Sloan, choosing his words with care.

'Not what the Italians call *Una Bella Morte* then,' said the superintendent, whose attendance at an Italian language class had been brief but explosive even by emotional Italian standards. His view of Omerta had upset teacher and class alike.

'So,' went on Sloan hastily, 'Crosby's just making sure that the distance of the chair from under the body measures up.'

'It would be a help if you could make sure that Crosby measures up too,' said Leeyes tartly. 'I don't know that we'll ever make a copper out of him.'

The rapid approach of a car heralded the arrival of Doctor Dabbe and saved Sloan from having to respond to this. The pathologist stepped briskly inside the cottage, followed by his taciturn assistant, Burns. He took in the grisly scene at a glance. 'I can't tell you anything about the sort of knot, Sloan,' he said, circling the dependent body. 'Not from here and not yet. The neck is too engorged. There are all the superficial signs of death by asphyxiation, though, especially in the face.' He shot the inspector a perceptive glance. 'How did you come to find him?'

'We came here in the course of making some enquiries, doctor,' said Sloan sedately.

'You did, did you? I see.' The pathologist gestured to his assistant who was rootling about in a black bag. 'Burns, are we booted and spurred yet?'

'I'm just getting the gloves out, doctor.'

'Then note the ambient temperature, please.'

As Burns took out a thermometer Sloan ventured to say, 'It would help a lot, doctor, to know the approximate time of death.'

'I daresay that it would,' agreed Doctor Dabbe affably, 'but it's too soon to say. Much too soon. I'll do my best when I've measured the post-mortem lividity and had a good look at him on the table. Rigor mortis seems to have been and gone so we're talking at least sometime last night. That much will have to do you for the time being.'

Detective Inspector Sloan nodded, while Detective Constable Crosby laboriously wrote down some measurements in his notebook. It became obvious to the others that Crosby had not yet mastered the art of doing calculations without the tip of the tongue sticking out of the corner of the mouth.

Sloan voiced something that had been bothering him. 'My constable tells me that the back door was unlocked when he arrived, doctor, and there is no immediate sign of a key.'

'Not my field, Sloan.' The pathologist was still circling the body. 'The actualities of the scene of death are all yours.'

'What I meant, doctor, is that we will be very interested to know if the deceased had a key in his pocket. One would have thought that normally he would have locked the back door before – er – suspending himself.'

'Normally doesn't come into it, Sloan. You should know that. And pathologists can only tell you what the brain looks like after death. Not what's been in it before the subject died. You want a psychiatrist for that.' He shot the policeman a quizzical look. 'If the deceased had been up to no good, which I presume was on the cards since you two are here in the first place, then all I can offer is that old truism that shame asks for punishment.'

'If you ask me this is a very funny way to go about it,' said Crosby, straightening up and indicating the deceased.

'And tell you both also that – as Shakespeare put it so well – "there's no art to find the mind's construction in the face",' the pathologist took another look at the hanged man and went on thoughtfully, 'especially when its oxygen supply has been cut off by a rope.'

'Applied by himself or someone else,' pointed out Detective Inspector Sloan, taking a close look at several scratches on the beam.

'I don't see how anyone else could have got him up there,' objected Crosby. He had taken up a position over by the sideboard, about as far away as he could from the dead man.

'There are ways and means,' contributed the pathologist obscurely.

'Surely he must have stood on the chair with the rope round his neck and then kicked the chair away,' persisted the constable.

Doctor Dabbe glanced up at the beam. 'All anyone else

had to do was toss the rope over the beam and haul away. That right, Sloan?'

'That's right, doctor.'

'But then he'd have to have been dead first,' said the constable.

'Or unconscious,' voiced Sloan.

'Exactly,' said Doctor Dabbe. 'Now, Burns, pass me an oximeter. We must get on . . .'

The four men already packed inside Norman Potts' old fisherman's cottage in Berebury were soon interrupted by the arrival of the Force's two forensic photographers, Williams and Dyson. Set about with equipment, the pair could be heard clattering down the narrow lane as they approached the cottage. Crosby admitted them and, with the addition of two more men, the room suddenly became very crowded.

''Ullo, 'ullo,' said Williams, the senior of the pair, looking round, 'what have we here?'

'That's my line,' objected Crosby indignantly. 'You've pinched it.'

Sloan sighed.

'What we seem to have,' explained Doctor Dabbe precisely, 'is a simple suicide. What we actually have may well not be.'

'Go on, doctor,' said Sloan, his notebook at the ready.

'Well, if I was a Scotsman,' said the pathologist, 'I would say that "I hae ma doots". Take a look at his mouth.'

'For why, doc?' asked Crosby insouciantly.

Sloan winced. That this was no way for a detective

constable to address a consultant forensic pathologist during the course of a case went without saying. He started to apologise but Doctor Dabbe cut him short.

'That's all right, Sloan,' Doctor Dabbe said amiably. 'No need to stand on ceremony. Not where crime is concerned.'

'Crime?' pounced Sloan. 'Here?'

'The skin doesn't look normal, especially round the mouth and eyes,' said the pathologist absently, still studying the hanging man and in no way put out by the constable's comment.

Detective Inspector Sloan said crisply to Williams, 'I'd like some photographs of the face, please.' Dyson was already setting up an arc lamp at the other side of the room.

'Say cheese,' said Williams, approaching the hanging man with his camera.

Sloan took a deep breath. He was about to bring all and sundry to order when he changed his mind and said nothing. His old mentor when he was a rooky constable – that highly experienced Station Sergeant – had more than once lectured him on the importance of levity in the face of tragedies: only other people's tragedies, that is, not your own. It was sometimes, he would say, better than various other ways of not coping, including kicking the cat, taking it out on the children and having nightmares. Detective Inspector Sloan was the first to admit that the dead man here was not a pretty sight and he therefore kept his peace.

Doctor Dabbe, at least, remained totally professional. 'There are burn marks on the face and you can see evidence of lachrymation which has coursed down the cheeks prior to death.'

'Tear gas,' concluded Sloan immediately, his mind starting to run along quite new lines. The atmosphere in the room changed suddenly when he murmured softly, 'It's not called Captive Spray for nothing, is it?'

'It is more than a possibility, Sloan. I might be able to confirm it at the autopsy,' said the pathologist. 'Tear gas can sometimes leave traces in the body after death.'

'If you do find . . .' began Sloan, a possible whole new scenario begin to flood into his mind while the phrase 'assisted suicide' took on a whole new meaning.

'And I'll check up on the knot too,' promised Doctor Dabbe. 'I daresay we'll find it the usual Hangman's . . .'

'Send the rabbit round the tree and then down the hole, up and round again. Twice,' chanted Crosby. 'Then send the knot up the line.'

'Thank you, Crosby,' said Sloan stonily. 'We all know how to make a Hangman's Knot.' Now he came to think of it, perhaps not everybody did, but it was beginning to look as if there had been someone about who not only knew how to tie a hangman's knot, but how to use CS gas. He motioned the photographers to record the upturned chair lying on the floor near the dangling man and the beam over which the body had been suspended.

'He was quite a small man,' Sloan said, unconsciously thinking aloud, 'so he wouldn't have been too heavy to haul up.'

'We'll be weighing him, won't we, Burns?' promised the pathologist.

The ever-silent Burns nodded.

'Render him temporarily unconscious, put the rope round his neck, throw the other end over the beam and heave away,' suggested Sloan.

'Could be done,' agreed the pathologist.

'Crosby,' ordered Sloan, 'measure the height of the seat of the chair from the floor – without touching it, mind you.'

'Yes, sir.' The constable bent over it and extended a metal tape.

'Now measure the height of the body from the floor,' ordered Sloan.

'Bingo,' said Crosby.

'By which I take it you mean they are the same,' said Sloan frostily.

'Yes, sir. Sorry, sir.'

'And then, Crosby, you can rustle up the Scenes of Crime people.'

'Charlie Marsden and his Merry Men,' said Detective Constable Crosby. 'Will do. I'll ask for a few portlies too, to guard the back lane.'

'And after that, Crosby,' said Sloan, rising above this slur on the uniformed branch, 'you can go round and chat up the landlord at the Railway Tavern before he finds out what's happened. We'll need to set up an incident room and I'll alert Tod Morton that we'll be needing a hearse when we're done with the body here. I'll be in touch with the Coroner myself.'

Doctor Dabbe said so would he. 'When I've done the post-mortem,' he added. 'And examined the hands properly to see if he put up a fight.'

'And what I will want to know, among other things,' said the detective inspector, 'is whether or not the deceased knew whoever came in . . .'

'Always presuming that someone did,' pointed out the pathologist. 'Remember it's too soon to say for sure, Sloan.'

'Friend or foe,' said Crosby, looking round. 'That's what we want to know, isn't it?'

'Whichever way you look at it,' observed Williams, the photographer, 'it can't have been a friend. Not if he ended up swinging like this.'

CHAPTER EIGHTEEN

Detective Constable Crosby slid into the saloon bar of the Railway Tavern as instructed after the manner born. The landlord stopped polishing glasses and asked him what he was having.

With a fine show of ignorance, Crosby asked him what the local brew was.

'Stranger in these parts, then?' The landlord waved his hand in a gesture designed to take in the whole area.

'Sort of,' said Crosby obliquely. 'I've just come over from Pelling.'

'Try our best bitter.'

'Will do,' said the constable, temporarily putting to the back of his mind all he had been told about not drinking on duty. He waited until it had been drawn and he had taken a first sip. He nodded appreciatively and then jerked his shoulder in the direction of Norman Potts' house.

'What's going on down the road? There's a load of police cars outside one of the houses there.'

'Where?' The landlord shot to the door and looked out. 'Well, I'll be blowed. That's Norman Potts' house. What's he been and gone and done now, I wonder?'

'What does he usually do?' asked Crosby, taking another sip.

'Make trouble,' said the landlord briefly. 'Big trouble, usually.'

'Bit of low life, is he?'

The landlord shook his head. 'No, not that, but he'll pick a fight with anyone over anything, if he can. Combative, if you ask me. Or do I mean aggressive?'

'What about?' asked Crosby, burying his face in his glass of beer.

'Money and family,' said the landlord. 'In that order. He owes me. Had to throw him out last week but he still came back. Wanted to borrow some more to tide him over.' He snorted. 'At least, that's what he said. Me, I think it's the gee gees.'

'Some wives,' advanced Detective Constable Crosby, bachelor, trying to sound wise, 'will spend every penny a man's got.'

'It's not that,' said the landlord. 'He had a wife but she took off. Or threw him out. I don't know which. Don't blame her myself. He must have been a real pain to have around. No, it's horses with him.' He paused and then said after some thought, 'Not that they're any more reliable than women.'

'They don't answer back,' observed Crosby.

'No more they do,' agreed the landlord. A smile split

his features. 'And some of them are faster. Only some of them, mind you. The ones you don't put money on.'

Crosby grinned appreciatively and said he'd have another half. 'Got a lot on the slate, has he?'

'Too much,' said the landlord grimly. 'Said he was working on something new out in the country and would pay me back soon but if you ask me, he wasn't working on anything.'

'Not up and about?'

'Not up at all, I should say. Lazy beggar except on race days.'

'And when he did work was it anything to do with flowers?'

The landlord gave Crosby a curious look. 'Funny you should say that. Do you know him, then?'

'No,' said the constable truthfully.

'He was always going on about his stepfather doing him out of his share of a nursery. I wouldn't have thought he'd know one end of a daisy from the other myself. Not until he starts pushing them up.'

Resisting the considerable temptation to say that that was just what the late – and apparently unlamented – Norman Potts would be doing quite soon, Crosby drank up and took his leave.

In his day Detective Inspector C.D. Sloan, like all policemen, had done his time as a breaker of bad news. Sometimes it was as the unhappy herald of sudden death after a road traffic accident, sometimes as the deliverer of an unwelcome arrest warrant. Only very occasionally did the harbinger bear intelligence that the recipient was pleased to hear. The finding of a live lost child was one of them although the tracing of an aged demented relative who had gone walkabout usually only occasioned modified rapture.

Thus responses normally ran the gamut from grief to joy and Sloan had gradually become inured to them all. What he hadn't experienced before, though, was such an equivocal reception to the information given.

'Norman dead?' echoed a bewildered Marilyn Potts when the two policemen arrived at Capstan Purlieu Plants with the news. 'Are you sure?'

'Quite sure, madam,' said Sloan steadily.

'Tell us more,' said Anna Sutherland, standing protectively behind her friend. 'Where, for instance?'

'At his home in Berebury,' said Sloan, telling the truth but not the whole truth.

'What on earth from?' asked Marilyn.

'That we don't know for certain,' said Sloan even more truthfully.

'But he wasn't even old,' protested Marilyn.

'That we don't know either,' said Sloan. The age of the asphyxiated man hanging from a beam in a cottage had not been easy to assess from his face. 'Not for sure.'

'So you're just telling me that he's dead, are you?' said Marilyn Potts truculently. 'Is that all?'

'Why are you telling her this anyway?' intervened Anna Sutherland brusquely. 'He and Marilyn were divorced. She told you that yesterday. Good grief man, you haven't come here to ask her to identify him, have you?'

'Not at this stage,' said Sloan cautiously. Mortuary technicians could work wonders but it took time.

Marilyn Potts began a low keening.

'What's it got to do with Marilyn now in any case?' demanded Anna Sutherland only just short of belligerently.

Sloan took refuge in police-speak. 'There are certain anomalies surrounding the death.'

'What does that mean?' demanded Anna roughly.

'That there are some enquiries still to be made about the deceased . . .' began Sloan. These days the duty of candour was enjoined upon the medical profession but not, thank goodness, on the police.

Yet.

'The deceased . . .' Marilyn Potts choked on the word. 'It's poor Norman who you're talking about, remember . . .'

'What enquiries?' asked Anna Sutherland.

'The provenance of some orchids is one of them,' said Sloan.

Marilyn Potts stared at him. 'Orchids? Are you joking, Inspector?'

'Certainly not, madam. I am quite serious. I understand you were at Staple St James giving a talk on the subject yesterday evening.'

'What about it?'

Detective Inspector Sloan, all policeman now, turned to Anna Sutherland and said, 'And you, madam? Where were you?'

'She was with me,' said Marilyn Potts quickly before her friend could speak.

Anna Sutherland said quite calmly, 'I was with Marilyn in the sense that I drove her over to Staple St James but I stayed in the car outside the hall while she spoke.'

'Why?' asked Crosby.

The older woman replied, 'You probably don't understand, constable, but it's quite difficult to deliver a lecture when there's someone you know well in the audience.'

Detective Inspector Sloan didn't need telling that. His wife, Margaret, knew it too. There had been that trying time when he had been lured into giving a talk to her Tuesday evening club, when to his relief she had fled to the kitchen. He hoped the ladies had forgotten the occasion but he hadn't. He asked the two women at Capstan Purlieu instead, 'Have you any other orchids here apart from the damaged ones we saw yesterday?'

Anna Sutherland muttered, 'The dead ones, you mean,' under her breath.

'Of course I have,' said Marilyn with dignity. 'I brought some back from Staple St James last night after I had given my talk.' She waved a hand. 'They're in one of the sheds over there.'

'With the door closed,' said Anna Sutherland drily.

'I'm keeping them for Enid Osgathorp,' said Marilyn. 'She's bound to ask for them when she gets back.'

'Bound to,' contributed Anna Sutherland. 'No flies on old Enid. If she's paid for them, then they're hers.

Detective Inspector Sloan said that he would like to see them.

'No problem.' Marilyn Potts led the way to a shed behind the cottage and flung the door open. 'Here we are, Inspector. Six orchids. All different. They're Enid Osgathorp's by rights, you understand.'

Detective Inspector Sloan, who wasn't sure that he understood anything at this point, nodded.

As they entered the shed, Sloan pulled his mobile phone out of his pocket and summoned up a photograph of the two orchids on the sideboard in Norman Potts' house. He compared them with those in the shed. Neither bore any strong resemblance to those standing on the decking in front of him. 'These orchids,' he said, 'which you presumably collected from Jack Haines for your talk last night . . .' If he remembered rightly their provenance had cropped up when he was over there yesterday.

'That's right,' sniffed Marilyn Potts. 'I did.'

'How many did you take with you last night to your talk?' he asked.

'Six,' she said, 'and I brought six back.'

Sloan ran his eye along the row. There were four orchids there.

'I'm sure I brought them all back,' she began, looking more worried than ever. She turned to her friend. 'Didn't I, Anna?'

'You did,' said Anna Sutherland, staring at the four orchids. 'I helped you carry them in.'

Detective Constable Crosby looked up and said brightly. 'She counted them all out but she didn't count them all back.'

'Oh, yes, she did,' Anna Sutherland contradicted him flatly. 'Six of them.' She pointed to the photograph in Sloan's hand. 'I saw them too – including two Dracula orchids just like those.'

'Dracula was a vampire, wasn't he?' remarked Crosby to nobody in particular.

'Yes,' said Anna Sutherland. 'A blood-sucker.'

'I brought six orchids back with me,' insisted Marilyn, looking troubled. 'I know I did. You'll back me up on that, won't you, Anna?'

'Oh, yes,' she said, adding enigmatically, 'but we're both heavy sleepers.'

The police car had scarcely faded from view at Capstan Purlieu Nursery before Marilyn Potts turned to her friend Anna Sutherland and started to speak. She seemed to be having some difficulty in forming her words.

'Anna . . . .'

'What is it?'

'Last night.'

'What about last night?'

'When we were over at Staple St James . . .'

'What about it?' said the older woman discouragingly.

'You wouldn't come into the Hall when I was speaking.'

'You know how my being in the audience puts you off. You're always saying so. I must say I myself don't understand why you feel that way but . . .' she opened her hands expressively, 'there you are.'

'No,' said Marilyn.

'No what?'

'No, you weren't there.' Marilyn flushed and went on awkwardly, 'I came out, you see. Someone in the audience wanted one of our plant lists and I'd forgotten to take them into the hall with me so I said I'd get one for him from the car.' Her voice trailed off and she said miserably, 'And you weren't there.'

'No more I was,' agreed Anna Sutherland easily. 'I'd gone for a bit of a potter round, that's all.'

'I thought we were saving petrol now we're so broke.'

'I didn't go far.'

'You took your time about it then.'

'How do you know?'

'I came out again later on and you still weren't there.'

'I was there when you were ready to come home and that's all that matters.'

'No,' said her friend, looking troubled. 'No, it isn't, Anna.'

CHAPTER NINETEEN

'Four orchids and not six?' exploded Superintendent Leeyes, sounding tetchy. 'Is this a criminal case or a flower show, Sloan? What on earth is going on at Capstan Purlieu and in Berebury too, for that matter? First blackmail and now a doubtful death.'

'I don't know exactly, sir,' admitted Sloan, 'but Norman Potts had connections over there.'

'And what about that old party missing from Pelling? Is she connected with of all these floral shenanigans too? Or the death here in Berebury? And where does her blackmailing come in?'

'I don't know that either,' said Sloan, spelling out what he did know about Enid Maude Osgathorp's connections with events to date.

'Was she blackmailing Norman Potts too?' the superintendent enquired with interest. 'He presumably once lived at Pelling since he's Jack Haines' stepson and so she would have known his medical history too.'

'We're already looking into that, sir. The deceased was certainly said to be short of money,' said Sloan. 'At least the landlord of the Railway Tavern told us he was.'

'I wonder what unmentionable lurgy he had been suffering from?' mused the superintendent. 'That's if the missing person was blackmailing him too.'

'I couldn't say, I'm sure, sir,' said Sloan astringently. What he himself really wanted to know was what exactly had been wrong with Benedict Feakins that could account for behaviour bordering on the bizarre.

'There you are, then,' said Leeyes ambiguously.

'We have reason to believe that the six orchids were Enid Osgathorp's in the first place,' he began carefully. 'Ordered by the missing person from Jack Haines . . .'

'Whose nursery was broken into the night before and orchids damaged,' the superintendent reminded him. 'And who also has connections with Norman Potts.'

'But used in a demonstration by someone else because the woman wasn't around to give it herself . . .'

'Not around for reasons which we don't know,' interrupted Leeyes, 'but have reason to suspect.'

'We don't know that yet,' put in Sloan swiftly – and promptly wished he hadn't. It was the sort of rejoinder that his superior officer didn't like and with his Personal Development Discussion pending . . . He belatedly added 'sir', by way of amelioration.

'And it would seem two of the same orchids were probably used by some joker after that,' finished Leeyes for him. 'That's what you're trying to tell me, isn't it?'

Joker wasn't a word Sloan would have used. There had been nothing at all funny about the figure of the man hanging in his kitchen in one of the less attractive neighbourhoods of Berebury. 'We have no way of proving yet that they are the same orchids, of course, but it would seem to be the case. Especially since they were of a variety called Dracula, a name with all its connotations with blood-sucking.'

'Blackmail,' said Leeyes bleakly.

'We're checking on the fingerprints of the two ladies at Capstan Purlieu and those on the pots the orchids at Berebury are in.'

'Is someone saying it with flowers?' asked Leeyes, demonstrating that advertising had reached an unlikely audience.

'That I can't say, sir, not at this stage,' said Sloan regretfully, 'but I think the variety and the gesture must have a meaning. I just don't know what it is.'

'Then find out,' ordered the superintendent grandly. 'And while you're about it, you'd better find that missing person too. Since they were her orchids in the first place she might be able to throw some light on the whole business – if she's still alive, that is. Blackmail is a very dangerous undertaking.'

'We've put out a general alert for her but there hasn't been any response so far. She had a pre-booked return railway ticket for that journey to Wales but it hasn't been handed in there or anywhere else on the route. The Transport Police have been showing her photograph to passengers on the Berebury to London trains.'

'Give 'em something to do,' growled Leeyes at his most

curmudgeonly. He didn't like other police of any sort on his patch.

'But no one remembers seeing her that morning.' Sloan hadn't been surprised at that. His own mother frequently said that grey-haired old ladies were as good as invisible to the general public.

Leeyes grunted. 'And you still don't know whether the deceased here at Berebury was murdered or took his own life.'

'Not yet, sir. A post-mortem is being arranged. We're waiting to be told the time at attend.'

The superintendent sniffed. 'Medical evidence isn't everything.'

Detective Inspector Sloan was the first to agree with him. His own doctor was being quite equivocal about a persistent rash on Sloan's left leg; hesitant about giving him a diagnosis, the physician had merely prescribed a succession of ointments to no avail. Subconsciously reminded of the itch, Sloan now rubbed one leg against the other.

'But let me know what he finds,' said his superior officer.

'We are also very aware,' persisted Sloan, 'that there are connections between the deceased at Berebury, Jack Haines at Pelling and Marilyn Potts at Capstan Purlieu – if not with Enid Osgathorp. We're going back to see Haines at Pelling next.'

Leeyes waved a hand. 'Put it all in your report, Sloan.'

'And then we propose to check up once again on everyone whose plants were damaged by the frost in the greenhouses just in case there is a link somewhere along the line with whoever turned off that greenhouse thermostat. Someone might have wanted to damage a particular customer's plants rather than just Jack Haines' business generally.' He had Benedict Feakins in mind but he didn't say so.

'A scattergun approach, you mean?' Leeyes grunted again. 'Odd way of carrying on, if you ask me.'

'Some of the dead plants,' ploughed on Sloan, 'were for the old admiral and some others for that young couple in the village who had the bonfire as well as those we already know about for the Lingards and Anthony Berra, their garden designer.'

'What does one of those do?' enquired Leeyes with interest. 'Some sort of glorified gardener, is he?'

'A garden designer is,' said Sloan unkindly, 'in my opinion something between an architect and a cookery presenter.'

'Takes all sorts, I suppose,' said Leeyes.

'And to be on the safe side, sir, we'll be checking up on Haines' competitors in the nursery business.'

'That's what I like to see, Sloan,' said the superintendent, unconsciously using a horticultural metaphor, 'you leaving no stone unturned.'

Mandy Lamb had reached the office at the nursery at her usual time that morning but there had been no sign of Jack Haines there when she arrived. It wasn't long though before Russ Aqueel came in looking for him.

'Boss not about then?' the foreman said.

'If he is, he's not here. As you can see,' she added pointedly.

'Well, he's not outside either or I wouldn't have come in here looking for him, would I?'

'Probably not,' said the secretary ambiguously. Rather late in the day she asked if there was anything that she could do for the foreman.

'Bob Steele's been in asking if he could pick up some Penstemon Blueberry Fudge if he came over for them.'

'Again?' Mandy Lamb raised her eyebrows.

'Again,' said Russ.

'Trade, of course,' she said.

'Naturally.'

Mandy Lamb sighed. 'I expect, knowing him as we do, that Jack would say yes.'

'That's what I thought.' He turned. 'I'll get back to Bob and tell him.'

Just then the telephone in the office rang and as Mandy picked it up the foreman slipped away. She listened carefully and then said in the impersonal tones of the perfect secretary, 'I'll tell Mr Haines when he comes in.'

It was another half an hour before Jack Haines arrived at the office. 'Sorry to be so late, I slept in,' he said, flopping wearily into the chair at his desk.

'You don't look as if you've slept at all,' said Mandy, making for the kettle. 'And you've cut yourself shaving.'

He brushed a hand over his jowl and stared bemusedly at the blood on it. 'Any messages?'

'The police are on their way.'

'What for this time?' He didn't sound particularly interested.

'They didn't say.'

He turned over his post in a desultory way. 'Anything else?'

'Anthony Berra's coming in to pick up his new plants for the Lingards.' She indicated a couple of crates on the floor. 'And Benedict Feakins said he was going to bring his cacti in this morning for you to look at but he hasn't turned up yet.'

Jack Haines grunted.

She went on, 'As the admiral's still in hospital Russ hasn't brought the load of bedding plants he ordered inside. It's going to upset our Anthony anyway. He's trying to wean him off them.'

'Tough.'

'And Russ says Bob Steele wants some more plants from us.'

'He does, does he?' It wasn't clear who Jack Haines meant by this.

'But Russ thought you would agree and so he's gone to ring him.'

'Oh, he has, has he?' It was quite clear that the nurseryman meant the foreman this time. He accepted the coffee gratefully. 'I've got a helluva headache.'

'I can see that,' she said, noting the black shadows under his eyes. 'You look like you've had a night on the tiles.'

'Only in a manner of speaking.' He gulped his coffee down.

'Not under them anyway,' she concluded neatly. 'You need some sticking plaster on that cut, by the way.'

'What I actually need is some more coffee before the police arrive.'

Mandy Lamb looked up as a car drew up outside the window. 'Too late. They're here.'

'I understand,' stated Detective Inspector Sloan, with some formality, 'from what you told my constable and myself earlier that you know a man called Norman Potts.'

Jack Haines said, 'I do. Only too well.'

'Do you mind telling me when you last saw him?' Detective Inspector Sloan, a man well-versed in the many pitfalls associated with dealing with potentially injured parties as opposed to suspects, kept his questioning as low-key as possible.

The nurseryman shrugged his shoulders. 'Weeks ago. Like I told you. He came round to see if I could tell him where his former wife was. I told him to push off. Why do you want to know? What's he done now?'

Sloan was not deflected. 'Why should he have come here looking for her?

'I trained her,' said Haines briefly. 'It's where she first met him and he thought I might know where she was.'

'And did you?'

'Yes.'

'Did you tell him?'

'No.'

Sloan nodded and made a note. Unexpanded responses were only one stage removed from the proverbial 'No Comment' and usually about as helpful. Sloan's eyes, gardener that he was, strayed in the direction of the two crates in the corner of the room. The plants looked top-notch – he spotted evergreen shrubs and some roses. They would be ready for planting – in fact the roses would be better for being in the ground by now. 'Tell me, this Norman Potts – would he have had any reason for damaging your plants?' With an effort he took his eyes off the crates, both full to overflowing, and brought his attention back to what Jack Haines was saying.

'No, but he probably thought he had.'

Sloan nodded. 'Quite so.'

'Matrimonial causes,' put in Crosby without quite knowing what the phrase meant.

'I'll say,' said Haines.

Deliberately lowering the temperature of the interview still further, Detective Inspector Sloan pointed to the plants. 'Someone's got some good stuff coming their way.'

'They have indeed,' said Haines, sounding cheerful for the first time, the nurseryman in him rising to the fore. 'They're for the Lingards – some replacements for what was lost in the break-in. We had a bit of trouble getting hold of some of them but I don't think we've done too badly in the circumstances.'

Sloan walked over and read some of the labels aloud. 'Abelia, Philadelphus, Ribes, Syringa, Cistus, Osmanthus . . .' He stood for a moment, something stirring at the back of his mind. He waited for a moment for it to surface and when it didn't he turned a label over on one of the plants. 'Here's one I don't know – Japanese Bitter Orange.'

'Can you eat it?' asked Crosby.

'Not if you've got any sense,' growled Jack Haines, 'but it does well in lime.'

Detective Inspector Sloan, still looking at the plants, asked absently, 'And Marilyn Potts at Capstan Purlieu?

Would Norman Potts have had anything against her?'

'I imagine he thought so.' Haines sounded almost indifferent, certainly not alarmed. 'Norman was like that.'

'Interesting lot of plants you've got there,' Sloan said, producing a photograph of the two orchids found at the house in Berebury and asking Jack Haines if he recognised them.

The nurseryman held it in his hands and said, 'Orchid Dracula andreettae. I sell quite a few.' He handed the photograph back to Sloan who folded it away carefully in his notebook. 'Want some?'

Sloan shook his head and then asked casually as if it was of no consequence, 'Last night, sir, do you mind telling me where you went after work?'

'Home,' said Jack Haines.

'Home alone?' intervened Detective Constable Crosby involuntarily.

'My wife died some years ago,' said Haines with dignity.

'Thank you, sir,' said Detective Inspector Sloan as if totally satisfied by this and getting up to go. He saw no point in revealing at this stage that Traffic Division's number recognition system had noted that Jack Haines' car had been recorded stationed outside Berebury Garden Centre for some time before travelling back to Pelling in the early hours of the morning.

That nugget of information could wait.

CHAPTER TWENTY

Inspector Harpe had been quite adamant on the matter. Two members of Traffic Division had spotted a car parked outside the grounds of the Berebury Garden Centre in the early hours of the morning with the driver sitting at the wheel. They had seen it again an hour or so later, still there.

'You're quite sure, aren't you, Harry?' asked Sloan, back at the police station again.

'I'm not, but they are,' responded Inspector Harpe promptly. He was known throughout the Calleshire Force as Happy Harry on account of his never having been seen to smile. He on his part maintained that there had never been anything in Traffic Division to make him smile. 'They couldn't think what an old codger like him was doing out and about at that hour of the night so they kept an eye . . .'

'He's a bit past "taking without owner's consent", a

man of that age,' agreed Sloan, glad that stolen cars didn't come within his own remit.

'Twocking's a young man's crime,' agreed Harpe, experienced in the matter. 'Even so my boys fed the number of his car through our trusty number recognition system and decided he was the registered holder all right and properly insured.'

'But you don't know what he was doing out at the time?'

'Sorry, Seedy.' Harpe shrugged his shoulders. 'You know how it is. The man's driving was OK, he wasn't speeding, he wasn't even on a mobile phone which makes a change from some of the young ladies we come across. They had no reason to suppose he was drunk in charge so they couldn't very well breathalyse him. His car seemed to be all right too, so my lads couldn't think of anything to stop him for.' The inspector sounded faintly regretful.

'Where exactly was he when they saw him?'

'Sitting outside the place. That's all.'

'Got any times?'

'Is that important?'

'It might be,' said Detective Inspector Sloan, adding fairly, 'on the other hand it might not.'

Inspector Harpe has just given them to him when Sloan's telephone rang. He listened for a moment and then said 'Sorry, Harry, go to go. A post-mortem . . .'

Detective Constable Crosby did not like attending post-mortem examinations. This was made manifest by his seeking the furthest point in the mortuary at which he could stand and still be nominally part of the proceedings.

232

Detective Inspector Sloan did not exactly relish having to be present at post-mortems either but took good care not to allow this fact to be evident to Doctor Dabbe or the pathologist's reserved assistant, Burns.

The doctor welcomed them to his domain as if the place was his home. Perhaps it was a good as his home, thought Sloan, some men being more married to their work than others. A vision of his own wife, Margaret, in their own home rose unbidden into his mind. He banished it as he realised that Doctor Dabbe was talking to him.

'We've done his blood picture for you, Sloan,' said Doctor Dabbe, adding somewhat unscientifically, 'Alcohol levels pretty well ringing the bell at the top. He must have been as drunk as a monkey.'

'What about drugs?' As far as Sloan knew monkeys had more sense than to get drunk.

Doctor Dabbe shook his head. 'No evidence of anything else found as yet. We'll be doing more tests, of course.'

'According to the pub landlord,' said Sloan, 'the deceased hadn't been in the Railway Tavern last night but there was a great heap of empty cans out the back.'

'They should have been recycled,' observed Crosby censoriously.

The pathologist spoke some numbers into the microphone that dangled above the post-mortem table at mouth height, adding in an aside to the two policemen, 'He's more than a bit underweight which compounds the effect of alcohol.'

Sloan regarded the body on the post-mortem slab. 'He was quite a small man in the first place.'

Doctor Dabbe pinched a fold of the dead man's skin

between his gloved fingers and said with professional dispassion, 'Undernourished too, but not dehyrated.'

'Heavy drinkers don't eat well,' said Sloan.

'They don't usually eat at all,' said the pathologist, peering round the puny body. 'I'll be surprised if we don't find that he's got an enlarged liver too.'

'Quite so,' said Detective Inspector Sloan, who would have liked a little less of the 'we' in these particular surroundings.

There was a slight movement at the edge of the laboratory indicating that Detective Constable Crosby had put two and two together. 'A small, unwell man who was as high as a kite wouldn't have been able to put up much of a fight if someone came into his house late at night,' he said.

'A very drunk man of any size wouldn't have been up to tying a rope over a beam and tying a noose round his neck of the right length, let alone clambering up on a chair and then kicking it out of the way,' pointed out Sloan. 'That's right, isn't it, doctor? We're not talking suicide here, are we?'

'Not like that poor lady over at Pelling,' remarked Crosby brightly.

Doctor Dabbe looked up. 'Oh, you mean the rector's wife? Oh, no, no doubt about that one. Open and shut.'

That wasn't a simile Sloan liked in the mortuary but anything that had happened in Pelling interested him just now and so he asked, 'Had she been treated for depression or didn't that come out?'

'It did and she hadn't,' said Dabbe pithily. 'At least she hadn't consulted her general practitioner because he was called to the inquest.'

Sloan searched in the recesses of his mind for a name. 'Doctor Heddon?'

'No, not him. He'd died by then. A new fellow. I forget his name. Pity she didn't go and see him rather than taking an overdose.' Dabbe looked solemn. 'Did you know that some early Christians used to feel that illness was sent by God and it was impious to attempt to cure it? Now they blame the doctors for not being able to cure everything.'

Detective Inspector Sloan, policeman to the last, took a deep breath and said, 'I didn't know that.' The parallel that crime might equally have come from the Devil shouldn't in his view stop a law officer from trying to prevent it or trying to bring the culprit to justice.

'Perhaps she was one of those,' said Doctor Dabbe. 'Not,' he added judiciously, 'that you could do much about disease in those days so it probably didn't matter anyway.'

'How exactly did she do it?' asked Sloan. One thing he did know was that suicides tended to follow a pattern. Copycat, like some crimes. And sometimes catching.

'Overdose of paracetamol,' said the pathologist succinctly.

Detective Constable Crosby chanted softly to himself, 'Why are there no aspirins in the jungle? Because the "parrots eat 'em all".'

Sloan elected not to hear this.

So did Doctor Dabbe, who said 'Paracetamol makes for the liver like a homing pigeon.'

'The Coroner brought in a verdict of suicide anyway,' said Sloan.

'Don't talk to me about Coroners,' said the pathologist.

'Delusions of grandeur, most of them,' said Crosby.

'What they say goes,' said Sloan, who wasn't sure if that was the same thing.

'What they say gets reported in the press without the benefit of correction,' said Doctor Dabbe ineluctably. He turned back and resumed addressing the microphone hanging above the deceased. 'Macroscopic examination also shows burns on the face, lips and mouth consistent with the use of a control spray at close quarters. Further superficial signs include bruised fists and an appendix scar.'

Detective Inspector Sloan knew all about bruised fists in heavy drinkers, the pugnacious ones, that is.

Doctor Dabbe said, 'My man, Burns, has got all the photographs of the knot that we need but I can't tell you much more about it at this stage.' The pathologist reached for something approximating to a saw while Crosby looked away.

Sloan asked, 'If he didn't tie it himself could someone standing behind him do it the same way without that showing?'

'I'm afraid so. No help there but there's no doubt about the facial burns. Or about the death being by suspension.'

Why this sounded better than hanging Sloan didn't know.

CHAPTER TWENTY-ONE

'The pathologist,' began Sloan, reporting back, duty bound, from the mortuary to Superintendent Leeyes, 'has advised me, sir, that he is minded to say that in his opinion the late Norman Potts did not take his own life.'

'Then find out who did take it, Sloan,' said Leeyes in his usual peremptory manner, adding for good measure 'And why.'

'The "how" might be a little easier to discover than the "who",' ventured Sloan more than a little tentatively. 'Or even than the "why".'

'Means, motive and opportunity,' the superintendent chanted the three essential constituents of crime perpetrated by the sane as if it was a mantra, which perhaps it was.

'A rope, a beam and bit of know-how might do for the means,' said Sloan, putting the old phrase 'a rag, a bone and a hank of hair' firmly to the back of his mind, although now he came to think of it a hank of hair – well not so much a hank as just a hair or so – had turned up at the break-in of Enid Osgathorp's cottage. He mustn't forget that. Or the blood on the glass of the broken pantry window. He mustn't forget Benedict Feakins' interview either. He shot a surreptitious glance at his watch. 'As for motive, sir, it's a bit too soon to say. It would appear that the deceased was a less than ideal husband and stepson but whether he was the one who destroyed their orchids and therefore either his former wife or his stepfather . . .'

'Or both,' said Leeyes, a man capable of complicating any situation.

'Or both,' said Sloan compliantly, 'took their revenge in a tit-for-tat way . . .'

'This isn't playground stuff surely, Sloan.'

'No, sir, I'm aware that sounds highly unlikely.'

'But you never can tell,' agreed Leeyes. 'There was that woman who could have been done in for a hatpin.' The superintendent's encounter with the dramatic works of George Bernard Shaw had foundered very early.

'Quite so, sir,' said Sloan, hastening on, 'As for opportunity, no one seems to have seen or heard anything near his house down by the railway here.'

'Two orchids scarcely amount to Birnam Wood coming to Dunsinane,' said Leeyes.

'Beg pardon, sir?'

'Macbeth,' said the superintendent vaguely.

'According to Doctor Dabbe,' said Sloan, making for firmer ground, 'the death took place either side of midnight last night.'

'The bewitching hour,' grunted Leeyes. 'At least

Cinderella got the time right. You knew where you were with her, timewise.'

'The doctor won't say further than that at this stage,' said Sloan stolidly. There was a school of thought that held that both nursery rhymes and fairy stories were rooted in crime, citing Little Red Riding Hood and the Babes in the Wood, but this was no time to be advancing the theory.

'Doctor Dabbe never will say,' grumbled Leeyes. 'He's too fly.'

'And we don't know at this stage either whether time was of the essence.' There would be someone in the background whom he hoped was already establishing a timeline of events and alibis for him to work on later.

'It doesn't take us any nearer the "who" anyway,' said Leeyes unhelpfully.

'No, sir,' agreed Sloan.

'Well, don't hang about, Sloan.'

'No, sir,' he said, making for the door.

The superintendent stopped him when his hand was on the door handle. 'I did say that your Personal Development Discussion was on Friday morning, didn't I?'

'You did, sir,' said Detective Inspector Sloan, adding in an even voice. 'I hadn't forgotten.'

It was later when Sloan saw the superintendent again. 'I don't know which is worse,' said Leeyes morosely.

'Sir?' Sloan was surprised. Admissions of doubt from his superior officer were few and far between.

'Blackmail or murder.'

Detective Inspector Sloan didn't know either. Blackmail, he thought, because there were sometimes – only rarely, of course – extenuating circumstances for murder, such as when the murderer was driven to commit it by the victim. That happened. Mercy killings came to mind too. He said, 'We seem to have both, sir.'

Leeyes sniffed. 'Blackmail is the worst, I think. Not that it's in the Ten Commandments.'

'A nasty mixture of power and greed,' said Sloan, surprised. The superintendent usually only quoted the criminal law, not the moral one.

'What we don't seem to have, Sloan, is another body. That is if someone's done for your lady blackmailer.'

'What we do seem to have, sir, in Norman Potts,' he advanced tentatively, 'is a victim of unlawful killing. He may or may not have any connection with either the missing person or blackmail but would seem to be involved somehow with orchids.' So, he thought, were Jack Haines and the two ladies at Capstan Purlieu but he didn't know how or why.

Yet.

'Would seem, Sloan?' echoed Leeyes derisively. 'Surely when two blooms of the same variety, said to have been supplied by one nursery and missing from another, are found sitting on the deceased's sideboard after he's been murdered it's more than just chance?'

'It's subject to proof,' murmured Sloan. He wasn't at all sure how he was going to bring that about, one plant of a species being very much the same as another – as presumably nature intended.

'And the aforementioned blooms known,' added

Leeyes for good measure, 'to have been the property of the missing woman.'

That too was subject to proof but Sloan thought it prudent not to say so.

'And of a variety named after a bloodsucker,' sniffed Leeyes. 'You'd noticed that, I take it, Sloan?'

'Yes, sir.' Sloan went on to murmur vaguely that horticulture did seem to come into things somehow but he wasn't sure quite how.

Superintendent Leeyes, no gardener, responded with something that would have greatly upset Capability Brown.

'Quite so, sir,' said Sloan hastily. 'In the meantime the Scenes of Crime team are going over the deceased's house and I am about to question Benedict Feakins under caution to see if I can get any further with him.'

Simon Puckle of Puckle, Puckle and Nunnery, who was sitting beside Benedict Feakins in the interview room at Berebury Police Station, was presenting a very different side of his work to the three other men there. Gone altogether was the professional family solicitor solemnly advising a client on probate matters. Gone too was the urbane man of the law and public citizen demonstrating helpfulness in response to a legitimate police inquiry. In its place was something more akin to a she-wolf protecting her young.

'My client,' he began formally, 'has duly attended here for interview under caution in response to the written request delivered to him under the Police and Criminal Evidence Act of 1984.'

'I didn't need to come,' said Benedict Feakins, sounding sulky. He pointed to his legal adviser. 'But he said I ought to.'

'Quite so,' said Detective Inspector Sloan, administering the caution without delay.

'What I advised my client,' murmured the solicitor, choosing his words with care, 'was that he was not obliged to accept the police's invitation to attend . . .'

'Some invitation!' echoed Feakins scornfully.

'But,' continued the solicitor smoothly, 'I also advised him that if he did not attend as requested, his refusal to do so could be brought to the court's attention at the time of any sentencing.'

'Sentencing for what?' howled Feakins, starting to leap up in his chair and then falling back in pain from his back.

'For whatever you'd done,' said Detective Constable Crosby in the manner of one spelling things out to the young.

'I haven't done anything,' protested Feakins. 'You're just setting me up.'

'On the contrary,' said Sloan stiffly, 'we are primarily interested in establishing further lines of enquiry in matters that have arisen in the village of Pelling.' In the opinion of Detective Inspector Sloan what Benedict Feakins needed was a nursemaid, not a solicitor.

'Why didn't you call it a summons in the first place if that's what it is?' exploded Benedict Feakins.

'Because it isn't,' repeated Detective Inspector Sloan austerely.

'I must explain to you, Mr Feakins,' said Simon Puckle, turning to his client, 'that had you been served with a summons you wouldn't be being questioned any further.'

Unsure what this meant, Benedict Feakins sat back looking mutinous.

Detective Inspector Sloan took the lead. 'It is an interview under the caution I have just read you. It is an occasion to give you the opportunity to comment on some matters that have been brought to our attention.'

'Such as?' challenged Feakins in spite of an admonitory look from Simon Puckle.

'I do think, Inspector,' intervened the solicitor, 'that it would be a help if you could possibly be a little more specific.'

'That's right,' said Feakins, sitting back and folding his arms across his chest.

'Such as exactly what you had put on your bonfire,' said Sloan.

'I've told you already,' said Feakins. 'All my father's old things.'

'Including some cremated ashes,' said Sloan. 'You didn't tell us about them.'

'Why should I have done?' Feakins came back quickly. 'It's not a crime what I did with them. They've got to go somewhere, haven't they?'

Simon Puckle bent towards Benedict Feakins and said something under his breath to his client.

'All right then,' said that young man ungraciously, 'but I don't see why I should say anything.'

'Because we have grounds for suspicion that an offence has been committed,' Sloan proceeded patiently.

'Over a bonfire?' said Benedict Feakins, while Simon Puckle leant forward attentively.

'Over a breaking and entering at Canonry Cottage, Pelling, at an unknown date,' said Detective Inspector Sloan in a steely voice. He pulled a sheet of paper towards him and went on, 'During which it is alleged that you scratched your head on some broken glass on a window, the property of Enid Maude Osgathorp, leaving traces of blood and hair on it.'

There were two quite different responses in the interview room to this. One was from Simon Puckle who said something sharp to his client but inaudible to the two policemen. The other was from Benedict Feakins himself. 'I didn't . . .' he began and then fell quite silent.

And would say no more.

Not even when Detective Inspector Sloan advised him that his silence would be deemed to be a refusal to answer questions and recorded as such; and definitely not after Detective Constable Crosby had remarked in conversational tones that he had always understood that silence constituted consent.

'Not in this instance,' said Simon Puckle suavely. 'I can if you wish quote the precedents.'

It was only after the detective constable had been rebuked for making the comment and told he was out of order by Detective Inspector Sloan that a faint smile crossed Feakins' face. Simon Puckle merely shook his head sadly, but at what it was quite impossible to say.

The atmosphere at Capstan Purlieu Plants was still somewhat strained but it had been considerably relieved by the arrival there of Anthony Berra. Declaring himself in search of even more plants, he looked from one to the other of the two women at the nursery before saying, 'What's up, Marilyn? Is there something wrong, Anna?'

'No,' said Anna Sutherland. She shrugged her shoulders. 'Well, yes, I suppose, in a way.'

'Yes, there is,' said Marilyn Potts tearfully. 'It's Norman.'

'Your Norman?' asked Berra, giving a cough.

'He's not her Norman any more,' insisted Anna. 'Hasn't been for ages.'

'What about him?' persisted Berra.

'He's dead,' gulped Marilyn.

Anthony Berra sat down on a bench. 'What's happened? Tell me.'

'We don't know,' said Anna. 'The police have been round but they wouldn't tell us anything much.'

'Except that he was dead,' wailed Marilyn, aping police-speak and adding in a solemn voice, 'in circumstances that have still to be established.'

'Whatever that might mean,' said her friend.

Anthony Berra looked blankly from one to the other. 'But he wasn't an old man.'

'And he isn't going to be one now,' said Anna Sutherland grimly. 'And you won't be either, Anthony, unless you get something done about that cough of yours.'

'Come on, Marilyn,' urged the landscape designer, ignoring this. 'For heaven's sake, fill me in.'

'I can't,' she said. 'I don't know anything more.'

'Yes, you do,' her friend Anna contradicted her. 'Some person or persons unknown nicked some of Enid's orchids from our shed after we got back from Staple St James last night.'

'She won't like that,' said Anthony Berra immediately. 'Enid's always very particular about anything that's hers.'

'You can say that again,' said Anna.

'But why would anyone want to steal two of her orchids?' he asked, clearly puzzled.

'Search me,' said Anna. 'But the police were looking for whoever did it all right.'

'And what – if anything – has that got to do with Norman dying?' frowned Berra. 'I don't get it.'

'The police didn't say,' said Anna in a detached manner. 'In fact they didn't say very much at all.'

'We don't even know where they are – the missing orchids, I mean,' put in Marilyn. 'They didn't tell us that either.'

'Or Norman, come to that,' said Anna. 'We don't know where he is either.'

'Except that he's dead,' said Marilyn, showing signs of bursting into tears.

Anthony Berra asked hurriedly, 'What about Jack Haines? Does he know about Norman?'

Anna Sutherland shrugged her shoulders again. 'I couldn't say but I expect the police have been to see him too.'

'They have,' said Marilyn tremulously. 'I rang him and he's as puzzled as we are. Jack wondered if he'd committed suicide from remorse.'

'Could be, I suppose,' commented Berra, 'if he was the one who opened Jack's greenhouse doors.'

'And ours,' pointed out Anna vigorously.

'All the same it seems going a bit far,' said Berra. 'Suicide, I mean.'

'He always was a bit unbalanced,' said Anna.

'I hope Jack has told Russ Aqueel too,' said Marilyn. 'He and Norman were pretty thick when Norman lived and worked at the nursery.'

'So they were,' said Anthony Berra slowly. 'I'd quite forgotten that connection.'

'So I expect he knows, all right, by now,' said Anna.

'Bad news travels fast,' said Berra sententiously, getting to his feet. 'And I'll have to get going too. I've got to get back to the Lingards at the Grange and do some watering.'

Anna Sutherland gave something approaching a chortle. 'Can't very well ask your lady employer to do it for you, can you? Not her.'

'Not likely,' said Anthony Berra. 'She might get her feet wet and I daren't begin to think what her shoes cost. They're Italian jobs.'

CHAPTER TWENTY-TWO

Mary Feakins took one look at her husband's face as he hobbled out of the police station at Berebury and made for their car. She waited while he parted from Simon Puckle – apparently without saying very much – and then she hurried round to open the front passenger door and help him in. As he lowered himself with great care onto the car seat she asked breathlessly, 'Well, how did it go?'

'I think the police believe I've made away with Enid Osgathorp,' he said hollowly.

'Never!'

'Apparently she's been missing for over three weeks now. At least, that's what they told me.'

'Don't be silly, Benedict. Why on earth would you want to do a thing like that?'

Her husband seemed to sink between his own shoulders. 'They say they found some blood and hairs on a broken window at her cottage and want to test them against mine. Simon Puckle said I should agree to samples being taken from me as it would look bad if I didn't.'

'But you hardly know the woman,' she protested, the real import of what he'd said not yet registering in her mind.

'She knows me though,' he said elliptically. 'Well, the family, anyway.'

'What exactly does that mean?'

'I can't tell you,' he said miserably.

Her eyes widened. 'You mean you really did break into her cottage, Benedict? I don't believe it! Are you mad? Didn't you think that she might have been in there and that it would have frightened her?'

'They say I knew she wasn't there. Don't you remember she told us she was going away? And anyway it wouldn't have frightened her,' he added bitterly. 'Nothing would.'

'But whatever for?' she asked, still bewildered.

'I was looking for something she said she had.'

'Something of yours? Why should she have anything of yours?' She swung the car out onto the road to Pelling, hardly paying any attention to other road users. 'And why should you have gone looking for it, anyway?'

'Not of mine. Dad's.' He pushed his foot down hard on the floor of the car as if braking. 'Watch it, Mary. You'll hit something in a minute if you're not careful.'

'Your father's?' she said, taking her eyes off the road to stare at him.

He nodded speechlessly, keeping looking straight ahead and not meeting her eye.

She tightened her hands on the steering wheel until the

knuckles whitened. 'I don't understand anything, Benedict. Anything at all. And whatever it is, you haven't told me.' Her voice sunk to a whisper. 'Don't you remember? We promised not to have any secrets from each other.' Even if her husband didn't realise it, Mary Feakins knew that they had just crossed the Rubicon in their marriage. It was borne in on her too, that she didn't like being on the other side of that particular river.

Benedict Feakins had other things on his mind altogether. 'Apparently they've got me recorded on one of those street cameras in Berebury High Street too.'

'What about it? You often go in there.'

'It was on the day Enid Osgathorp disappeared not far from the station. They say I was photographed coming out of the ironmongers two doors away from the station with a spade.'

'That's the one you bought for digging the border,' she said promptly. 'Oh, God . . . they don't think that you . . .'

'I don't know what the police think,' he said shakily. 'They don't ever say, but I know they wouldn't stop asking me questions. Like whether I'd been a patient of Doctor Heddon's. Well, of course I hadn't because the old boy had died before we came to live in Pelling.' He frowned in recollection. 'The inspector seemed to lay off a bit after that.'

'That's something, anyway.'

'But it's not all.'

'Go on.'

'They asked if I'd got anything left of Dad's. Anything at all. And I said I hadn't. They didn't like that for one minute, I can tell you.'

'Benedict,' she was the one looking straight ahead now and not meeting his eye, 'there is one thing in the house left of his.'

'What's that?' he shot at her. 'Tell me.'

'His photograph. The one of him in the silver frame that was in the sitting room. I put it somewhere safe before you could put it on the bonfire.'

To her surprise he greeted this with a hollow laugh and a shaking of his head. 'You don't understand a single thing that this is about, do you, Mary?'

'No,' she said bluntly. 'I don't.'

'That photograph's not my father's.'

'Don't be silly, Benedict. Of course, it is. I knew him, remember?'

'It's only a picture of him.'

'That's what I just said.'

'But it's not his in the sense I'm talking about, which is a very different thing.'

Mary Feakins sighed. 'I still don't understand, Benedict.'

'And I can't explain,' he said unhappily.

Police Superintendent Leeyes was more sympathetic about Benedict Feakins having kept silent than Sloan had expected. 'Happened to me once,' he said gruffly. 'I kicked up rough about the interviewee not speaking and got told pretty sharpish that the solicitor can tell his client to keep schtum if the interviewing officer hasn't disclosed enough about the nature of the case against the suspect for the legal-eagle to advise him properly. Or her,' he added belatedly. He didn't like female solicitors or, come to that, female criminals.

'The trouble, sir, is that we don't know quite enough about it ourselves to disclose very much more,' admitted Sloan. 'Besides, I didn't want to show my hand too soon.'

'But you say two separate entries have been made to that property at Pelling and the old party hasn't been seen since,' rumbled Leeyes.

'Yes, sir.'

The superintendent shot a suspicious look in Sloan's direction. 'You're not holding off because she might have been up to no good, are you?'

'No, sir.' This was true. Somewhere at the back of his mind the line about 'Theirs not to reason why . . .' surfaced. He knew what his job was and he would do it; crime was a hydra-headed monster and he knew too that a policeman should not select which parts of it to tackle. A crime was – and remained – a crime.

'The missing person must be somewhere,' rumbled on Leeyes. 'Dead or alive. Not that you can dig up half Calleshire to look for her.'

'No, sir. We have good reason to believe that she was a blackmailer, though,' said Sloan. 'I've got a reliable witness whom she tried it on but who wouldn't play ball.'

'But presumably no actual proof,' pointed out the superintendent, a genius for finding the weakness in a case. 'You can't prove a negative, you know.'

'Yes, sir, I remember you saying,' said Sloan. This, he knew, was a legacy from some evening class or other that the superintendent had graced. Had it been Philosophy? Or was it Logic, a class abandoned by the superintendent over a difference of opinion with the lecturer about the nature of Occam's Razor? He couldn't remember and went on hurriedly, 'I have high hopes that Admiral Catterick will be prepared to testify to this. But we still don't know whose ashes were on that bonfire of Benedict Feakins – and as far as I can see we have no means of finding out since DNA doesn't survive cremation.' He put wild thoughts of Enid Osgathorp having been cremated under a false name out of his mind as being quite impractical, the clerical work involved in certifying death being what it was.

'We may never know short of this fellow Feakins telling you,' said Leeyes.

'And being truthful about it,' said Sloan, making for the sanctuary of his own office as soon as he could. There was a pile of reports waiting for him there. So was Detective Constable Crosby.

The first was a message from the forensic pathologist, Doctor Dabbe, stating that as a result of further tests he could now confirm the presence in the body said to be that of Norman Potts, deceased, of a substance consistent with its having come from a so far unidentified variety of control spray. Sloan tossed the report over to Detective Constable Crosby.

'Bit wordy, isn't he?' said Crosby.

'You may say he's dotting the *i*'s and crossing the *t*'s, all right,' agreed Sloan, 'but remember what he says has got to stand up in court. Mind you,' he added, 'he's quite possibly proving murder on the way but by whom and why we don't know.'

'Yet,' said Crosby optimistically.

Sloan ignored this touching faith in their ability to find a murderer and picked up the next message. It was from

Inspector Harpe of Traffic Division. None of his squad had spotted a small runabout truck registered in the joint names of Anna Sutherland and Marilyn Potts of Capstan Purlieu Plants in or around Ship Street in Berebury the night before.

Or, indeed, anywhere else.

'Not that there's any reason why either of them would want Norman Potts knocked off,' said Crosby when he too read this.

'No reason that we know of,' Sloan corrected him, 'but it very much looks as if those orchids came from their shed.'

'And from Jack Haines' place before that,' said Crosby.

'Much, Crosby, as I dislike being manipulated,' Sloan said acidly, 'I can see that someone, somewhere, is behaving as if they wanted us to make the connection – and with Dracula – but exactly why escapes me for the moment. Anyone could have picked those flowers up from that shed after the two women got back from that precious lecture of theirs. It wasn't even locked.'

'Which lecture Marilyn Potts was delivering instead of Enid Osgathorp,' Crosby reminded him.

'I know, I know,' said Sloan, picking up the third report. It was from the police constable whose beat included Pelling and several other villages out that way. As requested he had kept a watchful eye on Russ Aqueel, foreman at Jack Haines' nursery. But at a distance.

'A bit of a drinker,' ran the text, 'and not too discreet. Keeps dropping hints in the pub that he might be getting a better job soon. Visits the Berebury Garden Centre a lot, usually taking trays of plants over there. Insists to all and sundry that he doesn't know who left the greenhouse doors open but that it wasn't him. His mates aren't so sure.'

Sloan tossed the paper over to Crosby. 'If Bob Steele at the Berebury Garden Centre is thinking of making a bid for Jack Haines' place then lowering its value would certainly help,' he said. 'And a fall in its value must definitely have happened big time after he lost two greenhouses full of plants – especially at this time of the year. With or without the assistance of Russ Aqueel, who may or may not have been promised a better job by him.'

'Steele could have been aiming at making Jack Haines bankrupt instead,' offered Crosby. 'Keep the price down a treat that would. He could buy at a fire sale.'

'Or even just destroying all those baby orchids so he could sell his own instead,' mused Sloan. 'A shortage could then be met from the Berebury Garden Centre, not Haines' nursery. That would explain the trouble at Capstan Purlieu as well. Even so, we'd better see this man Steele and have another word with the foreman at Pelling.'

'Turf wars, I bet,' pronounced Crosby. 'Fits with garden centres, doesn't it? They sell turves, don't they?'

Detective Inspector Sloan ignored this and replaced the last of the message sheets on his desk. 'That it, then?'

'In a manner of speaking, sir.' The constable was toying with yet another piece of paper, reading and re-reading it. 'There's one here that I don't understand.'

'From Forensics?' Sloan hazarded a guess. They were a section that tended to speak in tongues of their own devising.

'No, sir. It's from Admiral Catterick's daily woman

at the Park. She rang to say that she's heard from the hospital that the admiral has answered Gabriel's call. Who's Gabriel, sir?'

'An archangel, Crosby,' said Sloan, well-brought up son of a churchwoman.

'An archangel?' Crosby sounded mystified.

'I'm very much afraid,' said Sloan slowly, 'it's her way of saying that Waldo Catterick has been transferred to Ward 13 at the hospital.'

The detective constable looked quite blank. 'So?'

'Ward 13 is a euphemism for the hospital's mortuary,' said Sloan sadly. 'It sounds better if the patients overhear the porters being sent for.'

Crosby's face cleared as unconsciously he used yet another euphemism. 'Oh, he's popped his clogs, then. Bad luck.'

'It's bad luck for us all. Our operation and his. His must have been too much for him.' Sloan paused and added thoughtfully, 'Especially in his state of health.'

CHAPTER TWENTY-THREE

'Right, Crosby, we need to get going out to Pelling to interview Jack Haines again now we know a bit more background.' Detective Inspector Sloan was just shovelling some papers into his briefcase when the Coroner's Officer, PC Edward York, put his head round the office door. 'And then get back to Norman Potts' house,' said Sloan.

'Got a minute, Inspector?' York asked.

'Have a heart, Ted,' pleaded Sloan. 'I've only just got back from reporting to the old man on the outcome of conducting an interview under caution to do with a missing person.' He didn't suppose for one moment that the Coroner's Officer was interested in missing persons. Not until they had been found dead, that is. 'And you know that I can't even begin to write my own report for the Coroner on the Potts' case until the doctor's done his. I haven't had a full report from Charlie Marsden yet, either. The SOCOs are still at the house.'

'I can see you're busy,' said the other officer calmly.

'Yes,' put in Crosby importantly, 'besides we think we're into murder.'

The Coroner's Officer said, 'Oh, really? No, I don't need anything more about Norman Potts. Not just yet, anyway. The Coroner'll only be taking formal evidence of identification when the inquest comes up, which won't be for a bit.'

'And that'll be adjourned while further enquiries are made,' chanted Crosby in mocking tones.

'That's right. To give you guys time to get on with finding out who did it,' rejoined York amiably. 'No, it's not him I've come about.'

'Who, then?' asked Sloan in tones that he hoped implied he didn't have all day.

'The rector of Pelling's been in touch.' As Coroner's Officer, Edward York was quite used to being seen as the friendly face of the constabulary and approached as such.

'Mr Beddowes?' Sloan's head came up and he turned to his constable. 'That reminds me, Crosby. We need a photograph of Norman Potts so that we can see if any of the street cameras picked him up in Berebury as well as the others the day Enid Osgathorp disappeared. See to it.' He turned back to the Coroner's Officer and explained. 'We caught the rector on CCTV in Berebury that day too. What does he want now?'

Edward York carried on, 'He thought he ought to tell somebody about a letter that's come to the rectory and being a clergyman he wanted to do the right thing.'

Sloan forbore to remark that he had known a number of men of the cloth who had done the wrong thing, clerical errors not being unknown to the Force. 'Tell us what exactly, Ted?'

'He's had a letter – or more accurately, a letter came addressed to his late wife – which naturally he opened. It was from the Calleshire Adoption Support Agency over at Calleford.'

'Ah,' breathed Sloan, light beginning to dawn.

'The agency said it was providing intermediary services for an unnamed male applicant of theirs. They were asking on his behalf for Mrs Ann Beddowes' consent to tell them her name and address and for permission for the person concerned to make contact.'

'Bit difficult that, seeing she's dead now,' remarked Crosby.

'That explains a lot,' Sloan let out a long breath. It probably explained why the rector's wife hadn't been at the presentation ceremony on her retirement to Enid Osgathorp too.

'Like what?' asked Crosby, clearly mystified.

'Like why she committed suicide, I expect,' said York, adding sapiently, 'A permanent solution to a temporary problem, that's what suicide is.'

'Like why she was being blackmailed,' said Sloan grimly.

'Apparently,' York continued on his current theme, 'the system is that at any time after its eighteenth birthday an adopted child can attempt to get in touch with its birth mother through the Adoption Agency. They can only go ahead, of course, if they know who she is and has previously agreed to it.'

'What if she hasn't?' asked Crosby.

'I think,' frowned York, 'the applicant can be given some sort of info – whether the birth mother's in good health . . .'

'But not good wealth, I hope,' said Detective Inspector Sloan, policeman first and last and all the time.

'News of general well-being I think is as far as it goes,' said York. 'But not her name or her whereabouts. They can pass on some relevant information, though, such as details about a hereditary disease or an inheritance.'

'Circumstances alter cases,' observed Sloan dryly.

'Some you win, some you lose,' said Crosby.

'But it doesn't work the other way round, does it?' asked Sloan, rapidly reaching a conclusion. 'Not vice versa?'

'The birth mother can ask but the child doesn't have to respond,' said the Coroner's Officer. 'If the child doesn't want it, there's no way round. All she can do then is deposit her name and address with the adoption people, leaving the initiative to make contact entirely with the son or daughter.'

'Fair's fair,' said Crosby.

'And that's only after they've been given professional assistance and counselling,' said York, adding wisely, 'They could be opening a can of worms all round.'

'If you've made your bed, you've got to lie on it,' said Crosby with all the assurance of the young and inexperienced.

Detective Inspector Sloan asked the Coroner's Officer

what the rector had had to say about the contents of the letter, if anything.

'Oh, yes, he said something all right,' replied York promptly. 'It was a quotation. He sounded very sad and said "Thy Mother's son! Like enough, and thy Father's shadow". He told me it was from something Shakespeare wrote but I wouldn't know about that myself.'

'If we look smart about it, Crosby,' said Detective Inspector Sloan, taking a swift look at his watch, 'we could interview Bob Steele before we go back to the crime scene.' Clearing away the undergrowth as you go along was one of the superintendent's great maxims. 'It'll give Charlie Marsden time to give the place a going-over.'

Nothing loth, Crosby turned the police car in the direction of the Berebury Garden Centre.

'We should probably have done it before,' said Sloan. 'There's something going on there but I don't know what. Norman Potts or Russ Aqueel might have known more about it than we do and taken action accordingly.'

'Or Jack Haines might have done,' said Crosby. The Berebury Garden Centre was on the outskirts of the market town and there were no open roads on the way, just winding streets with Anglo-Saxon origins. He negotiated these with virtuous attention to all the road signage. It was only when Sloan spotted a Traffic patrol car hidden up behind a school that he realised why.

Bob Steele received the two detectives civilly and without any apparent anxiety. 'Jack Haines? But I've already told you I know him. What's up now?'

'We are making enquiries into another matter that's cropped up.'

'Another matter . . .' The man caught sight of Sloan's face and said, 'I see, and you aren't going to tell me what it is. That right?'

'If you would just answer our questions, sir, it would be very helpful.'

'I'm sure,' said the other man roughly. 'Go ahead.'

'Russ Aqueel, the foreman at Jack Haines' nursery, would appear to be a frequent visitor here.'

Bob Steele visibly relaxed. 'That's no secret. If I run out of plants I buy them from old Jack. If Jack wants anything from me I do the same and Russ brings them over. Custom of the trade. We all help each other.'

If Bob Steele heard the little snort that escaped Crosby at this he gave no sign of having done so.

'I pay him on the nail, Inspector,' went on Steele, 'if that's what's worrying you. Ask that secretary of his over there – Mandy somebody. She wouldn't let anyone get away without.' He sniffed. 'Proper watchdog, she is.'

'And when exactly,' asked Sloan, 'did you last see Jack himself?'

Steele's eyes narrowed. 'Ah, so this is what this is all about. Well, if you must know I spotted his car outside here pretty late last night. As you're detectives I expect you'll have worked out that I live on the premises.'

'We were not unaware of the fact, sir,' said Sloan, whose mother had taught him that politeness could be as sharp-edged a weapon as any knife. 'What was Jack Haines doing?'

'Besides sitting in his car,' put in Crosby.

'Waiting for Russ Aqueel to come out of my house I expect.'

'And what was Russ Aqueel doing in there?' asked Sloan patiently.

Bob Steele spread out his hands in a gesture that included two thumbs-up. 'Promising me he was going to hand in his notice to Jack Haines next Friday and agreeing to come to work for me instead. If you must know we were having a drink on it. Or three,' he added after a moment's thought. 'Russ can put them away, all right.'

'Thus,' said Sloan regretfully, reporting back to Superintendent Leeyes when he'd checked everything out, 'apparently giving all three of them an alibi for Norman Potts' death last night.'

'That's if the pathologist's got the estimated time of death right,' said Leeyes, a last ditch man by nature.

'There's one thing the doctors have got right, sir,' said Sloan, a sheet of paper still in his hand. 'Benedict Feakins' blood group has been confirmed by the haematologist. It matches the specimen on the window at Canonry Cottage. We'll be charging him with breaking and entering.'

Detective Inspector Sloan, head of the Criminal Investigation Department of 'F' Division, was at a loss to explain why he was not gripped by this information.

'And they're in the process of seeing if they can confirm his DNA from some hair they collected from the scene,' he added, equally unexcited by this.

As Anthony Berra's car disappeared down the road from Capstan Purlieu Plants nursery, Marilyn Potts took a deep breath and announced to her friend that she was going over to Pelling to see Jack Haines. 'I want to talk to him, Anna.'

'He may not want to talk to you,' responded Anna Sutherland trenchantly. 'He never did. Well, at least not since you married Norman and then started your matrimonial causes action or whatever it is they call it these days.'

'Divorce proceedings,' she said pithily, adding, 'but this is different.'

'Of course,' suggested Anna thoughtfully, 'we mustn't forget that Jack may know more than we do.'

'And what exactly is that supposed to mean?' demanded Marilyn.

'Those orchids you used last night came from his place the other day.'

'But, Anna, the police didn't say anything about where the ones they had had come from.'

'Cagey, weren't they?' said her friend pleasantly.

'You don't think that Jack had anything to do with Norman's death, do you? Not Jack, surely.'

Anna shook her head. 'Frankly, I wouldn't have thought he was up to anything as strenuous as killing Norman, not with his figure. Too much tummy.'

Marilyn stared at her. 'Who said anything about Norman being killed? The police only said that he had been found dead.'

The other woman shrugged her shoulders. 'Stands to reason, doesn't it? Me, I couldn't see Norman killing himself. Not no way. He was a man with an eye for the main chance if anyone was.'

'He certainly looked after number one first,' admitted Marilyn sadly. 'Even after we were married.'

'Well, all I can say is that if someone has killed him then he didn't look after himself well enough, number one or not.' She stood up. 'Now I must get on with some potting up. Besides, I've got a phone call to make. I've got a lot to do today.'

Jack Haines barely looked up when Marilyn Potts came into his office. 'Back again, Marilyn.'

'Like the proverbial bad penny, I keep turning up.' Uninvited, she pulled a chair up and sank into it.

'What is it this time?' he asked.

'Call it curiosity.'

'Dangerous thing, curiosity,' said Haines.

Mandy Lamb slid a couple of mugs of coffee before them and remarked, 'It killed the cat too. Sugar?'

'What's to do with Enid's orchids, Jack, and come to that, what's to do with Enid?' Marilyn Potts waved away the sugar. 'There's been no sign of her for weeks. She should have been back before now.'

'Search me. I don't know that either.'

'Nobody tells him anything,' said Mandy Lamb ironically.

'Look here, Marilyn,' said Jack Haines, stirred by this, 'we don't know that there is anything to tell.'

'Oh, yes, we do,' she said with unusual firmness.

'Speak for yourself, my girl.'

Marilyn Potts took a deep breath. 'Two of Enid's orchids were taken from our shed last night after we got back from my talk and they've been found by the police somewhere but they won't say where. They had a photograph of them.'

'Two Dracula,' said Haines. 'The police have been here too.'

'Checking,' contributed Mandy Lamb from the sidelines, 'like they do.'

Marilyn Potts sighed. 'I don't know what's going on, Jack, but I know I don't like it.'

'Me neither,' he said, 'but I can't think what either of us can do about it.'

Marilyn Potts sat in her chair, twisting her hands together. 'Why should it be two Dracula that were taken?'

Mandy Lamb leant over the table that the other two were sitting at and remarked that Count Dracula was a vampire. 'Vlad the Impaler, they called him.'

Jack Haines shrugged his shoulders. 'For heaven's sake, Mandy, it's only the name of an orchid – that's all.'

'A bloodsucker,' the secretary persisted. 'Perhaps Norman Potts was a blackmailer and someone was trying to tell you something about him.'

'Two orchids . . .' said Marilyn, frowning suddenly.

Jack Haines stirred irritably. 'For God's sake, Marilyn, stop going on about them.'

She pushed her chair back and got to her feet, struggling to wrest her mobile phone from her pocket. 'I must ring Anna. It's important. Very important.'

CHAPTER TWENTY-FOUR

Although the photographers had long left Norman Potts' house in downtown Berebury, Charlie Marsden and his team of Scenes of Crime experts were still examining the place when the two policemen arrived back there.

'We've done a preliminary search, Inspector,' said Charlie Marsden as the two detectives stepped inside the door. 'Not a lot of real interest,' he jerked a finger in the direction of the sideboard, 'unless you count those floral offerings over there.'

'We're looking for a true artist in crime here, Charlie, remember.' It was something that Sloan was only just beginning properly to appreciate himself. The choice seemed wide enough. He cast his mind back to Anna Sutherland, effortlessly humping heavy loads about at their nursery. She could have hauled the body of an unconscious Norman Potts over a beam easily enough –

and she hadn't liked his treatment of Marilyn, her friend. Benedict Feakins, bad back or not, was young and had the strength. So also did Russ Aqueel, although where he came into the equation was what the mathematicians called an unknown factor. Bob Steele of the Berebury Garden Centre, who had insisted he didn't know Enid Osgathorp, would certainly have known Norman Potts and Norman Potts might have had some legal leverage on Jack Haines' business through his late mother's estate, thus thwarting Bob Steele's ambitions. It was something he would have to look into.

'We've checked the plant pots with the orchids in, Inspector.' Charlie Marsden interrupted Sloan's thoughts.

'And?'

'No joy. Handled with gloves on. By the way, you might like to know that we got some DNA off a bit of a toothbrush that wasn't completely burnt on that chap Feakins' bonfire over at Pelling. The report's on its way.'

'Bully for you,' responded Sloan absently.

Marsden sniffed. 'Can't imagine why he didn't want us to find it.'

'Neither can I, Charlie, but that'll have to wait.' Sloan put the information at the back of his mind for the time being. It wasn't by any means the only thing that he couldn't explain. What he really wanted to know was where those dead orchids came in – well, not only the orchids – all the plants that had been destroyed by frost. As a keen gardener, he, Christopher Dennis Sloan, could blame Jack Frost for a lot; as a policeman, he, Detective Inspector C.D. Sloan, still couldn't see where a low temperature in March came into the picture. What he could see, though, was that there was undoubtedly a scheme of things in the background. And it was this scheme that was so puzzling.

It was easy to see who had lost out in it, not least Norman Potts, but there didn't seem to be an obvious answer to the opposite question beloved by detectives of 'Who benefits?'

'What's that, Charlie?' he asked, suddenly conscious that the Scenes of Crime Officer had gone on speaking to him.

'Bit bizarre in a place like this, if you ask me, those orchids,' said Marsden. He waved an arm in a disparaging gesture at an unlovely and uncared for domestic interior.

'Lacks a woman's touch,' agreed Sloan in an unconscious tribute to his wife, Margaret, as he mentally compared his own early bachelor surroundings with his present home comforts.

Charlie Marsden grinned. 'No signs of a lady here at all. First thing we checked. No signs of much else either really.'

'Cupboard bare?' suggested Crosby.

'The deceased doesn't seem to have gone in for eating much at all,' said the Scenes of Crime Officer. 'There's the odd tin of baked beans and half a loaf but that's about it.'

'"A Little Bit of Bread and No Cheese",' chanted Crosby.

The other two men stared at him.

'Birdsong,' stammered the constable, abashed. 'The yellowhammer. We did it at school.'

'The only sort of birdsong that I know about,' said Charlie Marsden heavily, 'is called Twitter.'

Detective Inspector Sloan ignored them both while he

gave some thought to the possibility of Norman Potts' meagre lifestyle being the end result of blackmail rather than alcohol or slow horses. This man too must at some stage in his life have been – when he had lived there with his mother – on the medical list of the late Doctor Heddon of Pelling and thus any weakness that he might have had surely been known to Enid Osgathorp. Although Doctor Dabbe hadn't mentioned discovering any unmentionable disease at the man's post-mortem, he would have to check back with the pathologist. Sloan sighed. He should have thought of that before but at this moment he felt like a juggler struggling to keep one ball too many in the air.

And therefore risking dropping the lot.

Was the near-squalor of these tawdry surroundings really down to the demon drink, a penchant for slow horses, or had Norman Potts too been subjected to blackmail? Sloan turned to Charlie Marsden. 'Any money in the house?'

'Not a lot,' said the worthy. 'The odd note in a teapot, that's all.'

'All of a pattern,' murmured Sloan, although it was another pattern he was trying to visualise – one that took in a still unexplained entry into Canonry Cottage with a key, a unloved missing person, the blackmailing of more than one poor soul, the probable suicide of one of them, the odd, naive behaviour of a maker of bonfires, inexplicable goings-on in the horticultural trade and, cast into the mixture for good measure, the destruction of hundreds of infant orchids.

To say nothing of the murder here of a man whom it appeared nobody liked much either. As soon as Norman

Potts' face could be made recognisable he would get on with having the CCTV records scanned for him on the day Enid Osgathorp was last seen in Berebury.

If she had been, that is. That was something else that had to be considered too.

The river, that swift carrier of bodies down to the sea, wasn't very far from the house where they were now. A body could have easily been slipped out unnoticed into the estuary on a dark night on the ebb of a spring tide, unnoticed by anyone – anyone that is except possibly Norman Potts. A watery burial would at least explain the absence of a body – and if he had observed it, perhaps the subsequent death of Norman Potts. That was if he hadn't carried it out himself. Sloan didn't know.

Not yet.

And where on earth did all those orchids come in – well, not only the orchids – all the plants that had been destroyed by frost? At least some of the plants for Anthony Berra's clients, the Lingards, were already in the way of being replaced, well not so much replaced as substitutes found. Idly he wondered why the substitutes meant for the Lingards' garden at Pelling Grange that he had seen in Jack Haines' office had been so different from the ones he'd been told had been destroyed by frost. Sloan stiffened as he realised that they'd changed from being lime-hating plants to lime-lovers . . . His pulse quickened: all detectives had been well schooled in one of the important functions of lime.

Charlie Marsden started to draw his attention to something else he'd found in the house but Sloan wasn't listening. Something that the superintendent had said had swum into his mind, something about the police not being able to dig up half Calleshire. He'd agreed that they couldn't, but it came to him that there was someone who could dig up at least some of the county without arousing suspicion.

'Not now, Charlie,' he said. He was trying to remember something that Crosby had said too. What had it been? Something about making your bed and lying on it – that was it. He breathed out very slowly, a picture of great villainy suddenly becoming very clear to him.

Before he could even begin to think this through and take action, the telephone in his pocket started to pulsate against his thigh. It was Superintendent Leeyes. 'That you, Sloan?' he barked. 'I'm told there's a woman called Marilyn Potts who's been on the line screaming that we should get over to Capstan Purlieu Plants urgently. She says she can't reach her friend on her mobile and she's frightened for her. I don't see why myself,' he harrumphed, 'that that constitutes a police emergency.'

'I do, sir,' said Sloan grimly. 'Now.' He cut the superintendent off without ceremony and turned. 'Come along, Crosby. We need our time.'

As it was the two policemen got out to Capstan Purlieu Plants only just in time to stop Anthony Berra from strangling Anna Sutherland.

CHAPTER TWENTY-FIVE

'I guessed it had to be Anthony,' said Anna Sutherland, anger and shock fighting for supremacy in her voice, leaving it reduced to a quaver. She was still shaking slightly. 'It was when he obviously knew that it was two orchids that were missing that I thought it must be him. It had to be. You see, we hadn't told him how many and I suddenly remembered that.' The woman had the grace to look a bit sheepish. 'I do know I shouldn't have rung him but I did.'

'No, you shouldn't,' exploded Marilyn Potts, who had just arrived hotfoot from Pelling. 'He might have killed you too.'

'He very nearly did,' said her friend hoarsely, fingering her bruised throat. She looked awkwardly at Sloan and said, 'I should be thanking you.'

'You'll have to unfriend him now,' put in Detective Constable Crosby, a recent convert to online connections.

Marilyn Potts had just realised something else. She looked enquiringly at Sloan and said, 'Are you saying Anthony killed poor Norman, then?'

For one moment it looked as if Anna Sutherland was going to bridle at the mention of 'poor Norman' but then she must have thought better of it because she sank back in her chair instead and held her peace.

'We think he must have done,' said Sloan, although Crosby had so far devoted all his energies to arresting Anthony Berra on a charge of the attempted murder of Anna Sutherland and hadn't had time to think of anything else at all. The constable had warned the handcuffed man that further charges might be preferred but he only got a cough in response.

'Why?' demanded Marilyn. 'Why on earth Norman, I mean? He hadn't done anything wrong, had he?'

Anna Sutherland had now recovered sufficiently to snort at this.

'Not that we know of,' said Sloan cautiously.

Anna Sutherland suddenly looked up and gave Sloan a very intelligent glance indeed. 'And what,' she said in a voice still croaky, 'about Enid Osgathorp?'

'We think we now know exactly where to look for her,' he temporised before turning away. 'Come along, Crosby, we're going there next.'

'And I need a stiff drink,' announced Anna Sutherland. 'Whatever you say, Marilyn, I am going back to the King's Arms at Staple St James,' here she cast a meaningful look in the direction of her friend and went on, 'where I am not unknown.'

* * *

Charmian Lingard, who until now had thought her social skills equal to any occasion, discovered for the first time in her sheltered life that they weren't. 'You want to dig up the Mediterranean garden?' she echoed as a squad of police officers in workmen's overalls turned up on her doorstep. 'Anthony won't like it.'

'And remove the statue,' supplemented Sloan.

'But it's all planted up,' she protested, 'in time for the flowers to be ready for the garden party.'

Oswald Lingard took in the scenario more quickly and limped forward and took his wife's arm. 'I think you'd better come indoors, my dear,' he said, leading her away.

Detective Inspector Sloan thought he heard her still protesting about Anthony's plants as she left the garden but his mind was elsewhere. 'Start here,' he ordered the men with spades. 'And go carefully.'

Their leader waved at the statue of the goddess Flora presiding over the long border. 'What do you want doing with the lady, sir?'

'That lady I want taking away. The other one I want finding,' said Detective Inspector Sloan. 'Carefully. Oh, I'll be wanting some soil samples too, although I think I know what you'll find. A lot of lime.'

CHAPTER TWENTY-SIX

Mary Feakins had helped her husband out of their car and back into the kitchen at The Hollies, settling him back in what he insisted was the only chair in the house that he found comfortable. Then she went upstairs to the airing cupboard and retrieved the photograph of her father-in-law. She set it down on the kitchen table in front of her husband and said in a tone that brooked no refusal, 'Tell me why this photograph doesn't matter and all your father's other belongings did.'

Benedict Feakins passed a hand in front of his face as if he was clearing away something from his mind. 'You won't understand.'

'Try me.'

'It's that awful woman.' He struggled to speak her name. 'Miss Osgathorp.'

'What about her?'

'She said I wasn't who I thought I was.'

'Don't be silly. You're Benedict Feakins.'

'You don't understand, Mary,' he said earnestly. 'She said I wasn't.'

'But she didn't know you. She can't have done. We've only just come to live in Pelling and she'd never seen you before.'

'She knew Dad.'

Mary Feakins frowned. 'Go on.'

'She said she knew from his medical record that Dad was impotent. She said Dad had had mumps when he was a lad and that he was unable to have children because of that. She told me that therefore he couldn't possibly have had me.'

Mary Feakins bounced back, light dawning. 'And I suppose she wanted some money to keep quiet about it?'

'I had such a lot to lose,' he said dejectedly. 'This house, you perhaps . . .'

That roused her. 'Me?' she said on a rising note of indignation. 'What about that bit in the marriage service about for better or worse, or weren't you listening at the time?'

'I didn't hear any of it,' he confessed simply. 'I was looking at you.'

'Oh, Benedict, you're hopeless.' She was struck by something else. 'So this is why we're so skint and can't pay the bills. You've been giving her money.'

He stared at the floor. 'She was quite remorseless.'

'And I suppose it never occurred to you to go to the police? Blackmail's a serious crime, you know.'

He hung his head. 'I just wanted us to be happy here.

If I wasn't Dad's son, then I had no claim on this place. Besides . . .'

'Besides what?'

'There's young Benedict . . .'

'Benedict the Third,' she reminded him meaningfully.

'I didn't want him to grow up not knowing who he was either.'

Mary Feakins sighed. 'And I suppose it never occurred to you to demand some proof from the woman?'

He looked really uncomfortable at that. 'No, but I did try to find it.'

'So you did break into her cottage, then?'

Shamefaced, he confessed to this. 'I wasn't a very good burglar and I couldn't find anything there anyway.'

She shook her head. 'You took all this nonsense from someone you ought to have known you couldn't trust? And at face value?'

He wouldn't meet her eye. 'She was very convincing. Well, plausible, anyway. How was I to know whether it was true or false?'

Mary Feakins sat up, another thought crowding into her mind. 'You realise that would have meant your mother had been playing around before you were born?'

'Yes,' he said, his despair evident. 'Mind you, she was very beautiful when she was young. I did check that I hadn't been adopted, though. And I hadn't,' he added.

'So,' she deduced logically, 'you set about systematically destroying everything that might have had your father's DNA on it so that whatever it was that this woman was alleging couldn't be proved. Hence the bonfire.'

'That's right.'

Mary Feakins abruptly got to her feet and went upstairs again. Her husband could hear her moving about in their bedroom above. She came downstairs carrying a mirror. Placing it on the table she commanded him to turn his head to the left.

'Why?'

'Do it,' she said in a tone he hadn't heard her use to him before.

Obediently, he moved his head as instructed. As he did so she brought the photograph of his father alongside the mirror. She smiled at his expression. 'You silly fool, Benedict, you're too gullible for words but I love you. Where else do you think you got that nose?'

'I love you too,' he said humbly. 'I should have told you all this before.'

'So you should,' she said briskly, 'and now the woman has gone missing. No wonder the police are suspicious. Anyone would have been.'

'I don't care what happens to her as long as she stays away.'

'But the police care,' she said, exasperated. 'They have to. It's what they're for. Hasn't it dawned on you that that's why they've been after you? After all, they must know that you've been behaving pretty suspiciously.'

He was almost indignant. 'I didn't kill her, Mary.'

'Then,' she said, 'I suggest you ring that detective inspector and tell him what you have been doing and why.'

He hesitated. 'Are you sure?'

'If you don't,' she said implacably, conscious of having crossed yet another river in the marriage process, 'I will. Here's the phone.'

Minutes later he put it down and said to her, 'They say that Detective Inspector Sloan is very busy just now. They promised he'd get back to me.'

Detective Inspector Sloan was indeed very busy. He was back at the police station in Berebury, dictating to Detective Constable Crosby the first of the charges to be preferred against Anthony Berra. 'The assault on Anna Sutherland for starters,' he said, 'but warn him that further charges are to be preferred in due course.'

'Like killing the Osgathorp woman?'

'Just like that, Crosby. And Norman Potts too. Those Dracula orchids were a nice touch to divert blackmail – otherwise blood-sucking – in Potts' direction and away from the major blackmailer. A very clever move.'

Mention of blood stirred Crosby. 'You're quite sure, sir, aren't you, that he's not infectious?'

Anthony Berra had not gone quietly but had proved no match for two trained police officers.

'Quite sure, Crosby. His doctor assures me that although Berra is HIV Positive you are not at risk. Berra's marriage would have been, though,' Sloan added, 'if his future wife or her family had ever found out about his having AIDS.'

'That woman'd got him over a barrel, hadn't she, sir?'

'I'm afraid so and he knew it. Now, Crosby, what I want you to do next is to search the accused's house for the key to Canonry Cottage. I think you'll find it there while I've got to report to Superintendent Leeyes.'

'No doubt about the identification, then?' asked Leeyes when Sloan arrived.

'None, sir. The body is that of the missing person, Enid Maude Osgathorp, all right. Her luggage was buried in the flower bed there with her and her handbag too. Her name's on both of them.' While the woman's luggage and handbag had withstood three weeks under the soil quite well, her body was not a pretty sight, the insect world being no respecter of persons – especially dead ones.

Leeyes grunted.

'Berra made the commonest of mistakes and buried her in quicklime,' carried on Sloan. 'Murderers will do it.'

'The amateurs, anyway,' said Leeyes grandly. 'They read too much crime fiction.'

Sloan agreed. 'They all think that it destroys bodies. And slaked lime's even worse,' he added. 'It's only got to rain . . .'

'So you reckon she never got as far as Berebury that day?' said Leeyes.

Sloan had been thinking about this. 'I think Berra gives her a lift – he almost certainly knew her holiday plans . . .'

'That fool of a bonfire boy did,' interjected Leeyes, 'so I expect Berra did too.'

'Feakins was talking his way into being a prime suspect,' admitted Sloan, 'but he's off the hook now.' He took a deep breath and went back to talking about Anthony Berra. 'So he picks her up at the bus stop, quietens her with a few doses of control spray if she gets difficult while he drives her to the Grange. The Lingards are in Italy and so he's been able to prepare the ground in the long border in his own time . . .'

'If you mean dig a hole, Sloan, say so.'

'Yes, sir. He kills her there . . .'

'Weapon?'

'Edge of a spade, probably. Doctor Dabbe is nearly sure but he won't commit himself until he's had a really good look at the post-mortem.'

'Par for the course,' said Leeyes, a weekend golfer. 'He never will commit himself if he doesn't have to and leopards don't change their spots.'

Sloan ploughed on. 'If she screams the peacocks there'll get all the blame. He covers the body with quicklime and then soil and hightails it over to Berebury as quickly as he can.'

The superintendent flipped over an earlier report. 'He says here that he visited a few charity shops there first . . .'

'Which don't have automated timed tills,' Sloan reminded him. 'So we couldn't check on his timing until he got to the bank and cashed a cheque. Then he ends up having lunch at the Bellingham Hotel. We did check on that.'

'Busy, busy,' said Leeyes.

'That's right, sir, but he's still got a lot to do. He doesn't dare plant any of the lime-hating plants he'd got on order from Jack Haines because they'll die if he does and that wouldn't do. Besides, the ground would have needed time to settle and he needs to be able to smooth it out and delay the planting without anyone commenting. Well, not anyone – Mrs Charmian Lingard, to be precise.'

'Ah,' exclaimed Superintendent Leeyes, light dawning, 'so he breaks in and causes mayhem at Haines' nursery. Clever.'

'Exactly so, sir. By killing all the orchids there and all those over at Capstan Purlieu as well, he muddies the waters nicely. Everyone thinks the damage is all to do with the orchids – not what's in the other greenhouse.'

'You can get away with a lot as collateral damage,' pronounced Leeyes, sometime soldier.

'He loses all the plants he doesn't want and at the same time gets a chance to order new . . .'

'And different ones,' concluded Leeyes smartly.

'Precisely so, sir. Plants that do well in lime.'

'So where does Norman Potts come in?'

'I reckon,' said Sloan, 'that he caught sight of Berra driving into Berebury without a passenger in his vehicle. Don't forget that they would have known each other from Haines' nursery and Potts was living in Berebury. It was the only real risk Berra took but we're a long way from Pelling here and the chances were pretty slim that he would have been seen by anyone who knew him before he got to the railway station. I expect he actually stopped outside that sandwich shop for a moment or two to add a little local colour to his story.'

'Verisimilitude is the word you want,' declared Leeyes.

'Thank you, sir,' said Sloan humbly. 'I think it was just bad luck for both of them – Berra and Potts – that Potts spotted him. I daresay the silly fellow tried a little blackmail on his own account.'

'Dicing with death if you ask me,' said Leeyes. 'The biter bit.'

'Very unwise, I'd say.'

'It's what we call evidence of system, Sloan,' said the superintendent loftily. 'Especially when you've got means, motive and opportunity like Berra had.'

'A dangerous thing to do, anyway,' said Sloan. As

far as he was concerned, if there was evidence of system anywhere it had been in the behaviour of Enid Maude Osgathorp. He wondered how many other people in Pelling there were who would sleep more soundly tonight knowing that a blackmailer had literally gone to ground.

For ever.

They would never know.

Not now.

'Sorry, sir, I didn't quite catch that.' He realised that the superintendent had been speaking to him.

Leeyes sounded tetchy. 'I said you haven't forgotten your annual assessment and Personal Development Discussion on Friday morning, have you, Sloan?'